# *Though Space and Time*

## *To the Grave*

**Zakary Darnell**

Zakary Darnell

| | |
|---|---|
| **Chapter 1** | **4** |
| **Chapter 2** | **9** |
| **Chapter 3** | **15** |
| **Chapter 4** | **25** |
| **Chapter 5** | **35** |
| **Chapter 6** | **44** |
| **Chapter 7** | **54** |
| **Chapter 8** | **64** |
| **Chapter 9** | **74** |
| **Chapter 10** | **85** |
| **Chapter 11** | **95** |
| **Chapter 12** | **108** |
| **Chapter 13** | **117** |
| **Chapter 14** | **127** |
| **Chapter 15** | **136** |
| **Chapter 16** | **145** |
| **Chapter 17** | **154** |
| **Chapter 18** | **162** |

| | |
|---|---:|
| **Chapter 19** | 170 |
| **Chapter 20** | 179 |
| **Chapter 21** | 188 |
| **Chapter 22** | 197 |
| **Chapter 23** | 206 |
| **Chapter 24** | 214 |
| **Chapter 25** | 222 |
| **Chapter 26** | 229 |
| **Chapter 27** | 237 |

# Chapter 1

Alan Po's bloodshot eyes snapped open. He looked to his right toward his clock to see a dim blue "7:32". A wave of terror rushed over him as he realized he had slept through yet another alarm. *Daniel is going to kill me*, he thought. Daniel, his current boss, had already informed him showing up late one more time would mean termination.

Alan jumped out of bed with a force that sent his blankets soaring. He ran from his bedroom, down the hallway, and into his small bathroom. His cat, Kipsy, exasperated by being so unceremoniously thrown from the bed, hissed and ran frantically from the room. As Alan undressed from his usual sleepwear, a pair of worn pajama pants and one of his dad's old shirts, he turned the shower handle all the way to hot. Hot was just the thing he needed to wake himself up after a late night.

*Don't let your mind wander, Alan*, he thought to himself as he stepped through the shower door. As focused as his exhausted mind would allow, he lathered himself with soap and cleared off the suds. He glanced at his watch and noticed it was now 7:34. *You have successfully showered in less than two minutes. Congratulations,* he said to himself in a slightly sarcastic tone. Quickly, he dried himself off, thinking about how long it might take him to get to work.

The mirror had fogged up significantly from the short shower. Alan swept his hand across so only his face and shoulders were visible. For a moment, he stared at himself. His deep, brown eyes shot from his untidy short brown hair to his patchily shadowed fuzz some might call a beard. His hair was easy enough. Untidy though it was, there really was no need to run a comb through because it was just short enough not to matter. He'd have to forego shaving, though.

Grabbing his toothbrush, he squeezed out what little toothpaste was left in the tube and started brushing vigorously. The only extraordinary aspect of Alan was his white smile. It was, in fact, the only thing that he was ever complimented on, which made him feel good about himself. Needless to say, he worked hard for that enviable grin.

Still conscious about time, he glanced at his watch again: 7:37. Knowing it would take him 21 minutes or more to get there, he spat and rushed to get dressed. In his room, Alan looked at the growing pile of dirty laundry. *I'll have to wash these tonight*, he thought as he rummaged through them to find a pair of jeans.

Shirt on and tucked into his jeans, he set off on his bicycle. Pedaling hard and fast, he tore down the street toward the center of Denver. Traffic was unusually hectic for a dull Sunday morning. Alan turned to the right and cycled down an alley to one of the side streets. There was much less traffic away from the larger roads, like Alameda.

Street after street passed like a blur. He had never ridden this fast in his life. "Three more streets to go," he said to himself. But just then, he heard the blare of a truck horn. Time seemed to slow to a crawl. Alan lifted his head and pushed hard off the pedals for a jump. He soared backward and away from his bike, which wobbled furiously and tumbled into the road. As he struck the ground, time seemed to revert back to normal again, and the truck collided with the upright bike. He looked across the street and saw the white pedestrian symbol with a flashing 04, 03, 02, 01.

The truck stopped about twenty yards down the street, and the driver jumped out. He began to yell at Alan for not paying attention, but Alan just pointed at the now flashing yellow numbers. The driver snorted from defeat and said "Good luck getting anything in court. I work for-" But Alan had stopped listening. Glancing back down at his watch for the final time, he saw it had cracked and stopped working. It may not be working any more, but it clearly showed 8:04 on the hands.

The next three blocks seemed more like a mile as he walked carrying his bicycle. He had never noticed how heavy it was before. Daniel met him at the door and started the usual tirade about being late.

"Why can you never be on time?" Daniel hissed. "Time and time again. I've given you more second chances than you deserve. What's your excuse this time? Did you pop your bike tire again? Or maybe you slept through your alarm. No matter what the excuse is, this is the last straw. Gather your things and go home."

Alan hung his head. "Actually, I almost died just now. A truck nearly hit me and smashed up my bike," he said in a low somber tone. "I don't suppose you'll look past this one."

"No, I don't think I will. Do you really think I believe your story about a truck? Not after how many times you've been late. I bet you're sorry to lose your job by oversleeping again, though."

Alan didn't want to listen to Daniel any more. He strode away toward his desk passing several empty cubicles on the way. *It must be about that time of the year*, he thought. Christmas was only a few weeks away, after all. As he arrived at his cubicle, his neighbor and one of his best friends, James Gatre, peered over the wall.

"Everything alright, Alan? I heard the man throwing it down again."

Alan looked at James from over the wall. He was a stocky man about five inches shorter than Alan. His face was surprisingly round for such a lean man, but it did not take away from his features. His kind eyes always seemed to brighten the mood of anyone with whom he spoke. Alan looked down slowly. Not wanting to admit the truth, he smiled and said, "Everything's just fine. Just a bit late is all." Alan's right hand instinctively scratched the back of his head as he gave a light chuckle at the dim situation.

"Cool beans, bro." James looked back at the screen in front of him. "Here I was worried something bad might have happened." Noticing nothing of interest, he looked back at Alan with a devilish grin. "Want to go back to that bar tonight? That girl might be there!"

Alan glanced quickly around. "Shut up," he whispered, urgently. Alan had never met the girl in question, but prying ears were always a concern of his. "We can go, but let's not talk about it here, capisce?"

James raised his eyebrows, amused. Speaking just slightly louder, he said, "Sure, sure. I won't talk about your little crush in the work place." A smirk crossed James' face, and his eyes glinted. Alan smiled and sat down at his cubicle.

The truth was, James always knew how to make Alan feel better. Any situation seemed less stressful with him there. *I sure am glad James is around*, Alan thought.

"Hey, James?"

"Yeah, broski?"

"I was fired today. Thought you shou-"

"Say no more!" James said, in the most auspicious tone he could muster. "We are going to get you a date tonight, and that's final."

As Alan gathered what few things he had in his cubicle, his only thoughts were that of the girl with whom he had fallen in love.

# Chapter 2

With one last look at the building in which he used to work, Alan turned, laden with his broken bicycle, and walked slowly back to his house. The passersby didn't even seem to notice him, as he strode slowly forward. One by one, they became a blur of faces. Even if Alan looked directly at them, he would only see vague shapes and figures.

Eventually, Alan crossed onto his own barren street. *Everyone seems to be at work. At least no one will know for a while longer.* He passed by the various privacy or picket fences until he came up to his own fenceless front yard.

The house was not dingy, but its quality was substandard for the neighborhood in which he lived. The paint definitely needed to be redone, and there were a few chores that should be done. As he looked on, he thought about what his parents would have thought, had they known what kind of person he turned out to be.

*They definitely wouldn't be impressed. That's for sure.* With his head hung low, he crossed the walkway, finding cracks he hadn't noticed before. *I wonder if those have always been there.*

Alan reached into his pocket and stopped in his tracks. *No no no.* Scrambling and fumbling through the rest of his pockets, hopelessness dawned over him like a waterfall. *Why did I never make that extra key, god damn it?* He cursed himself for never having the sense to lock the deadbolt.

Keeping his fingers crossed in hopes of his own senselessness, Alan reached for the knob and jiggled it. The door did not budge. Sighing loudly, he walked around the side of the house to his quaint patio and looked at the sliding glass door. *I don't remember locking it, but who knows at this point.* Alan grabbed the handle and pulled slightly harder than he had intended.

The glass door slid quickly along its guide, hitting the opposing jamb hard and jumping off the track. As the frame hit the concrete, the glass splintered from one corner, and fractures formed outward until they reached the frame. Alan's hand did not move from the handle as the door fell back against the jamb and the glass poured out over the ground. All Alan could do was watch. For several minutes, he stood, flabbergasted by what he had inadvertently done. When his senses finally returned, Alan opened the screen door carefully and entered.

His house was slightly cluttered with trash and unwashed dishes from the previous day. Kipsy was on the dining room table meowing incessantly. "I know, Kipsy. Give me a minute, and I'll clean it up." She seemed to understand completely and jumped from the table to the chair and to the floor to follow Alan through the archway which separated the dining room and living area. Alan sat on the age worn loveseat, and Kipsy jumped into his lap and purred softly while circling for a comfortable spot.

"I don't know what we are going to do, baby girl." He said as she curled up with her front paws over her face. He looked lovingly at her and stroked her long soft black fur. Alan cherished these moments with Kipsy. She lay on his lap every day after work for roughly twenty minutes. She was a bit old and set in her ways, so Alan didn't upset her routine often. As he stroked her fur, he began to contemplate what he might do, now that he didn't have a job or any prospective job opportunities lined up.

*I could go to the job fair. I think it's only a few weeks away.* He pondered for a few more minutes, and then slowly and carefully reached into his pocket for the phone on which Kipsy was laying. Managing to get to his phone without so much as a stir from her, Alan began to search for a new job.

At only twenty six, he did not have tons of experience working. In fact, the only job he had ever had was the only one from which he'd ever been fired. It wasn't the best job, but it did pay well. He had a bachelor degree in marketing, and it landed him right in the middle of a midlevel telemarketing job. It wasn't bad for just having graduated, but four years with no promotion made it seem unbearable. Alan may not have been the best employee for attendance, but he had the absolute best marketing statistics for the second year running. *Being fired was definitely not the best thing for career advancement, Alan.*

Kipsy lifted her head and looked straight over Alan's shoulder for a few moments and stood, stretching every muscle as she did so. Alan stopped stroking her fur, and she lightly leapt off his lap to her perch atop the cat tree next to the love seat. She stared out the window with her bright yellow eyes, and gave small chirps for every bird she saw. Alan got up and walked back through the archway into the dining room. He grabbed a broom and dust pan from the pantry next to the sliding door and stepped outside.

He grabbed the broken door and carried it to the grass and out of the way. The glass was surprisingly compiled nicely together. As he swept the glass, Alan contemplated all of the jobs to which he applied. One in particular stood out in his mind. He'd applied the instant he saw because it was his dream to be an advertising designer. How could he pass up that opportunity?

It took Alan several trips to finish dumping the glass in the bin, but he didn't mind the work. He looked at his watch and saw the time was 10:33 a.m. *How has it already been two hours since I was fired?* He went inside and immediately decided he was going to clean this mess of a house at once. Cleaning never was Alan's strong suit, but he had a new found dedication to keeping up with the house chores stimulated by the possibility of finally meeting the girl of his dreams.

One of his few strange favorite things to do was washing dishes. Most people he'd met hated the job, but for Alan, it meant time to think about everything that's been going on in his life. With dishes stacked high from around the house, he was in for a good hour and a half of thoughts. After a short time, his mind drifted to the girl he knew from that bar. *What was it called? Oh, yeah, O'Barron's.*

Alan could picture her face perfectly. She had long auburn hair, deep, piercing sapphire blue eyes that shimmered gloriously, and just the right amount of freckles on each cheek. From the very first time he saw her, he had been desperate to meet her. Unfortunately enough, Alan was socially awkward to the extent of potentially fumbling over his own words and spilling his drink upon his first encounter with her. Thus, he had never been confident enough for a first encounter. He had simply watched her from a distance, waiting for the right time to eventually come around. Thinking about her now made a thin smile come across his face. He never wanted to stop the thoughts.

Alan then became suddenly aware of a dull pain in his hand. His thoughts snapped back to reality, and he looked down to see a billow of bright red in the midst of the pure white bubbles in the sink. He had somehow cut his finger open on the only knife he owned. *How does that even happen? Today could not get any worse.* Pulling his hand out of the soapy water, he grabbed a towel from the oven handle and wrapped his finger.

He walked across the kitchen to the hall leading to the bedrooms and bathroom. *I don't remember where I put that first aid kit.* Kipsy weaved in and out of his legs meowing softly with concern. "I'm okay, Kipsy. It's just a small cut." The elderly cat scampered with dedication to his bedroom and to the desk in the corner. Meowing softly, she rubbed her head on the second drawer repeatedly.

Seeing this strangely specific notion from Kipsy, Alan walked to the desk and opened the drawer. There in the corner under a small pile of books was the first aid kit. Alan looked at Kipsy, to the first aid kit, and back at her. Kipsy jumped to the top of the desk and sat on her haunches, licking her front paw. Alan watched her, queerly, and said "Thank you, Kipsy. You are the actual best kitty cat I could ever ask for." As weird as it was to have her show him anything in such a specific fashion, he wrote it off as a coincidence. *Things like that don't really happen.*

He peeled the bloodied towel off his hand and found that the cut was worse than he had originally thought. It went straight through to the bone and was bleeding profusely. *I can't really afford to go to the hospital, right now.* Loading his finger with antibiotic infused gauze, he wrapped it tightly with a bandage. *Okay, now that I have thoroughly injured myself, I might as well make some tea.*

Tea had always brought him comfort when he was feeling down or hurt, and this seemed the perfect situation for just that.

Alan rose from his desk chair and looked at the clock beside his bed. The time on it read 3:47 pm. *Time seems to have gotten away from me. James should be off work by now.* Alan walked back down the hallway to the kitchen and looked at his phone. *No messages. That's a bit odd.* He dialed James' number and listened to three rings.

James picked up the line with a keen, "Heyo."

"What's up, man? Just wondering if we are still going out for drinks tonight."

"Sure thing, dude. I'm about home, so I'll come by your house later and pick you up. Kay?"

"Sounds good. See ya later."

He pocketed his phone and went back to the dining room. *I wonder what I'm going to do about that back door. I can't just leave it broken.* One of the bad parts about owning a house was being responsible for all the repair costs. *I don't have much buffer in my savings fund for things like this.* He breathed in and out with thought and decided it was a necessary expenditure, so while he brewed some tea, he found a glass service and called.

# Chapter 3

After he finished setting up the appointment for a replacement door later in the afternoon the next day, Alan rested his head on the back of the love seat and closed his eyes. The company through which he would replace the door was going to charge more than he could afford, but there was absolutely nothing else he could do. As these thoughts processed in his mind, Kipsy sat atop her perch watching him with her blazing yellow eyes. Alan opened one eye and looked up at her. *What is up with her today?*

A look from Kipsy wasn't unusual, but her eyes looked straight through him on all of those occasions. This look was more focused. Kipsy stood up and stretched her haunches and back, but her eyes never moved from Alan. Alan closed his eyes and heaved a sigh. "Okay. What am I going to do about my hand, Kipsy?" Kipsy gave a light chattering meow and jumped onto the love seat beside him.

Feeling the impact, Alan opened his eyes and lifted his head to see Kipsy sitting next to him with the same look as before. Her eyes glistened softly, and she gave another chattering meow. This one was more forceful than before. Alan tilted his head in confusion. "You are awfully vocal today."

Kipsy placed her paw on his unhurt right hand. A small shock came from her paw, and the effects made shivers emanate from the spot and spread rapidly all over his body. *What is actually going on?* He thought, almost frantically. His left hand throbbed slightly, and he looked at it. Blood was visible under the bandage. Kipsy nipped his hand with her teeth, and he looked back at her in wonder. Although she did not hurt him, she started licking his hand on the spot. Her scratchy tongue tickled his hand slightly, and he chuckled a little.

Kipsy looked straight into his eyes and cooed a small mew. Alan raised his hand and placed it on Kipsy's head. He scratched behind her ears and under her chin. Kipsy's eyes squinted with pleasure, but her gaze never faultered. She started purring. Alan was not used to this much attention. Kipsy usually sat on her perch most of the day to watch the birds and people outside.

"Okay, baby girl. I have to get a new bandage going." He said, taking his hand off her head and getting up from the love seat. She jumped off and followed him into the bedroom again. Wrapping his hand once more, he looked at Kipsy butting her head against his legs. *What are you trying to tell me?* His stomach rumbled. Alan looked at the clock beside his bed and realized it was half past five.

"I bet you're hungry. We haven't eaten today."

Kipsy stopped rubbing against his leg, looked straight into his eyes, and meowed loudly. He had never had such a definitive answer in his life.

"Alright. Let's eat."

Back in the kitchen, Kipsy licked her chops as he opened a small can of her favorite salmon fillet dinner and placed it on the dining table. She licked politely at the juices and purred loudly.

"That's all well and good for you, but what am I having?"

She looked at him briefly, unconcerned.

"You are tons of help."

After a small sigh, Alan opened the refrigerator and shuffled his feet slightly. It wasn't usually this bare, but he hadn't exactly planned on being fired. He stood for a moment, contemplating, and decided on scrambled eggs with salsa. *It's not much, but it will have to do.* He grabbed the last two eggs and a jar of homemade salsa.

While cooking, Alan's phone started buzzing in his pocket. Grabbing it, he saw James' face appear on the screen, and he answered.

"What's up, James?"

"Not much, man. Are you ready to finally get a date with that girl?"

Alan paused for a second. *Does he really think I stand a shot at that?*

"Hell yes, dude."

"Good stuff. I'll be there in t-minus 12 minutes."

Alan smiled. The dorky way James always acted never seemed to get old to him.

"Cool beans, bro."

"Hey, now. That's my phrase. I can't have you going around stealing my thunder."

Alan and James chuckled and said farewell.

*James will be here, soon. I suppose I don't really have time to eat.* It felt like such a waste to have cracked two eggs and not use them for something. Deciding to give them to Kipsy as another snack for later, he cooked them up. Kipsy watched with curiosity as he scrambled the eggs and cooked them to perfection. Her brilliant yellow eyes never so much as flinching. As he finished and placed the eggs into her dish, she dropped from the table and scampered into the hall to the bedrooms. Alan, curious, followed her into the spare bedroom whose door was slightly ajar. *How did this get open?* He pushed the door gently, and it swung stiffly open with an audible creak from the hinges. Kipsy was sitting with fixated eyes on the closet door.

Alan entered the room and flipped the light switch. A stale white glow flickered from the bulb on the ceiling fan, but the light dimmed to almost nothing. With a small pop, the bulb went out. Crossing the room by the light emitted through the shades, he found the lamp on the bedside table and turned the knob. Light blazed out of the small lamp and filled the room, slightly blinding him in the process. He blinked several times and followed Kipsy's gaze. There were very few clothes left in the closet. Most had either been sold off or donated to some sort of charity.

Alan took a brief look around his parents' old bedroom and felt a small lump form in his throat. The last time he had been in here was shortly after his parents had died nine years prior when he had taken all of the possessions which had no sentimental value to the Salvation Army. He looked back into the closet and saw at what Kipsy had been looking. In the middle between two tattered garment bags was his father's old suit. Alan always loved the look of the old thing. It always somehow avoided having any dust particles from clinging to the fine fabric. Without a moment's thought, he grabbed the suit and put it on. *I haven't tied a tie in years. Maybe I've still got it.* It took five full minutes to get it right, but he reveled at himself in the mirror, afterward. Kipsy gave a yawn of approval and left the room.

At the instant Alan closed the spare bedroom he heard a knock at his front door. Straightening his tie ever so slightly, he set off and opened the door to see his friend and wingman, James.

"Hot damn, man. You look spiffy!" James said, coolly.

"Thanks, bro. You look good, yourself." Alan said.

James was wearing a sleek blue blazer, a solid white button-up shirt with the first two buttons undone, and khakis. Alan had no clue how James' sense of style came about, but it seemed uncanny for such an uncouth person.

"I'll be home sometime later, Kipsy. You're in charge until I get back" Alan said, looking to where she had roosted on her perch. Kipsy looked over her shoulder and meowed faintly. Taking this as a sign of acknowledgment, he locked the door and stepped across the threshold.

"You got your keys this time?" James said, patting Alan on the shoulder before he closed the door.

Alan then realized he hadn't actually ever grabbed his keys from the bedside table, he said, "Oh, good call." He swiftly went back to retrieve his keys, and they were off.

James' car was one of the nicest in which Alan had ever been. James had been born into money, though Alan had never asked how much, and this allowed him to purchase a new vehicle every few years. Each one was astoundingly more lavish than the last. This particular one was top of the line from Germany, and it had many riveting new additions. The heads up digital display, which projected onto the windshield just above the steering wheel, fascinated Alan more than any other feature.

"I wish I had one of these," he said in a marveling tone. "How much did it cost again?"

"You know I don't like to brag, but it was only $75,000" James laughed a little and pushed the start button to the right of the steering wheel. The engine hummed into life so quietly Alan had to strain to hear.

"Are you ready for this?" James said with a smirk.

"Ready for wha-"

James pushed the accelerator to the floor, and the car lurched into life. The tail end moved back and forth slightly as the tires squealed. James released the emergency brake, and the car pelted forward after traction was made. Alan's head was pushed back into the seat. His heart fluttered excitedly. There was no way to tell if the pounding in his ears was from blood pressure or excitement. Whatever it was, Alan loved every minute.

James was driving masterfully. The way his hand moved the gear shift almost completely eliminated any shutter from the transmission. *This is smoother than any of his other cars,* Alan thought as James rounded a corner. Alan had to grab the passenger assist handle to keep him from slinging to the left from the force.

"The engine has twelve cylinders." James had raised his voice to overcome the furious, but muffled, roar of the engine. "It gives the extra oomph I've been looking for."

"Don't you think we should go a bit slower on these side streets?" Alan bellowed back, a little louder than had been necessary. His stomach was starting to feel compressed with sickness. That was precisely the reason he only ever rode his bicycle.

James looked over at Alan with one eyebrow raised. "I suppose you're right. I wouldn't wanna hurt anyone." With one quick motion, his foot moved from the accelerator to the brake, and the car began to decelerate quickly. Once they had reached a reasonable speed, James looked back at Alan and smiled.

"That was still pretty damn fun, right?" He asked, enthusiastically.

"It really was," said Alan. He still clung to the assist handle and looked through the passenger side window. They turned from the quiet side streets onto Colorado

Boulevard. This street was bustling with activity, but it still seemed so peaceful compared to his mind. Alan looked on and was quiet for the rest of the twenty minute ride to O'Barron's.

Upon arrival, Alan could make out the distinct aroma of alcohol. He loved that smell. He never was one to drink excessively, but the scent always instilled a feeling of comfort and the ability to be whoever he couldn't otherwise be in public. The parking lot was not quite full, yet, and Alan wondered if she was here or not.

The girl was almost always here when Alan and James came together, so Alan hoped beyond hope she would come tonight. The two friends exited the car and approached the doorman. They flashed their IDs to him, and he gave a small nod of approval. Alan went through first. The door was heavy but swung easily. As he entered, Alan noticed the pungent odorous musk that always accompanied large groups of people. It overpowered the bittersweet fragrance of alcohol he had first smelled outside.

James and Alan visited this bar often enough to have a regular seat. However, James frequented far more often than Alan ever did. Alan held the door for James and followed him to a table close to the bar on the opposite side of the seating area from the door. When James was firmly sat in his regular spot, he raised his hand to beckon a waitress to the table.

A strawberry blonde girl of medium height strutted over to them. Her low cut shirt accented her breasts, and Alan had to look down at his drink menu to keep from staring. This bar was particularly known for the skimpy outfits worn by the waitresses, which attracted many of the local male population. *It's a great way to increase business, but I don't see the point*, he thought, flipping a few pages of the menu to seem indecisive.

"Hey, James! The usual tonight?" she said. Her tone was almost gaudy but also pleasant.

"Absolutely, Kaiya. And my friend here will have the same." James gestured to Alan with a wave of his hand.

"Well, hiya, James' friend. I'm Kaiya." Her enthusiasm was strange, almost seductive. There was a slight tinge of a southern accent, but it was barely noticeable. She put out her hand.

Without looking at her, he greeted, "Hello. I'm Alan. It's nice to meet you." He shook her hand and noticed she had a fairly firm grip.

"Alright, fellas. I'll have your drinks right out." She turned to leave, and as she did, Alan caught a whiff of her perfume. For the slightest of moments, he was intoxicated by the fragrance. *What even was it? It reminds me of...* His mind returned to him like a snap when he noticed James looking his way. *Did he notice that?*

His stomach rumbled, reminding him that he hadn't eaten yet. "Do you want to get some wings?" Alan asked, slightly embarrassed.

James glanced at the menu for a second and said, "Eh. We had wings last time. What about some nachos or sliders?"

Alan quickly regained his composure at the mention of food and avidly raised his eyebrows. "Nachos sound good."

James always footed the bill on outings such as this. As unwilling as Alan was for hand outs, James always insisted. After the first few years, Alan became used to the gesture and marked it down as one of extravagant friendship.

Kaiya returned with their drinks on a tray. "Here we have two Long Island Iced Teas and two glasses of lemon water." She said with her cheery voice. "What else can I get for y'all?"

Alan looked down at and took a sip of his drink while James told her the order. He knew he should take it easy on drinking until that girl came in, but he needed something to calm his nerves. Kaiya held out her hand for his menu, and for the first time, Alan noticed her face.

He breathed in quickly for a gasp, but there was still some drink left in his throat. He choked and coughed. His knees hit the table as his abdominal muscles contracted into a coughing fit. James got up from his seat and started patting Alan on the back.

"I honestly didn't think he'd be this excited to see you," James looked at Kaiya, amusedly.

Kaiya looked at Alan with concern. "Are you going to be alright?" She asked him and placed her hand on his. The instant her hand met his, Alan's coughing fit curbed enough for a few breaths. He looked at her intense sapphire blue eyes and said with another small cough, "You."

Alan looked at James for some verification that this was, in fact, happening. James, with a cool, composed look on his face, said without falter, "This fine young woman has agreed to go on a date with you, broski."

Alan's eyes widened as he looked back at Kaiya. She smiled wide and shook her head, verifying James' claim. Alan was elated to the point of hyperventilation. The woman he'd been dreaming about for months had, for whatever reason Alan could not tell, agreed to a date with him. His heart pounded hard in his chest, and he just could not stop smiling. James gave him a solid slap of a high-five and a shot of the best scotch in the house. Normally, Alan would have refused a forty four dollar shot, but his mind was currently distracted by the idea of a date from the most beautiful girl on the planet.

# Chapter 4

Four hours and several drinks later, Alan and James planned out what exactly Alan would do on his future date. As it turned out, James had been coming to the bar every night for weeks trying to hook up Alan and Kaiya. With this and the fact that James was entirely more experienced at dating in mind, Alan appreciated his help in the matter of planning the date, even if he hadn't ever kept a relationship longer than half a year. Alan knew James was afraid of commitment, but it did not change his prowess at impressing the women he dated.

As a more intrepid person than Alan, James suggested seeing a horror movie. This idea sat well with Alan, since he did love the whole genre, but uncertainty pushed on the periphery of Alan's mind. He did not know if Kaiya would enjoy a horror movie or, more so, what kind of horror she would find appropriate. Both James and Alan looked through current movie show times and decided it would be best to watch the movie after dinner because that would allow attentions to be more on the movie and each other rather than rumbling stomachs.

"Are you sure we should see horror and not a romantic comedy of some sort?" Alan mused. Romantic comedies weren't necessarily his favorite, but he also wanted to show a more tender side to his movie preferences. After all, this would be his first date in 8 years. He didn't know what sort of protocol came along with the responsibility of showing a girl a good time.

"I'm actually fairly certain horror is a great choice. Nine out of every ten dates I take to horror movies end up successful." James said with a matter-of-fact tone.

Alan did not know what 'successful' meant, but whatever it meant, he wanted this date to be as rewarding as possible. Alan also knew that James was sometimes the type to sleep with many of his dates as soon as possible. Perhaps this is what James meant. Alan shook his head minutely at this thought, making up his mind at that moment to only consider the date a success if Kaiya agreed to another.

"What about dinner? Have you talked to her abo-"

"Way ahead of ya, buddy." James nodded, pointing his finger with a small shake. "Her family is Sicilian, but she really enjoys Japanese culture, since she spent a while in Japan with her family. Take her out for a nice sushi dinner, and ba da bing." James said the last part with his best Italian accent and put all of his finger tips together on one hand. Alan couldn't help but laugh. James never did well at impersonations. This one was particularly bad.

In truth, Alan would have preferred a good Sicilian or Italian restaurant to any sushi place, but if Kaiya loved it that much, he would eat all of the sushi in Denver with her. His mind started to wander toward her, but his daydream was cut short by James saying his name and beckoning with a whistle.

"You're not that drunk, are you?" James interjected. "Because you seem drifty in the eyes, dude."

Actually, Alan had started to feel hazy a while back. But of course, he'd drank more today than he had any other night in the last month and a half at least. "I feel fine," he said, unconvincingly. "I've just been daydreaming a lot." It wasn't altogether untrue, so he didn't feel as though he'd lied to James. Alan sipped on his water for a few seconds before continuing. "I can't seem to get her out of my head, ya know?"

James nodded and noticeably shot a look at Alan's hand. "I never did ask. What happened to your hand?"

For the first time since he'd left home, he looked at the bandage. The blood from his wound had surfaced on the gauze, but it wasn't noticeable at a glance. "I was washing dishes and cut it on a knife."

James, who had taken a drink, choked and spit with laughter, spraying water all over the tabletop. His fit subsided quickly, but he sniggered still as he said, "Don't you only own one knife?" He grabbed several napkins and started wiping away the mess he'd made.

Alan rolled his eyes and smirked. "That's exactly right. It wasn't a good day until you showed up," Alan explained. "I wrecked my bike on the way to being fired. Then I got home, broke my glass door, and cut the hell out of my finger. I was lucky you showed up when you did. I'd have probably ended up killing myself." They shared a laugh, and Kaiya stepped up to the table just as James had finished cleaning up.

"I get off in about ten minutes. Can I sit with y'all until ya leave?" Her voice echoed in Alan's thoughts. His mind was screaming silently at him. *Say yes. SAY YES.*

Jumbled with thoughts, the only response he could muster was an "Uh huh."

James jumped in and assured her that Alan would be more than pleased to have her stay. James, who had stopped drinking over an hour ago, cut off Alan from his steady supply of liquor, and they got back to planning the date. The details had to be hashed before Kaiya got off work. The entire occasion was going to be a surprise, other than following the loose guideline of dinner and a movie.

After much deliberation, it was decided that Alan would take her to the best sushi restaurant in Denver. It also happened to be the most expensive. They would also go to a showing at the IMAX for a horror movie Alan did not know. James seemed confident in its quality, however, so Alan did not argue. Throughout the process, James kept telling Alan not to worry about the cost. Since Alan did not have much money, it seemed completely illogical to not take such an important aspect into account. After all, Alan was currently jobless with a savings that was definitely not impressive, and James knew it.

Right after every detail was settled, from clothing to locations, James added slyly, "Oh, and I'm paying for the whole thing." Alan's eyes widened. There was no way he could accept such generosity.

"You have to be joking." Alan croaked. "I can't accept that. It wouldn't be right."

"And one more thing. You are taking my car, too." James looked unfazed by Alan's gasp of shock. "I just bought it yesterday, so it's got almost no mileage. Take her for a spin down 25." His tone was so relaxed that Alan took it for a joke, at first. He waited for James to come out and say 'just kidding.' A few too many seconds of silence passed, and Alan looked around for a clock and saw it strike midnight.

He spoke quickly, knowing Kaiya could show up any minute. "I can't take your car. I haven't driven in years. All this is too much. I can't accept."

"I'm not giving you the choice, broski." James waved his hand in dismissal. Kaiya approached and sat quietly in the seat next to Alan. "By the way, how much is it going to cost to fix your door?" James inquired, knowing Alan could not refuse the offer any more.

Alan's shoulders slumped. He had been defeated. *But, he thought, how bad could it be to take it?* "Hello again, Kaiya," he said, ignoring James' question. He was not prepared to let him offer to pay for anything more.

"Hiya," she beamed. Her smile pierced Alan's very being. Something was different about it, though. Alan could not quite place what it was. He cursed his willingness to drink. If only he had drunk less, perhaps he would be able to tell what it was. Curiosity itched at the back of his mind, but he decided not to dwell.

"What were y'all talkin' about?" She looked from Alan to James and back, still smiling. The diminished southern accent that had started to show more as the night moved on was much more prominent, now. Alan could not help thinking how absolutely delightful it was to hear it come out.

He smiled wide as she looked back at him and told her about his finger and the happenings beforehand. Her smile faded into a look of concern. "Don't worry, though. It doesn't hurt at all," he reassured her, but Kaiya's expression did not change.

"It's not that," she said, seriously. She took his hand into both of hers. "Do you mean to tell me you cut yourself on the only knife in your entire house?" Alan stared at her blankly. Her flat countenance gave him nothing to read. He began to worry, thinking ownership of only one knife was somehow wrong. She burst into laughter and looked at James. Alan looked at him, too. James convulsed with suppressed laughter with one hand over his mouth. Alan began to chuckle, faintly. He had not expected such a dry sense of humor.

Alan's chuckle quickly turned into a hearty laugh, and James could no longer suppress his laughter. The laughter sustained for a while, catching the attentions of other tables, but the trio paid no mind. After calming, Kaiya caressed Alan's hand softly and asked, "So tell me 'bout your kitty." For a few moments, Alan was distracted by how light and warm her hands were. His fingers tensed, nervously, and he felt hers respond by tightening into an easy hold.

Alan's nerves slackened, and he answered, "My parents got her when I was just a kid. She's always been my buddy. When I had my tonsils out, she laid with me on my bed until I got better. Since then, she's pretty much always slept with me." His eyes grew distant from reminiscence. Kaiya slid her thumb back and forth over his hand, and he blinked. "Anyway," he continued, "She completely ignores me when James is over. It's like she thinks I'm replacing her or something."

"It's true," James added, "She pretty much stays in his room the entire time I'm there. Always has." He and Alan both sipped from their glasses together, unintentionally. Alan, using his hurt hand, had to be careful not to wet the bandage with the condensation accumulating on the thick glass.

"What about you," Alan inquired, "Do you have any animals?"

Kaiya lowered her eyes and furled her brow in frustration. "I'm not allowed to have pets where I live," she said, obviously upset by the idea of being denied companionship.

Alan gripped her hand under his with understanding. "You can come over any time to pet Kipsy, if you want," he said without recognizing any implications his statement might have. Out of the corner of his eye, he saw James start sniggering again. With the realization, Alan raised an eyebrow and glared at James. "No need for a dirty mind."

Kaiya lifted her eyes, but there was no fault in her expression. In fact, she had a wide smile across her face that, to Alan, was the most exhilarating smile to ever be encountered. *Seems like she doesn't mind crude humor*, he thought. "That's awful nice o' you," she said in a soft, low voice. Her southern accent was definitely becoming more prominent, and he loved it more with each word.

Having become distracted by happenings and the sound of her voice, Alan had completely forgotten to ask her about the date. Thinking as quickly as his drunken mind would allow, Alan blurted, "What day would you like to go on that date?" *Smooth, Alan*, he thought, *real smooth.*

James folded his arms and leaned back into his chair. He really had put his all into landing this date for Alan. For that, Alan would be singing his praises for the next few decades. Kaiya's cheeks flushed pink. Her gaze went skyward with thought, and she hummed with concentration.

"Well," she started, "I have the next three days off, so when would you want to?"

Alan considered for a moment. He vaguely recalled having plans the next day. His brow furled with concentration, and he tapped his temple. The tap, tap, tap soon sounded a gong in his brain. He had almost forgotten about the appointment he had made with the glass company but had absolutely no other plans. He stopped tapping his temple and looked smugly at Kaiya. He inquired about Tuesday, and they decided it would work best for both of them.

Alan glanced at James. His chin was resting on his chest, and his eyes were closed. Alan looked at the clock behind the bar. It was only a quarter to one. "James," Alan raised his voice slightly. Not so much as a twitch. "James," Alan said, a bit louder. Nothing.

Alan looked back at Kaiya. She smiled, knowingly, and they both stood up. Alan walked around the table and put his hand on James' shoulder. At his touch, James jerked awake and said with a start, "I don't want burritos."

Alan and Kaiya laughed, and Alan patted James' shoulder. "It's time to go home, buddy," Alan said in earnest. He did not want to leave. His entire being wanted to remain here alongside Kaiya and just be. Responsibility always reigned, though. James stood groggily and yawned while stretching his arms high toward the ceiling. The yawn was long, and James smacked his lips afterward. Alan noticed the bloodshot redness in his eyes. *He must be exhausted.*

"What were you guys laughing at?" James asked, curiously. He blinked and lazily moved his red eyes from Alan to Kaiya. Once again, they tittered and exchanged glances. Alan grabbed James' chubby cheeks and pinched a little.

"You don't have to get burritos, if you don't want them." Alan jested. He let go of James' face, and James let out a long sigh.

"I was talking in my sleep, wasn't I?" James asked, sheepishly. His puffy cheeks brightened with embarrassment.

Alan rested a hand on James' shoulder. Speaking to Kaiya, he said, "James, here, used to fall asleep at work and have full on conversations with customers before waking up."

Kaiya let out a snort of laughter. James shrugged his shoulders and mused, "Hey, now. I've gotten better. Plus, it seemed to make the customers happy sometimes, so why stop?" All three snickered together as if they'd all been good friends for years. Alan noticed how well Kaiya fit in with them, and it made him glad.

After a not-so-drawn-out goodbye, James turned toward the exit and started walking. Alan knew he was giving them a chance to be alone together for a short amount of time. Alan scratched the back of his head nervously and looked at Kaiya.

"I don't think I ever got your number." He said. He could feel his ears turning red. This was the very first time in his life he had ever asked a girl for her number. But she had already agreed to a date. Why was he so nervous?

Kaiya touched his arm and said, "Oh, yeah. Probably important." She grabbed the pen from her waist pocket and a napkin. She scribbled her phone number onto the napkin and lifted it to her lips. Her ruby red lipstick left a perfectly shaped mark on the napkin. At once, the Alan noticed what had been different about her smile. She had put on lipstick.Kaiya handed him the napkin and beamed. As he took it, he saw how clean and beautiful it was for such a quick jot. *Is everything about this girl amazing?* He slipped it into his inside jacket pocket.

Without any warning, she hugged him around the middle. Instinctively, he wrapped his arms around her and held her to him. Her body was soft, supple. She pressed her face into his chest and squeezed him a little tighter. He noticed just how much shorter she was compared to him. From here, the fragrance of her perfume was overwhelming. Just as he started wanting to hold her closer, she let go. She straightened her outfit and said, "Thank you so much. I'll see you Tuesday."

# Chapter 5

The drive back to Alan's house was uneventful by comparison to James' hazardous display from before. James dropped Alan off, and they exchanged farewells. The street to one side was blazoned by the car's headlights. The street was so empty of life, but the neighbors were usually asleep by now. Still, the apparent desolation was eerie to him. The only sound was the quiet hum from the new engine of James' car. Alan watched the car ease away from him. As it rounded the corner, the street became dark and even more lifeless. There was no breeze, and the night sky had only a few visible stars. Times like these made Alan wish he lived in the countryside. The stars always fascinated him, but the city lights polluted the sky with dense haze.

Alan studied the sky for a few more minutes. Although the street was dark, the ambient light from nearby convenience stores made the thin clouds glow. The moon was a mere sliver and was almost unnoticeable behind one particularly thick cirrus cluster. The clouds' pale yellow luminescence filled the sky. As Alan's eyes began to adjust, the street, too, brightened to an assortment of warm and dull greys.

He turned to look at his house. The dark grey paint seemed even greyer in the night. Though the window, he could see Kipsy's yellow eyes reflect the glimmer eerily. The rest of her body was masked by shadows that played on her black fur. This gave the illusion of two ghastly, fiendish eyes in straight from a Wes Craven movie, but her long flickering tail had a pearly white tip and swished back and forth, giving away her benevolent nature. She sat on her perch, seemingly awaiting his return. He approached the door, and saw her eyes follow him.

Alan unlocked the door, opened it, and stepped through. He heard the soft patter of Kipsy landing on the floor from her perch. Flicking the light on, he closed the door and felt her head butt against his leg. She weaved between his legs and mewed softly with pleasure at his arrival. He scooped her into his arms, flipped her over gently, and scratched her belly. She purred so violently her entire body shook. Her eyes became slits, and she nestled into the crook of his arm.

"Are you ready to go to bed, baby girl?" He asked, scratching behind her ear and massaging her cheek. She let out a soft chittering meow and nipped his hand lovingly. He set her down and let his hand flow over her back as she moved toward the hallway. He turned the light back off and followed her down the corridor to his bedroom with his mind's eye. He heard the door creak with her entrance and the faint blue glow from his alarm clock illuminated his path. In the glow, he could make out the silhouette of Kipsy on his bed.

"Let me change out of this suit and get a new bandage going, alright?" He looked at her for a minute, but she didn't move or meow. He didn't even bother turning on the light before crossing the room to his bed. Her eyes followed him to and fro while he undressed and tucked the suit back into its bag. He decided that it should take residence in his own closet, which hardly had anything. With his closet now looking less barren, he sat in the office chair in front of his desk and undid the bandage.

Dried blood flaked off of his skin and clung to the gauze. Alan looked closely at the opening in his skin. The light was just enough to see that a nice thin clot layer had formed and held the cut together. All around, he thought he had done a pretty nice job at fixing himself up. Instead of a full blown gauze-laden bandage, he wrapped an adhesive bandage firmly around his finger.

Kipsy took cue to get off the blanket and sat staring while Alan flung it high over his queen bed. "I think we're ready," he said, flopping himself down and closing his eyes. Without moving, Kipsy meowed loudly. He opened one eye and knew precisely why she was upset. He hadn't given her a goodnight kiss. She absolutely could not sleep without first having a goodnight kiss. "What a spoiled cat you are," he smiled. She meowed at him. He gave her a kiss on the nose. Her nose was cool and moist to touch, and he smiled. That feeling was one he absolutely loved.

Satisfied, Kipsy circled in place on his chest and came to rest in a nice curled ball right under his chin, purring softly. He carefully reached over to turn off his alarm only to realize it was already off. *That must be why I slept through this morning.* No longer able to fight sleep, Alan's bleary eyes closed, and he immediately fell into a blissful slumber.

In his dreams, Alan usually found himself in a far off place with otherworldly creatures that he would defeat in some way or other. This one was different than usual. He became ethereal, ghostly. His physical body remained asleep on the bed, but Alan's consciousness was now extracorporeal. He looked down on himself. Kipsy still lay in a perfect ball of fluff on his chest. For only a moment, he looked on at his body somehow tethered by a natural attachment to himself. But his disembodiment intrigued him to carry on deeper into the mental fabrication. He never stayed put in his other dreams, so why should he stay in this one? He turned, and his particulate form passed through the wall of his house. He winced with pain, as though the wall itself was squeezing every atom that comprised him. Soon enough, he was on the other side, and he walked to the sidewalk.

Alan's eyes went skyward, and he was dazzled by the flowing rainbow of lights. Vaguely, he recalled knowing the name of such a beautiful sight. But such memories came from eons ago, and he could hardly remember. The lights danced with each other in a ballet of pirouettes and glissades. He wanted to reach out and touch them. He did, but there was no arm to extend. He could feel its existence. It was there. He looked down. His body was not visible, either. The pavement below him was completely visible, but he could feel nothing of the concrete on which he stood. Now, he was thoroughly confused. *What is going on?*

Despite his confusion, he continued. Alan walked to the end of the street. As he crossed the next side street, a car rounded a corner. He threw up his arms to protect himself, but the car negotiated through his body without resistance. Again, he felt the pain he had with the wall. As with the wall, the pain subsided as soon as the car had gone completely through him. Without delay, he walked on to Alameda and watched several cars pass. Despite the light from the sky above and stores all around him, everything seemed dim and dull as though he watched through a veil or filter.

Behind him, he heard a familiar chattering meow. Slowly, he turned. Kipsy stood a few feet behind him. She sat on her haunches and stared straight through his being.

It was as though she could tell he was there but not how far away he was. Alan crouched down and tried to call out to her, but his voice failed him. He could feel his lips move in sync with his inner voice, yet no words formed at their touch.

Kipsy let out another meow of longing. She stood up and pranced down the sidewalk toward Colorado Boulevard. Her tail swished back and forth with its own mind. Alan tried to follow her, but his movements were suddenly sluggish by comparison. Every step was strenuous. Trying desperately to keep up, he waved his nonexistent hands in a swimming motion.

His efforts did nothing to enhance his movement. He watched as she started to cross the street, her black sleek fur a disguise amongst the asphalt. Two cars were coming from that direction. Alan tried to call once more. Still nothing came. He wanted nothing more than to have those cars notice his best friend. He willed them to stop with every fiber of his being.

But they sped up. Kipsy stopped mid-lane and looked back at where he stood. She sat and licked her front paw serenely. The car closest to the curb passed straight over her. A dull thud filled Alan's ears and heart. He could not see properly, but he knew what had happened. As quickly as this form would allow, he walked over to her now lifeless, crumpled body. Her once vibrant yellow eyes were dim.

Alan's own inability crushed his spirit. Now kneeling, he put his airy fingers on her body but felt nothing. No heartbeat. He didn't even feel her fur between his fingers as he tried to grasp it. His cry of despair rang out in his ears. No one but he could hear the dismay. No one would care here. Alan was alone, now. He yelled at the top of his lungs and yelled and yelled.

Alan opened his eyes. His throat was dry and scratchy, and his breaths came in heavy rasping gasps of the dry Denver air. Frantically, he looked down to see Kipsy still on his chest. He rested his head back on the pillow and swallowed hard. Kipsy was warm and breathing lightly. For a few minutes, he watched her stomach rise and fall with each of her tiny breaths.

The dull blue light of his alarm clock flashed 12:00, so he looked at his watch, not remembering it had broken the previous morning. The hands were still stuck at 8:04. *The power must have gone out.* The crack between his window sill and the blackout curtain showed dim dawn light. Alan stroked Kipsy gently. She chattered and rolled onto her back for a belly rub. He scratched her tummy softly and lay contemplatively. He had never experienced a dream like that. It felt real, but all the while he knew it was a dream. It wasn't all around unusual for him to know when he was dreaming, but none of them had ever felt so real. He had also never had such a depressing dream.

After a few minutes thought, Alan decided to go back to sleep. His eyes were still bleary from exhaustion, and his lids grew heavier the longer he thought. He closed his eyes once more and fell fast asleep. He did not dream, or rather he was not aware of any dream. When he woke, Kipsy was no longer on his chest. He yawned widely and sat up, rubbing his eyes as he did so. Between his legs lay Kipsy soft and warm, purring softly.

For several minutes, he remained in that position. She seemed so calm, so serene. Her paws were over her eyes, and she was contorted onto both sides and her back. Alan often wondered how she could possibly sleep like that. It was one of her most favored positions to sleep comfortably. Almost as if she was aware of being watched, she uncovered her eyes and stretched her legs, with the biggest yawn. Her other eye opened to a slit, and she seemed to glare at him. He smiled, bent over, and kissed her cool, moist nose. She protested with another long stretch and got up.

"You're so cute," he simpered.

She peered at him with her yellow eyes. They appeared green in the blue glow from the alarm clock. Her sleek, slender body was outlined and only faintly visible. Even in this low light, Alan could see her undying stare. She wanted him to get out of bed, since he made her get up.

"Alright. Alright. I'm getting up. Happy?"

Kipsy looked unimpressed but gracefully jumped off the bed and waited next to the door. Alan tossed the blanket aside, stood, and turned on the light. He had to cover his eyes to keep from being blinded. Kipsy watched him patiently and occasionally licked her paws to clean her face, while he moseyed about the room looking for clean clothes. Finding none, he looked down at the pile of dirty clothes that had amassed in the corner of his room and realized he had not done laundry yesterday like he had wanted. From the pile, he picked a pair of sweatpants and a baggy cartooned shirt once owned by his father and loaded the rest into a laundry bin.

Alan opened the door and Kipsy trotted down the hallway. He strained to carry the heavy bin to the laundry room, adjacent to the kitchen. Laundry had always been his least favorite chore. Groaning and moaning on the way, he dropped the bin with a thud on the laundry room floor. He had just gotten a load separated and into the washer, when the doorbell rang. *That must be the glass place. I didn't know it was that late.*

Entering the living room, he saw the big company truck through his large picture window that overlooked the street. Kipsy was sat upon her perch keeping watch over all the happenings in the front of the house, chittering and chattering at passersby. Alan opened the door and was greeted by a tall, grizzly of a man with a dark complexion, pronounced jaw, and broad shoulders in a light blue button up shirt holding a clipboard.

"My name is Eimer. We have a work order to install a glass door. Is this the correct place?" The man had a fairly thick accent to match his complexion that Alan couldn't quite place, but his English was impeccable.

"Yep, that was me," Alan replied. "Need me to fill out any paperwork?"

Eimer handed him the clip board and said pleasantly, "If you will, that would be perfect." He grabbed a pen from his breast pocket, clicked it, and passed it to Alan. "Where is the door, sir?"

Alan had been distracted momentarily by the paperwork and had forgotten to tell him. "Oh, urm. It's around back. I'm sure you'll see it. Oh, and I know I was quoted $2600, but can you see what you can do to make it a bit lower? I'm pretty strapped for cash at the moment."

"Thank you, sir. Do you mind if I step inside?" Eimer gestured kindly with his hand, and Alan affirmed. Eimer walked purposefully through the house to the dining room and assessed the door. Alan followed dutifully, scribbling information down as quickly as he could manage while trying to remain legible.

Eimer came back to the living room and said, "I'll have to look into the pricing, but I'd say we could probably fix this whole thing for around $1300." Eimer pondered and scratched his chin. "It's not so bad, but the door is pretty banged up. That'll be the most expensive part. The track hasn't been damaged whatsoever, but we will still have to replace it to match the new door. All around, I'd say it could have been much worse." Eimer looked at Alan, who had finished the form, and took the clipboard back.

Alan nodded and conceded, "Thank you, Eimer. I appreciate it. But I'll get out of your way. You guys have free reign." Eimer went back to the dining room, opened the screen door, and started taking measurements. Alan sat on the love seat and turned on the television to keep busy. Kipsy still sat on her perch, chirping incessantly at the commotion outside. From the love seat, Alan could see through the archway into the dining room to watch over Eimer and his two helpers. Through the window, he could watch the entire western end of the street and most of his front yard.

# Chapter 6

The crew of workers finished installing the door after only thirty minutes of clanging and hammering. Kipsy kept firm watch over the front yard, while Alan glanced at the back door every few minutes. It was early in the afternoon, but it still felt like morning to Alan. He was groggy from the strange night he'd had. He had not been able to focus on the television, much. Between keeping an eye on Eimer and thinking about Kaiya, his mind had been completely full. He did not know if he was allowed to send Kaiya a message or phone her, since they had not yet been on their date. Instead, he decided to ask James.

James never worked on Mondays. Something to do with a religious position he held at one time or other. James had at one point been a part of some religion, but that was before Alan had met him. James still took advantage of the perks, though. On days that James did not work, he was often found doing some form of physically laborious activity. Rock climbing was one of his favorites, and Alan frequently enjoyed tagging along to hikes up the Rockies in search of a good rock wall whenever they shared a day off. Today was one of those days. James' responses grew rapidly more intermittent as the afternoon progressed, and Alan did not doubt he had found some sort of challenge to face.

Being an incredibly shy person made Alan always feel the need to work up to a question he wanted to ask of someone, even James. Otherwise, he felt as though he would somehow take advantage of their friendship.

Without help from James, Alan could be as clueless as a squirrel with an acorn in the middle of the ocean. Therefore, he did not mind waiting to ask or for any response James might give.

Passing time was usually easy for Alan. He always considered himself to be a professional procrastinator. However, anxiety about the upcoming date had taken root in his thoughts, which made time seem to crawl by at a snail's pace. He had tried playing games, searching for more job opportunities, and even unsuccessfully tried to nap once the back door was finished. His disquiet grew with each passing minute.

At last, Alan found his tension eased by James knocking on the front door. Once again, Alan had been in the laundry room. James seemed to be the only person who ever knocked. The button for the doorbell was not unnoticeable, but it was a quirk of James' that Alan found to be endearing. Alan often pondered whether James' age, being 11 years older than Alan, or his fanciful upbringing was the root cause to his insistence on knocking. Alan once asked why James chose to knock, but his only response was a shrug of dismissal. Perhaps he was as clueless as Alan.

Alan opened the door to James who wore a perfectly devious yet smug smile. Alan immediately knew he had been up to something and did not know whether he would enjoy whatever James had devised or regret involvement entirely. Nevertheless, Alan had felt bored since waking up and could easily go along with anything James had planned. No words were spoken. Alan merely kissed Kipsy on the nose in farewell, grabbed his keys, and the two were off.

"What are you planning on wearing to your date?" James queried after a long silence in his car.

Alan, who had considered his father's suit again but did not want to seem tacky or dress up too much, shrugged off the question with an, "I don't know."

"Good," said James. "That gives me options." Alan looked at James out of the corner of his eye. He knew this tone. Alan had not dressed for an occasion which meant meeting people, yet here he was, sitting in the passenger seat, regretting his life decisions. But James also did not have the sheen of perspiration that usually accompanies physical activity. *What is he planning?*

Alan swallowed his disapproval and inquired, "Where're we gonna go, then?" Wherever it was, he did not have much choice in the matter, now. The point of no return had long passed.

"You and I are going on a little trip," James said. He stroked his nonexistent beard and shot Alan a look. "It's good you didn't wear nice clothes, though. We are probably going to get a bit dirty."

Alan, now perplexed by the thought of anything being dirty about buying dress clothes, scratched the back of his head, nervously. Without missing a beat, James said, "Don't be nervous. This is going to help you out tomorrow. Give you some confidence."

Alan was moderately relieved by this. He did not want James to spend any more money than he already had. Plus, he had already taken $450 during the ride home the previous night for what James had referred to as 'date expenses.' No matter how many times Alan had asked, James never elaborated.

James drove for a long while, first up I25 then east on I70 until the mountains surrounded them. Snow started to float gently downward and was pelted out of the way by the speed of the car. Large flakes fell steadily harder until the roads and mountainsides were dusted in white.

The paved road onto which they exited wound steeply up the mountain side. The view from here was breathtaking. They rounded a particular bend, and the entire city of Denver and all of its suburbs could be seen clearly. James pulled off into a small dirt parking area and got out. Alan followed suit, and they sat on the hood of the car, now speckled with fine, powdery snow.

"I brought you up here because I wanted to talk to you about something, and I find it easier to think when I'm climbing." James went around to the trunk of his car and pulled out two seventy five foot coils of rope, several different carabiners, and a few other things of which Alan did not recall the names. James walked to the edge of the overhang where they parked and looked over the edge. "This looks good," he nodded.

James tied the rope through a locking carabiner and attached it to a metal loop under his car. He handed Alan the other coil of rope and locking carabiner. Alan repeated the process of tying the rope as he had many times before, and they threw the other end of the rope over the side.

Alan looked over the edge and became a little queasy. He had never been a fan of heights, and up until now, the only climbing he had done with James had a start point on the ground and had almost always been indoors. "Are you sure this one is safe in the snow?" Alan asked. Alan always had faith in James. He was strong, capable, and intelligent. They'd known each other for almost five years. Ever since the beginning, they had been the best of friends. Alan knew that, out of everyone on this planet, he could rely on James most, but that did not ease his thoughts.

James tossed Alan a harness and said, "Of course not, but let's try, anyway." James harnessed himself to the rope and started the descent. Alan, full of trust, did the same. As they slid down their ropes, they focused hard on placement of holds that would be sturdy enough to support their weight. The descent was, after all, the easiest part of the entire journey. The snow continued to fall like tiny feathers around them. It was good they both were used to this sort of weather, but Alan acknowledged the luck in the lack of breeze. Any sort of wind would have halted any climbing.

They came to a full stop about three quarters of the way down the rope and prepared for ascent. Alan stared at James for a few seconds. James poised readily. His face was etched with a determined smile that gave Alan inner strength. Alan had absolutely no idea what James could possibly want to talk about that brought them all the way out here, but the esteem Alan saw in him at this moment removed any qualms Alan had.

Alan glared at the summit with resolution. He and James took hold of the rock face and started the climb. James made climbing look easy. He hardly had to stop to search for foot or handholds. Alan tried desperately to keep pace, but his hands were clumsy. It seemed as though each place he grasped was wrong. *Maybe he wants me to be sure of myself.*

James stopped about twenty feet above him. Alan watched as James grabbed the rope and leaned back to look at him. "Everything okay down there?" James called. His voice bellowed off the cliff wall and echoed in Alan's ears.

"Sure," Alan yelled at the top of his lungs. The echoes of his own voice surrounded him, and he noticed how uncertain he had sounded with each resound. His muscles felt as though they were on fire. In his mind reverberated the thought, *just one more step*. He looked over his shoulder and saw the end of the rope. He hadn't even gone ten feet.

"It's all good. Just take your time, buddy," James reassured. He clung to the rocks effortlessly and looked around to the vast city of Denver. Alan climbed on, invigorated by James' confidence in him. His will to make James proud forced his muscles to carry his weight up to meet James. It felt like hours before he was able to look James in the eyes. Alan panted hard and fast. His heart pounded in his chest, and a stitch was starting to form in his side. Riding his bicycle was child's play compared to this climb.

James had found a small shelf Alan didn't notice on the way down. It was only the size of a dinner plate, but it seemed sturdy enough for a person. James gestured for him to rest there, and he did so. Alan's legs did not hurt at all, but the rest of his body ached intensely.

"Did you eat today?" James asked him, concernedly. With a hefty sigh, Alan nodded and leaned his head back against the wall to close his eyes. Words were failing him at the moment. Every ounce of energy he had left was focused on breathing. "Well, you look like death, bro. Here eat this." Alan opened one eye. In James' hand lay what looked like a granola bar.

Alan eyed it carefully and queried, "What exactly is it?"

"It's something a buddy of mine and I have been using for a while, now," James looked concerned but determined. "Just try it. I swear you won't die." James pushed his hand a bit closer to Alan. "Tastes like chocolate."

"Alright, fuck it," Alan said. He grabbed the bar, bit off about half, and handed it back to James. The substance was chewy, but it seemed to dissolve in his mouth after only a few seconds. There was hardly any taste at first, but the distinct aftertaste of cocoa appeared after Alan swallowed. Feeling as rested as he probably ever would on this cliff, Alan slid off the ledge. His muscles complained but supported him. He looked back at James and nodded approval.

Again, they set off up the face. Alan did not fall behind this time. His hands found support in each hold. It seemed as though Alan's hands had minds of their own. He glanced at James and saw him lose grip. Alan had never seen James falter in such a way. James' body seemed to lean backwards slowly. His hand grasped at empty air, and his face became a grimace.

Alan reached out a hand to grab hold of James' harness, but he was just out of reach. Helpless, Alan watched as James started to plummet downward. The rope jerked as James' belay loop caught his weight. His body smacked against the face, and several loose rocks tumbled down. For a moment, James dangled, lifelessly.

*He only fell five feet*, Alan thought. Unnerved, Alan rappelled downward to James' side and nudged his arm. It limply swung beside him. Alan looked at the ledge above him. Only fifteen feet remained, but he was not sure he could heave James' weight up that length. Alan grabbed the rope which held James and pulled him closer. Hurriedly, he looped part of the rope through his harness and to James' to keep James securely attached. It only took Alan five minutes or so, but it felt like hours to finally be prepared to keep going. With all the might he had remaining in his legs, he heaved.

To the Grave

James was heavier than Alan expected. Every step up took the wind out of him, but each step drew him nearer to the pinnacle. Once again, his muscles were on fire with pain. He couldn't stop. He couldn't lose momentum. He needed to get to the top. No thoughts entered his mind but those of reaching the car and driving James to the hospital. He pushed himself to keep going. *Almost there*, he thought over and over.

An eternity passed before Alan reached the top. His whole body screamed at him with displeasure. He mantled the ledge and pulled himself and James over. As he stood, his legs wobbled with weakness, and he had to catch himself on the hood of James' car. He quickly unbuckled his and James' harnesses and threw them to the side. He could not afford taking the time to put them into the trunk.

Alan could no longer carry James. His legs and arms were shaking too violently for that. Alan resorted to dragging him around the car. Alan grabbed James under the arms and lifted him into the car with considerable effort. Alan's head began to swim from the strain he'd put on his body, and an ache edged along the back of his head from ear to ear. He fished through James' pockets for the ring of keys and found them. Taking a moment to regain composure, Alan ran back around the car as fast as his tired legs would carry him. Once in the driver's seat, he paused. *Where is the key hole?* Confused, he looked desperately at James. James' once lifeless body started convulsing violently.

Fear flashed across Alan's face, and he whispered, "Oh, shit." He muttered this repeatedly as he recalled a snippet in the back of his mind from the night before. *How did he start this thing?* Alan stabbed the start button with his finger harder than necessary. The engine hummed into life.

Alan shifted the car into reverse, peeled backward, slammed it into drive, and tore out of the dirt parking area, rocks spraying behind them. The car lurched left or right around the tight, winding turns. Without regard for oncoming traffic, he sped around turns by cutting lanes. Once he was on I70, he revved the engine to its full potential. It roared, mightily, and the powerful V12 propelled them forward. He watched the speedometer go up swiftly. 40, 60, 80, 100, 120.

Scenery passed by them in a blur. The car bulleted by the few cars on the highway and weaved in and out of traffic without trouble. 140. The engine was letting out the high pitched whine of overexertion. 150. The large green signs were becoming too difficult to read, but Alan knew precisely where he was going. He pushed the brake, and the car tottered forward. He pulled off I70 and onto 6$^{th}$ avenue.

Alan stomped the gas again, and the car responded, loyally. Without hesitation, the speedometer shot upward. There was significantly more traffic on 6$^{th}$. He wound through a particularly large group of cars as quickly as he could. As soon as he had passed them, flashing red and blue lights appeared in the rear view mirror.

"Fuck me!" Alan screamed out. He did not stop. He was so close. Tears started to form in his eyes. He blinked them away, hard. He slowed and exited onto Union Boulevard and turned into St. Anthony's Hospital. He stopped and got out of the car. The police car stopped inches from his bumper, and the officer stepped out of his cruiser and put his hand on his tazer.

"Sir, I need you to put your hands on your head," the officer announced.

"I can't do that. My friend is dying." Alan pleaded. He ran to the other side of the car, and looked at the officer with tears streaming down his face. The officer hesitantly took his hand off the tazer and rushed over to help Alan. Together, they lifted James out of the car. The door behind them opened, and several nurses and doctors rushed out with a gurney. James was placed on top, and one of the doctors checked his pulse.

"He's critical," She said. Her voice only came in a high pitched whine, to Alan. He stood back from the crowd of people. There was nothing more he could do, but his own uselessness broke over him. Tears still falling, he watched the doctors and nurses take care of his mentor and friend.

# Chapter 7

The waiting room was cold. Outside the large picture windows, lights lit up a large parking lot past which darkness reigned over the vastness. Large white snowflakes still fell through the glows of the lights around the parking lot. Inside, bright fluorescent light panels dotted the ceiling. One sizable portion of the room was dedicated to seating, and the other was a wide reception area. In the seating area, a few dozen chairs lined the walls and formed two rows in the middle. Alan sat as close to the reception desk as he could have managed. A small corner chair, separated from the rest of the row by a side table stacked with magazines and a half empty box of generic brand tissues. A clock on the opposite wall from Alan's seat ticked loudly and incessantly.

About a dozen other people accompanied Alan in the waiting room, some sniffling or showing some other sign of sickness and others waiting for loved ones. He cradled his head in his hands and stared at the floor. This was the way he had remained since his arrival at the hospital. He had been forcefully told by several nurses that he could not go in with James to the intensive care unit. Several hours had passed since, but Alan did not know how many. It was dark, now.

Over and over, he played out in his mind what could have happened to make James fall as he did. In his mind's eye, the scene came in slow motion. The black dots on the cream colored tile danced in his vision to form the shapes of his memory. Alan could see James lose grip; his hand grasping for a hold but catching nothing. Even in thought, Alan could not bring himself to look James in the face. No matter how many times the scene played over in his head, he couldn't find any reason James might have fallen the way he did.

Alan wondered if he could have done anything differently. Perhaps he could have climbed faster. James could not have been that heavy. Alan shook his head. He had been unable to hold back tears. While at first they came in waves, they only dribbled every few seconds, now. Each one plopped on the floor and burst into thousands of even tinier droplets upon impact.

He closed his eyes, and the movie played again in his head. This time, he saw James falling. His feet left the rock face, and he toppled backward. His body turned sideways with the last contact from the cliff. The rope became taut and brought him back into the rocks, slamming his head and shoulder against them. He watched James bounce upward from tension on the rope. His torso folded obscenely and sprang back into relative normality. Each arm swung beside him.

"Mr. Po," a nurse called from the emergency room door. Alan's ears perked. Jerkily, he lifted his head to look over. A short pudgy woman stood holding the door open and looked around the room, intently. "Mr. Po," she called again.

Alan stood quickly and stumbled. His legs were still weak from the exertion through which he had put them, and, in his anticipation, he had completely forgotten. He caught himself on the chair and raised his hand to indicate he was coming. As rapidly as his tired legs would carry him, he walked across the long room and followed the nurse into a small office area behind the reception desk.

She motioned for him to sit, and he was greeted by a different woman than the one he had seen when he first arrived. A smiling petit black woman with the most impressive afro Alan had ever seen in his life sat at the desk behind the window. He stopped, stunned for a moment and marveled its size. *It must be three or four times the size of her head.* Alan shook off his surprise and sat in the chair issued to him, folding his arms across his stomach.

The woman across from him looked at her computer screen and back at Alan. "Your name is Alan Po?" Her voice was squeaky but pleasant. Alan nodded and clenched his jaw with anticipation. "And you were here upon Mr.…" She glanced back at the computer screen, "Mr. James Gatre's arrival?" Again, Alan nodded. "Mr. Po, I need to ask you if Mr. Gatre has any family to contact."

Alan opened his mouth to speak, but only a raspy breath-like noise escaped his lips. He cleared his throat a few times before continuing. "It's actually G-ah-tree," he corrected. "James' father lives in the Cayman Islands, and his mother lives in upstate New York," he croaked. "I don't have any of their contact information with me."

The woman hummed in understanding and looked back at her computer screen. "G-ah-tree. Got it. What sort of relationship do you have with him?"

"I'm his best friend," Alan muttered. This sounded like the sort of conversation he heard on doctor shows right before they announced a patient's death. It made him incredibly uneasy.

"Alright, sir. Do you know of any other relatives he might have or someone we can contact on his behalf?" Her voice was starting to edge on concern.

Alan shifted his gaze downward in concentration. "I know he had a lawyer that handled his money and stuff. Maybe him?" Alan scratched the back of his head, nervously. "I think his name is Steven Maher. M-a-h-e-r. Or is it M-e-y-e-r? I can't really remember." Alan's face screwed up in puzzlement.

"Alright. Thank you, sir. If you will, please follow Regina. She will take you where you need to go." Alan took notice of the small woman's surprisingly big hands as she pointed at the nurse Alan had followed over to her desk.

Alan took one last look at the lady's strikingly massive afro, turned, and followed Regina through the emergency room door. They walked through many corridors with big signs. Each sign had a colored label with words like 'radiology.' Regina turned down a hallway with the indicator 'morgue' on it, and Alan's heart sank deep into his stomach.

His mind started racing with the possibility that James was actually gone. *No*, he thought, *it can't be true*. He'd seen other words on the sign but had focused so much on 'morgue' that he could not recall what the others were. His feet became unbearably heavy. Each step dragged along and felt automatic, mechanical.

They came up to large double doors, and Regina pressed a small button next to a sign bearing a handicap symbol. Both doors opened mechanically, and they continued through into an even colder, dank room that smelled unusually and sickeningly sweet. On the opposite side from the door was a wall filled with large steel doors about two feet by two feet. In the middle of the room stood a man and a woman both dressed in long white coats. These two turned to look as Regina and Alan entered. With one long look around at all of the instruments in allotted spots on tables and shelves, Alan could tell his worst fear had been realized. They were in the morgue. *No. This can't be real.*

The woman in the white coat approached him and held out her hand. "Hello. My name is Caitlyn. First I'd like to offer you my condolences. We're all very sorry for your loss."

Alan did not look at her. Instead, his focus lay on the table which stood between the two doctors when they had walked in. *No.* On the top was a stocky, muscular man with a round face. More tears welled in Alan's eyes. *This has to be a dream.*

He couldn't take his eyes off of James, but he still did not want to accept that this could have happened. James was a fighting man. If anyone, he would pull through. With one sob, he swallowed hard. The female doctor, seeing his distress, touched his arm and said, "I truly am sorry." Her loss for words was made evident by an enduring awkward silence that filled the room. The only noise came from the occasional short sniff from Alan.

For several heart-tearing minutes, Alan stood, eyes affixed to the man whose jokes and smile had brightened almost every day of the last six years of his life. His brain could not seem to wrap itself around this situation. He could not believe that this could happen. James would never smile or joke again. Standing among strangers and feeling utterly alone, Alan fought the recognition of mortality until something inside him broke. First, he had lost his parents. Now, his best friend was gone and could never return. He shook and lowered his head. The nurse, Regina, stooped slightly and looked into his face.

"It can't be true," Alan whispered softly. One last bodily sob and Alan looked up at the female doctor. Her hand still rested on his arm. "How did he die?" Alan asked. His voice was shaky, and a lump started to form in his throat.

The man standing next to James stepped forward. "It seems as though his death was caused by a brain hemorrhage, but there are several fractures along his cervical vertebrae." His voice was cold and emotionless, a low monotone which screamed indifference. He continued, "Based on what we were told upon his admittance, he suffered head trauma from his fall on the cliff. This is likely the root cause."

Alan immediately hated that man. He wanted to grab something, anything, and throw it at the man's face. Alan's muscles tensed in fury, fists clenched, teeth gritted. Promptly, every taunt that had ever been said to Alan came bubbling up from his memory. Alan wanted to make the man hate himself as much as Alan hated him. He opened his mouth to shout these spiteful insults, but his voice cracked and crumbled into nothing. It wasn't the man's fault, and Alan had never been the type of person to let out rage on someone else, especially someone he didn't know. He let out a long sighing breath.

"Am I-" His voice cracked. He cleared his throat and tried again. "Am I able to leave?" Alan muttered through his despair. He did not want to be in this hospital, any more. The smell, that stupidly sweet smell, ate away at his insides and made him want to vomit. He wanted to run away from this place and never return.

The female doctor took her hand off his arm and said quietly, "Of course." Her voice was sweet, but Alan could tell she was just as empathetic as the man in white. Her feeble attempt at consolation only validated his will to leave more. No one in this place could possibly understand how he felt.

He missed Kaiya. He longed for her presence. Being around her had been the absolute happiest he had ever been in his life, and now he needed that. He turned, abruptly, and left the room. The long empty corridors were even more ominous when walked them alone. His heavy footsteps rang out as he walked. Choruses of humming and buzzing from machines of all kinds filled his ears. Soft intermittent beeping of heart monitors came from a few rooms he passed.

On his way out, he only saw a few people, mostly nurses in pale aqua scrubs. Back through the emergency room doors, Alan was met by a stately, balding man in a suit. "Why, hello. You must be Alan Po." The man was almost an entire foot shorter than Alan and spoke eloquently.

"I am," Alan confirmed, shortly. He was not in the mood to speak with anyone else.

Alan tried to step around the man, but he spryly sidestepped and said, "Ah, ah, ah. Not so fast. You and I must speak on the subject of James Gatre." The man's voice was zealous and fanciful, so Alan reluctantly conceded. It did not seem like the man would let him pass, anyway.

"Alright," Alan lamented. "What about James?"

"Splendid," The man said enthusiastically. "Now, I know it's been a troublesome time. Troublesome, indeed. But the fact of the matter is that James Gatre had a sizeable estate, and he wished for you to have it upon his untimely death."

Alan stared blankly at the man. He blinked. "What do you mean?" he asked.

"Well, now, I can't go into too many details here," the man handed Alan a small business card with 'Steven Maher – Financial Attorney' on it. Steven continued, "But why don't you come down to my office sometime tomorrow? We will discuss the matter further then, perhaps over a bit of brandy."

Alan looked at the card and back at Steven. He still could not quite comprehend what was happening. His mind was filled with racing fragments of thought which all seemed to collide together and jumble. "Okay," Alan responded, inattentively.

Steven offered a halfhearted sympathetic smile. "Splendid, indeed. That's a good lad," he said. His tone was almost condescending, but in a way that made him sound more concerned than anything else. Briskly, Steven walked around Alan and behind the reception area. Alan supposed he headed toward the desk with the woman with the afro. Alan interlaced his fingers on top of his head and leaned back his head in exasperation. He breathed in deep and closed his eyes.

At that moment, he remembered Kipsy. He looked at the clock in the waiting area to see it was already half past eleven in the evening. He had to get home. Without a second thought, he walked out the front doors and to James' car. The police officer had been kind enough to give Alan a warning. He had been clocked at 113 miles per hour, but the officer only wrote down the warning for 15 over the limit of 65.

Alan had also been requested to come to the station to give a formal statement of what happened. *But I can't do that, right now*. He decided to go the next day after seeing Steven. *I don't think I'll be able to make that date tomorrow*. He stomped his foot, which did nothing but make his leg and foot ache. *Hopefully,* he thought, *Kaiya will understand.* He had faith in her, despite only having actually known her for a single day. She seemed dependable to him.

Alan got into James' car and drove slowly back home. Mentally, he was weary. Alan parked in his driveway for the first time that night. It felt strange to him. This car which once belonged to his best friend now resided in his own lot. Never would James drive it again or feel the gusts blow against his face through its open windows. For a while, Alan sat in the vehicle and cried for this most wonderful of humans with which he had so luckily crossed paths.

In the light of the glowing green instrument panel, Alan could see himself in the rear view mirror. His eyes were puffy. He imagined they were also red, but the light didn't show that. He looked away and got out of the car. He couldn't look at himself any more. He walked inside and was immediately greeted by Kipsy. She did not rub against his legs, as usual. This time, she jumped immediately into his arms and nuzzled her face into his neck. Alan held her close and more tears streamed down his face. He carried her, still nuzzling, back to his bedroom, lay down on top of the covers, and cried himself to sleep.

Alan found himself looking down a long hallway with twelve doors incrementally placed on either side across from one another. Pillars decorated with unknown shapes and figures protruded from the walls. His body moved slowly, and he felt resistance in the air, like wading through water. He came up to the first two doors and opened the one on the left. As the door swung, it fell off the hinges and was swallowed by the blackness on the other side. He wondered what was on the other side of the blackness. He outstretched his arm to push through and found it to be the same ethereal way he remembered in his last dream. He turned his hand over and raised the other, unsure that he was actually in a dream. It felt real, again.

His arm pierced the blackness like a knife and he was pulled through by some unknown force. The other side was a vast open park full of flowers Alan recognized. In fact, this park looked familiar, as well, but he could not place where he would know it. Above him, the night sky glowed with the same aurora he had seen in his other dream. It glowed brighter this time. Among the burning and dancing lights, a single golden speck spun around above him. It spun faster and faster in tighter circles, until the speck appeared to remain still among the swirling lights. He saw the speck flicker gently and shoot straight into the sky and out of sight. Alan wished the speck luck on its travels. Though, something in him tore away at the moment the speck left. A new emptiness started to fill him as the speck grew farther away.

Alan turned around. He could see the doorway was still open, but the black film was gone. He passed back through and into the hallway once more. Across the hallway, he tried the door across from him. This door did not budge. Alan looked back down the hallway but was at once awakened by the sound of the doorbell.

# Chapter 8

Alan's eyes flickered open. His left arm was tingly from lying on his side all night, and he noticed Kipsy was balled up right next to his neck. She was purring softly but did not wake when Alan rolled onto his back. Alan had no idea if the door bell had been part of his dream or not. *What a strange dream it was.* He looked at the dim blue alarm clock on his bedside table. It was only 6:32 a.m.

For a few minutes, Alan remained still. His arm slowly regained feeling and lost its prickling sensation. His mind went over the previous day, again. He had been so distraught by James that he had forgotten to contact Kaiya. *She probably thinks I forgot about her*. Alan's heart started to feel heavy again.

Despair was not usual for him. Even after his parents had died in a plane crash while on their way back from a business trip to Chicago, Alan had recovered from his grief fairly quickly. This felt different, though. It was a deeper pain than Alan had ever felt in his life. Of course, he had never been very close with his parents. They were frequently called away on business or other errands and left him alone or with a babysitter. But what happened to James had cut him deep. An overwhelming sadness engulfed him, and he buried his face in his pillow, screaming. From the commotion, Kipsy stirred and meowed with irritation.

Alan lifted his head from the pillow to see her bright yellow eyes staring straight into his. She was standing right next to his head. He raised an eyebrow, and she turned slowly toward the edge of the bed. The doorbell sounded once more, and Alan shrugged.

"I might as well get up. Huh?" Kipsy looked at him over her shoulder, and yawned. "I don't get how you're so tired. You sleep all day and all night." She jumped down from the bed and waited by the door. Alan got up and realized he had not undressed the previous night. With another complacent shrug, he opened the door and walked into the living room.

Although he was curious as to who might be ringing his doorbell this early in the morning, Alan did not mind having been roused from such a strange dream. Through the picture window, he could see day had not broken quite yet. A purple, orange, and yellow sunrise had crested on the horizon and made beautiful the sky above with trickles of light edging over the clouds. The view was absolutely spectacular. Alan looked into the peephole to see two men in black suits standing in front of his door. *Now, that's unusual.* He furled his brow and opened the door a crack.

"Can I help you gentleman?" Alan asked, politely. He noticed a long white limousine parked by the curb.

"Mr. Po. Will you please come with us?" The man on the right was the one who spoke. His voice was deep and gravelly. But, his voice did not match his stature. As the shorter of the two, he was also much skinnier.

Alan poised himself a little taller. "What is this about?" he inquired, noticeably less polite this time.

The man on his left spoke this time. "Our employer would like to have a word with you, please." His voice was high pitched and screechy. It reminded Alan of nails on a chalkboard. He wondered how such a burly, tall man could sound so mousy.

Alan was unsure of what was going on, but he followed the two men out to the back of the limousine while keeping an eye on both of them. The tall burly one opened the door for Alan and motioned for him to get inside. The interior was luxurious. The seats were made of soft tan suede. On the side opposite the door was a long row of seats leading all the way up to the front portion of the car. As Alan's eyes followed the row, he noticed an older man in a flamboyantly maroon suit with a bright red and pink tie and large round sunglasses sitting on the far side of the vehicle smoking a cigar.

"Hello, Alan," the man said with a puff of smoke from his cigar. "It's been a long time. Come in. Sit down. I'd like to talk to you."

At first, Alan did not know who this man could be. He racked his tired brain for some sort of familiarity, but none came. Nevertheless, he stepped into the limo and sat down next to the door.

"Would you like a glass of champagne?" the strange looking man asked, waving his hand toward a bar Alan could not have seen from the doorway. Alan nodded, and the man poured some champagne into two tall, thin glasses. Without moving any closer to Alan, the man held out the glass for Alan to take.

Alan was forced to get up from his seat to come up to the man. Just as he did so, the limousine moved forward, and Alan fell back into his seat. The man did not budge an inch. Standing once more, Alan moved carefully up to the man and sat a few feet from him. From here, he had a better look at the man, and a queer sense of acquaintanceship sprouted in Alan's mind.

"It's good to see you again, Alan. It seems you haven't changed a bit. Still skittish." The man handed the glass to

Alan, who took it and sipped. The man's voice, too, was starting to pull on a memory in Alan's mind. He knew that voice from somewhere.

Alan's face remained contorted from confusion, and the man shook his head and laughed. "Do you really not remember me?" he chuckled. "I'd had you pinned as a particularly smart fellow. Ah, well. I'm James' father."

"O-o-o-o-oh," Alan burst out. It had been at least three years since he'd seen George Gatre. "The sunglasses really threw me off, and you look much more... uh... tan." George laughed again. "And what's with the two guys? And how did you get here so fast?"

"Well, it's not every day I come up from the Caymans. I wanted a couple chauffeurs." George said, waving his hand in precisely the same way James always had. "You know full well that I have my own private jet. It only takes me seven hours to make this flight. I never wanted to be too far away from my son. Speaking of. These are terrible circumstances to make a visit, though."

Alan looked down. He didn't know what to say to George. That he was to blame for James' death? George poured more champagne into his glass. Almost as though he could tell what Alan was thinking, he said, "Don't worry about it, kid." George's tone was remorseful but kindly. "I wanted to pick you up to ask you about the details of his death. What happened on that mountain?"

Alan looked back at George who had taken off his sunglasses. His eyes were the same hazel as James, but his face was slenderer. George had very little white or grey hair for a man his age. The tinges above his ears were almost perfect enough to have been professionally done, and, for some reason, George's appearance was making him anxious. Alan opened and closed his mouth nervously.

Alan did not want to relive those moments any more than he already had in the hospital, especially to James' father.

George studied Alan's face for a few seconds. He leaned back. Alan could tell George was not a sort of man to have masses of patience, and he felt incredibly intimidated at the moment. Feeling rushed, Alan gulped down the rest of his champagne and started telling George what had happened on the cliff. Occasionally, George would nod with understanding and pour more champagne into Alan's glass. Just as Alan finished recounting, George poured the rest of the champagne bottle into both of their glasses.

"It seems to me that you think this whole situation is somehow your fault," George said after a few seconds to contemplate. He tipped the glass upside down and gulped the rest of his champagne. After smacking his lips, he continued, "I'll have you know I've been to the hospital already. They seem to think he had a stroke, which caused his fall."

Alan peered over his glass at George. It was starting to become difficult to focus, and Alan began to think he'd had too much to drink. "What makes them think that, sir?" Alan asked with slight difficulty.

"It's a bit of a long story, but I'll stick to the details," George began. "It all started when I was a child back in the 60's. As you know, I grew up in Japan until my father brought me here to Colorado. When I was 7, I had episodic seizures. The family doctor couldn't figure out what was wrong, so my father took me to a hospital in Tokyo. Turns out, I was diagnosed to have an arterial disease called Moyamoya." At this, George paused for a moment to set his glass back into the rack from which it came. "Moyamoya causes the carotid artery to shrink. Usually, it only appears in children, but it also seems to be genetic. The fact is no one knows for sure."

Alan was perplexed. He had never even heard of this disease. His brow furled with concentration that usually comes from intoxication, and George continued, "Unfortunately, none of my family history followed me from Japan, and James never appeared to show any signs as a child, so I thought it wasn't ever worth mentioning. This was well before Moyamoya was found to occur in adults around the age of 35."

Alan was still confused as to why George was telling him this. Brow still furled, he asked, "But the doctor told me he died of a brain hemorrhage." Alan did not know why he purposefully left out the doctor mentioning James' head trauma as a possible cause. He just did.

"Yes, and as I've mentioned, I was at the hospital earlier," George interjected. "It seems as though James had a miniature stroke while you two were on a climb and fell. That is according to what you told the doctors and their own deductions. Once he struck his head, it caused a rupture in a cranial artery which caused the brain hemorrhage and, ultimately, his death."

The last part sounded as though George was reciting it out of a book, rather than from memory. Alan's mind still had some trouble piecing together the details, so he asked, "But what does that have to do with you and this mayo thingy?"

A small, sympathetic smile appeared on George's face. "Moyamoya," he corrected, "is often discovered because it causes mini strokes." The smile faded. George shook his head and closed his eyes. A single tear dropped down his cheek and fell into his lap. "It wasn't until today that I found out Moyamoya could occur later in life." He pounded his fist against the lush suede bench seat. "If only I'd known before."

Alan moved a bit closer and placed his hand on George's shoulder. George opened his eyes and looked at Alan. Alan could see the same look on Georges' face as Alan had in the rearview mirror the night before. Seeing the despair and remorse on this man's face made Alan accept his part in James' death.

Alan patted George's shoulder and consoled him, "I thought it was all my fault, too. But James died doing something he loved. I don't think anyone could've done anything different." The words Alan spoke came without cognition. As Alan spoke them, he realized they were completely true. There was nothing Alan or anyone else could have done differently for James. He smiled, and George's sad eyes formed half a smile in return.

For the next hour, they rode around and reminisced over past experiences with James. Some sad, most happy, but all were great memories. When they arrived back at Alan's house, George clapped him on the back with a great hug.

"It's been good to see ya, kid," George said over Alan's shoulder. "I think you should keep the car. It'll be good for you. Something to have of James'. I'll make sure to work it out with the lawyer."

At this, Alan remembered what the lawyer had said the previous day. "Mr. Gatre," Alan requested with an uncertain tone. "James' lawyer told me last night that he left me a bunch of stuff. I don't know why."

George released his hug and held Alan at arm's length. "I imagine it's because he thought so highly of you," he said with a wide smile. "Didn't have any kids or plans to have any. And I think he knew you always wanted a family. You seem like a family man, anyway."

Alan laughed nervously. He had no idea if George was good at guessing or if James had spoken to his father about him often. The two said their goodbyes and George left in the limousine with Alan waving on the sidewalk. The sun had risen considerably since he had been gone, but it was still low and shone a brilliant red-orange through the wispy morning clouds. Still feeling slightly intoxicated, Alan went inside and sat down to greet Kipsy. She curled up in his lap and fell asleep.

Alan took this opportunity to send a message to Kaiya. *A text message will be good enough*, he thought. He knew talking on the phone would end in disaster because he was not drunk enough to be confident in himself, but he desperately wanted to talk to her and see her face. Even something as simple as a dinner date would be a welcome respite to his current mood and situation. She responded almost immediately, which threw Alan off somewhat. He had not expected her to be awake so early in the morning.

They conversed through text for a few minutes. Kaiya did tell him she thought he had forgotten about her. Alan let her know something very important had happened, but he still wanted to take her out that evening. They agreed on a time to meet and decided that a movie was unnecessary. She did, however, still want to see one. Feeling glad at the fact she also wanted to see him tonight, Alan stroked Kipsy's fur and turned on the television for background noise.

Alan and Kipsy remained this way until the sun was bright and high in the sky, which lit the living room well through the large picture window. Alan did not know why Kipsy stayed on his lap that whole time. She was never quite so affectionate. *Maybe she knows. I don't know how she would, but maybe she does.* The sound of a lawn mower starting outside caught both of their attentions. Kipsy rose to stretch quickly and jumped to her perch to check out the dealings outside.

Alan also stood and stretched. A yawn forced itself upon him as he did so. It was time to go see the lawyer and settle the other unfinished business from the previous day. He took a set of clothes from the laundry bin next to the washer and noticed he still had several loads left to do. Not willing to commit to any chores at the moment, he put the thought in the back of his mind and showered.

This was the longest shower he had ever taken in his life. He mostly stood under the hot water to think about everything he had been through in the last few days. How had his life taken such a miserable turn? Alan did not believe in any higher powers, but it appeared they were testing his worth, if they did exist.

Alan stood in the shower for such a long time the water grew cold. Shivering, Alan turned off the water and stepped out. Once his teeth were brushed and he was dressed, Alan set off for the office of Steven Maher. The address on the card was not one he recognized, so he used the GPS on his phone to find his way and took James' car to save time. *I guess it's my car, now.*

Upon arrival, Maher's assistant greeted Alan warmly and informed him, "Mr. Maher is currently with a client, but he will be with you, shortly." Alan sat in one of the provided large leather reclining chairs and waited patiently to be called in.

The wait took barely long enough for Alan to have time to lean back to relax before the door to Maher's office opened and both James' parents, George and Olivia Gatre, walked through. Alan sat upright and stood quickly to meet them both. Olivia, tear trails still visible on her round face, rushed to Alan and hugged him tightly. Olivia had been much more involved with James' life despite living in New York, and Alan had gotten to know her quite well on her frequent holiday visits.

"Oh, Alan," she cried. "I'm so sorry." Alan hugged her back and comforted her. He could feel more tears fall onto his shoulder as the woman cried once more.

"You shouldn't be sorry," Alan told her. "I should be. It seems I've quite ruined the Christmas season for us all." Olivia smacked the back of Alan's head. "Ouch! What was that for?"

She raised her head from his chest, as she was almost a foot shorter, and looked up into his eyes. "This is not your fault at all," she exclaimed through a few tears. "And I will not stand for you blaming yourself. Hear?"

Alan smiled, softly, and let her go. "Yes, ma'am. And I know it isn't," he breathed. It was good to see her. She had been the only motherly figure in his life for over nine years.

Olivia shook her finger in his face with a stern, authoritative look. "You will come see us tomorrow. Hear?" She sounded so forceful, but Alan new it was a play.

"Okay," he chortled. "Are you staying at the Hilton on Colorado Boulevard you usually stay at?" Olivia nodded, and gave him one last hug. Alan shook George's hand, and each of them nodded. Over George's shoulder, Alan saw Maher wave for him to come in. Alan said goodbye to the two and went in.

# Chapter 9

Alan sat comfortably in a plush leather wingback chair. The inside of Maher's office was lavishly decorated with trinkets, many of which Alan could tell were expensive. Most resided on bookshelves which also housed masses of encyclopedic looking law manuals. On the wood panel walls, ten or more plaques were hung. Each one was etched with Maher's name and some sort of award for best this or highest rated that. At the center of it all was a framed degree with 'Universitas Harvardiana' at the top.

Steven Maher was seated in a black desk chair so large it looked to consume the small man. His chair seemed normal behind a massive, magnificent mahogany desk. The desk was organized neatly with small stacks of legal documents, pencils and pens in individual holders, an unblemished plastic mat inside which a calendar lay, and the largest laptop Alan had ever seen. Alan noticed the calendar was nearly black with scribbles of important dates or appointments. Though, Alan could not make out any of the writing from his seat. Alan began to suspect from the size of everything in Maher's office that he may suffer from a Napoleon Complex.

Maher interlaced his fingers and rested his elbows on the desk. "Alright, Mr. Po," he started. His face was hidden by radiant sunlight which blazed through the unshaded window behind him. "Thank you for seeing me today."

Unable to see anything but the silhouette of a man in the afternoon sun, Alan shifted his eyes away from the blinding light and nodded, complacently. Repositioning in his seat, he crossed his leg to appear more businesslike. The wingback chair made Alan feel compressed and surrounded, uncomfortable. As plush as it was, Alan longed for the reclining chair in the lobby. There was nothing welcoming here. Nothing cozy.

"As I've already told you," Maher said, rising from his chair, "James Gatre left you a sizeable estate upon the occurrence of his untimely death." He walked around the mahogany desk to a small round table in the corner beside the door. Three uniquely shaped glass bottles filled with differing shades of brown liquid sat on a glinting silver platter. Maher opened the decanter with the least contents and lifted it to his nose. He took a long, powerful whiff and sighed with pleasure. With metal tongs, he grabbed six pieces of most clear ice Alan had ever seen and placed three in each of two crystal rocks glasses.

Alan stared with one eyebrow raised as this small man brought one glass over to him. "Thank you," Alan said, taking the glass. Alan could smell the alcohol rise from the glass along with a sweet woody fragrance which lay subtly under the pungent fruitiness that Alan associated with the few wines he'd drank in his life. Alan took the minutest of sips and gagged. He tried, and failed, to stifle a cough.

Maher gave a chuckle and smiled, "Not a fan of brandy, I see. No matter. Drink as you wish." Walking back around the desk, he fell back into the giant seat and lifted his glass. "A toast to friends," he beamed.

Alan held his glass high and mentally prepared himself for the upcoming drink. Each lowered their glass to their lips and drank its entirety. Alan was surprised by how smoothly it had gone down. He looked into the glass and wondered how it could be possible. Alan looked back at

Maher whose eyes were closed and lips were moving in a whisper.

Maher opened his eyes and smiled heartily. "Splendid," he said, getting up once more to open one of the drawers in the desk. "James had a vast wealth in the sum of eight million three hundred fifty five thousand dollars and some change."

Alan gaped. He had known James was wealthy, but he was still surprised by how much. He blinked to regain his composure. Maher looked unfazed by Alan's look and continued, "That figure is, of course, after all the proper taxes and dues have been paid. You may refuse. James included a clause which would donate the vastness of his wealth to a specified charity should that be the case. However, know this. He named you as his sole heir because he loved you as a brother. He told me this just two weeks ago, when he asked me about a will."

Alan looked queerly at Maher for a moment. He thought it odd for James to have made out a will just two weeks before he died. He opened his mouth to ask, but before Alan could ask this question Maher interjected, "James found out about his condition just a few days before he made the will. As far as I had been informed, he was instructed to avoid strenuous physical activity. As we both know, he disregarded this instruction. May I ask, what did he say leading up to the incident?"

Alan's thoughts were a chaotic mess at Maher's words. *What were you thinking? How could you have been so stupid? What the fuck, James. What the actual fuck.* Alan stammered incoherently, muttering fragments of his thoughts to himself. The snap of Maher's fingers brought him back from his racing mind. "Oh, right."

"That's a good lad. Did he say anything that you might classify as strange?" Maher requested.

"Well, right as we were leaving my house he said 'this is going to help you out tomorrow. Give you some confidence.' I didn't think it was odd at all. He's always helping me out."

Maher stared at him, waiting for more. When nothing else came, he said, "He didn't say anything else out of the ordinary?" Alan shook his head and apologized. "No matter, I suppose." Maher looked down at a short stack of papers on his desk. Alan glanced at the stack, and Maher grabbed the stack and tapped it neatly to straighten the edges. "This is all of the paperwork. It's not much, but it may take a while to complete. I suggest you read as much as you can. I'm here if you have any questions." Maher handed the stack to Alan and sat down.

Over the next two hours, Alan read through every line in the thirty some odd pages twice and only understood half. He never bothered to ask any questions. Instead, he signed where Maher indicated, and the deed was done. Maher looked at Alan and nodded, "The entirety will be transferred to your account by the end of the day."

Alan could not find it in himself to be happy. He couldn't even muster a smile. Each page he signed and read made him feel like he was stealing from James in some way. In the moment of signing the last page, he hated himself beyond the hate he had for anything else in this world. He wanted to be out of this room. The smell of brandy filled his nostrils, and he started having difficulty breathing.

Alan walked out of the office and breathed in as deeply and slowly as he could. His next stop would be the police station to file an official report. The clock on the wall

77

in the lobby read 11:43 a.m. His stomach gurgled with displeasure, and he decided lunch was necessary. He went home and gave Kipsy many belly scratches and made sure she had her lunch before setting out once more to find somewhere quick to eat.

After lunch, Alan arrived at the police station and spent the next three and a half hours in a small white cinderblock room. The only decoration in the room was rectangular metal table which was almost big enough for a family of four. The hard metal chair in which Alan remained was uncomfortable at best. The officers offered him coffee, but he refused. The report was completed smoothly, since the hospital had already sent James' autopsy and medical records to the station for confirmation.

It was almost half past four in the afternoon, and Alan was determined to have a great time with Kaiya on this first date, especially considering the sort of day he'd had. On the way from the station back to his house, he talked himself into remaining calm. "Don't be nervous," he told himself over and over again. He knew that is what James would have said. Alan messaged Kaiya to let her know he would be there soon and dressed himself in the suit he had worn Sunday night and looked at himself in the mirror.

Kipsy, who stood by his side, stared at him with her bright yellow eyes. Alan could feel her displeasure in his appearance. He decided to take off the jacket and keep the tie. He looked at her. Her expression changed to one of acceptance.

"I'd pick you up and hug you, but I don't want to get hair all over the shirt," he explained to her without fear that she would understand him. Kipsy meowed loudly, jumped on his bed, and rolled over to expose her belly.

Alan smiled warmly and scratched her belly. Her purr was tremulous and shook Alan's whole arm. He gave her a kiss on the nose and said, "I'll see you tonight, baby girl. I love you."

Every ounce of him was shaking with nervousness, even after the talks he had with himself. Kaiya only lived a few streets away, but the drive took longer than he'd expected and made him a full ten minutes late. Nerves still racking, Alan parked in front of the apartment complex she described, stepped out of the car, and walked up three flights of stairs to the door marked 34C. Alan knocked three times and waited, hoping she wouldn't be upset by his tardiness.

From inside, Alan heard Kaiya call, "Just a minute." He rocked back and forth on his heels and tried to remind himself to not be a nervous wreck. He looked around at the apartment complex. It reminded him of the old buildings in the Harlem streets on those gang movies his dad used to watch. Paint was peeling off the exterior walls. The banister had copious amounts of rust, which compromised its stability and ruined its purpose. It was obvious that no one had taken care of this place in a long while.

The sun was already low enough in the sky to be completely hidden by the mountains. This gave the lot in front of the building an ominous tone. The snow from the previous day was already gone, except in patches under bare trees or in the shade of houses. A lone crow cawed in the distance. Alan was strangely reminded of an Alfred Hitchcock movie he'd seen with his dad when he was a kid.

He became aware he had stopped rocking on his heels. He heard the door handle turn and snapped to attention. As the door opened, Alan's jaw dropped to the floor. Kaiya stood before him in a glittering black dress which went down to her knees and black ankle strapped heels which showed off her already nicely toned legs. The upper half of the dress hugged her figure perfectly, and she wore a thin sparkling gold chain at the bottom of which hung a small diamond encrusted heart.

Her strawberry blonde hair cascaded in waves around her shoulders to just below her bosom. Her radiant dark blue eyes were accented by naturally toned eye shadow that made her eyes burst with even more color. Alan stood awestruck, mouth ajar. Kaiya blushed and looked at her feet. She held her hands behind her back and twisted one leg, nervously.

"You... You look amazing..." Alan said, breathlessly. He could not believe his eyes. The woman whom he once believed to be the most beautiful in the world had somehow become even more beautiful. She made it look so easy and natural. Kaiya flushed an even deeper pink. Alan wanted to kiss her spontaneously, but he refrained. Having only been on one date before, he did not know when the 'right time' would be. He hoped Kaiya knew.

Alan only knew what he'd seen in the old movies his father used to watch, so he held out his elbow for her to take. She looked up at him with glistening eyes and smiled wide. She took his arm gracefully, and he led her down the stairs and to his car. Alan noticed how lightly Kaiya stepped. She looked to be gliding across the pavement as she stepped around the car door he had opened for her.

She sat with her hands in her lap and smiled at him again. Alan's heart fluttered as he closed the door for her. It was late enough in the afternoon that traffic was starting to thin out from rush hour. The drive to the restaurant was awkwardly quiet. Alan did not know what to say, and he presumed Kaiya was in the same boat. Occasionally, he would exchange glances with her, and each would smile and look away sheepishly. Alan could not quite think straight with her right next to him. He was completely unprepared, vulnerable.

The restaurant was surprisingly packed for so late on a Tuesday night, which made finding a parking spot virtually impossible. After several minutes of roaming, Alan found a spot toward the back of the lot and opened the car door for Kaiya; she took his arm. She thanked him, and the crushing silence was broken. He guided her to the entrance around cars and across lanes of other cars searching for a parking place.

The place was so full the line was out the door and around the side of the building. Alan tapped the shoulder of a patron in front them. "Hey, do you know how long it's gonna take?"

"Last I heard it was thirty five minutes for the ones on the inside," the man shrugged.

Alan turned to Kaiya and asked her, "Do you want to wait? We can find another place."

She shook her head slightly and flushed pink in the cheeks. "I don't mind. I just want to spend time with you."

Alan's heart pounded hard enough to jump out of his chest, but he wanted to play it cool. Alan shrugged and offered, "Let's find somewhere else. As long as you're happy, I'm happy."

Kaiya smiled and hugged arm tighter. "Okay," she said, "Let's find an Italian place. I love Italian."

*Maybe James was a bit wrong about her, after all.* Momentarily, Alan reproached himself for thinking negatively about James, but Kaiya's tug on his arm thrust his attentions back.

They went slowly back to the car, arm in arm. She leaned her head against his shoulder and clung tightly to him. Back in the car, Alan brought out his phone to search for a good Italian restaurant nearby. Without hesitation, Kaiya suggested a place. It was a small, not so fancy place in Golden. Alan had been told by a few different people the quality of the homemade Italian cuisine and had wanted to try it. He agreed with her, and she clapped her hands and wiggled in her seat. *She's like a kid in a candy shop.*

They set out toward Golden, but Alan decided against taking any highways. Instead, he drove up Colorado Boulevard, down Colfax, and finally to South Golden Road. He wanted this feeling to last as long as possible. Kaiya's expression never changed as they neared the strip mall she pointed out. As Alan pulled into the parking lot, he let out a sigh of apprehension. It did not look like a place he wanted to bring a first date. The red brick building was home to several small establishments, many of which were decorated with signs advertising different deals or announcements.

Kaiya looked at him with excitement and squealed, "I love it." Alan raised an eyebrow. He was perplexed she could be so excited over a small Italian eatery. Once again, he exited the vehicle and opened her door. She seemed even squirrelier than she had at the other place. She squeezed his arm tight, and they entered.

The inside was immensely more impressive than the outside. The aroma of fresh garlic, fennel, and oregano was thick enough to taste, not just smell. Alan breathed in a gulp of it and immediately understood how Kaiya could be excited. They walked up to a counter directly in front of the kitchen area, and the hostess greeted them warmly.

"Hello. Would you two like a table or a booth?" She asked with a smile.

Alan glanced at Kaiya and held her a little closer to him. "A table, please," he requested. The hostess confirmed and led them to a cozy dining area. They noticed that the place, though not packed, was still relatively full. Each table was covered in a red and white checkered nylon cloth, which reminded Alan of the ones he would use on a picnic.

The hostess placed them at a table next to the wall. Alan pulled out Kaiya's chair and pushed her in close to the table. He caught the intoxicating fragrance she had worn in O'Barron's as she sat firmly in place. For a moment, Alan was overwhelmed by the scent and closed his eyes. He recovered with a miniscule shiver and seated himself across from her. The table was a four seater and had places set for four people.

Kaiya rested her chin on her hands and looked at Alan with a cute smirk. A new wave of warm nervousness shot down his body, and he could feel his palms starting to sweat. The hostess handed each a menu and said, "A waiter will be right with you." The hostess left in a trail of prying eyes from men around the restaurant and bar area, but Alan only had eyes for Kaiya.

His eyes were fixated on hers, and she stared straight back into his. He felt his stomach fill with butterflies. Kaiya raised an eyebrow with concern, and Alan realized his leg was quickly bouncing up and down with anxiety. His mind jumbled with words he wanted to say to ease his own tension, but none of them could formulate a complete thought. *I. Leg. Table. You. Bounce.*

Kaiya reached her hand over and placed it on his. She said in a smooth, soothing voice, "You don't have to be nervous. I'm already here. It's not like I can go anywhere." The sound of her voice eased the raging storm in his head. From the point of contact of her hand on his, he could feel the tension in his body release. Relief spread itself outward until Alan was calm enough to collect his thoughts. His heart was still in complete emotional turmoil.

A tall, lanky man with a pimply face and a thick brown moustache stepped up to the table. His demeanor was confident, and he spoke with a clean tone of authority, though his appearance did not support this. He turned to Kaiya and said quickly and without falter, "Welcome to Mannie and Bo's. My name is Kyle. What can I get you to drink?"

# Chapter 10

Kaiya quickly scanned the booklet of mixed alcoholic drinks for some options and pointed at the menu enthusiastically. "This one," she said, showing Kyle. Alan could not see the name, but it looked colorful.

"I'll have the same," he said, decidedly. "And two glasses of water, please?"

Kyle nodded his head and said, "Alrighty. I'll need to see some ID." He verified their age, and asked, "Can I start you guys off with an appetizer?"

Alan looked at Kaiya, and she shrugged. Clueless as to what sounded good, he responded, "What do you like?" Alan usually disliked asking someone else their opinion on food. He usually felt inclined to agree, even when he disliked the recommendations. This time, however, he was genuinely curious. He hardly ever went out for Italian cuisine, since James had been the only person to ever take him anywhere and James also hadn't been the biggest fan.

Kyle answered without hesitation, "I love the garlic sticks. They are delicious and simple. They're also only forty nine cents a pop." His answer piqued Alan's interest, despite Alan's initial unease.

"We'll take some," Alan said. "Four, I think. That sounds like plenty." Kaiya nodded in agreement.

Kyle smiled and jotted down their order. "I'll be right back with those drinks and your garlic sticks." With a whoosh, Kyle was gone.

Alan raised his eyebrows and looked at Kaiya. "That man does not mess around," he chuckled.

Kaiya giggled, "I guess not." Alan looked down and found Kaiya's hand was still resting on his. She followed his gaze and blushed. "Sorry."

She tried to lift her hand away, but Alan grabbed it, saying, "No, it's okay. You made me feel better." He clasped her slender hand between both of his. "I'm just not the best at this. It's been a long time since I've gone on a date or anything."

Kaiya studied Alan with caring eyes. Alan could not get enough of them. "I'm not really the best at this, either. All of my other dates have ended kind of abruptly." She gave a sort of half smile, like a woman who had been through so many disappointments in life that it became natural to accept them as reality. They looked at each other, and Alan began to think she might expect him to be like the 'other dates' she mentioned.

Moments passed. Around them, the clamoring of people in the bar area grew louder as a large group of men and women walked through and sat at a group of three tables at the center of the room in which Alan and Kaiya were seated. The commotion raised Alan's awareness of his surroundings, and he looked away from Kaiya for no more than a second to observe. When he looked back, she was holding her menu up to read it. Her face was half hidden.

Alan took the opportunity to look at his own menu, still holding her hand firmly in one of his. When this place had been recommended to him, the person had said their calzones were 'to die for,' but Alan was unsure. He had never had a calzone before, but, according to the menu, it looked like a pizza folded in half. *I guess I'll try one, if they're so good.*

Kaiya shifted in her chair and peered over with a small bite to her lip. "I can't decide," she whimpered. Her accent showed itself, and Alan melted a little. A shiver made its way up his spine. He couldn't help but smile.

"What about a calzone," he suggested. "They are supposed to be really good." He laid down his menu so she could see.

Kaiya's eyes widened and she moaned, "Omagoodness. That sounds so-o-o-o good. I haven't had a calzone in forever."

Alan chuckled, nervously. He hadn't expected that reaction. Together, they went over the twenty three ingredients which could go inside the calzone. Alan noticed that Kaiya liked almost all the same ingredients he did. She hated the taste of pineapple on pizza, but he could forgive her that. The two decided to each get something different and share.

Kyle came back with two absolutely massive chalice-like glasses. Inside was an yellow juice that blended evenly and beautifully into a cherry red blossom of nectar which wisped upward.

"That looks gorgeous," Kaiya exclaimed. She clapped her hands together, ecstatically. The glasses took over half the table top, and Kaiya took a big sip of hers with excitement. Her lips suddenly pursed, and her eyes tightened together.

Alan looked at her with concern. "Is everything alright?" he worried. While she recovered, Alan took a sip and immediately realized why she'd made such a face. The drink was remarkably sour. The alcohol was barely even noticeable through the explosion of strawberry pucker and lemon. His face tightened for a moment.

Kyle interrupted their reactions by pointing out, "Most people stir them up to mix the flavors, but I just love the sour part." They both aahed in understanding. He continued, "Have you decided on what you'd like to order?"

Alan looked at Kaiya, who was smacking her lips in preparation for another swig. "She will have a calzone with mushrooms, Italian sausage, bacon, jalapeños, and cheddar cheese." Kyle nodded and wrote the order on his small pad. "And I will have a calzone with chorizo, garlic, green chili strips, and tomatoes."

Again, Kyle jotted down the order, quickly, and said, "Alrighty. Thank you, guys. I will be right back with those garlic sticks." He jolted off as quickly as before, and Alan began stirring his drink. After a few whirls of the straw, Alan's beverage mixed from a yellow to red gradient to an amazing sunset orange. Kaiya did the same with her drink, and they both drank. The taste was splendid. It was not overwhelmingly sour like before. It was sweet and tart with a mixture of strawberry and mango flavors with only a hint of lemon. Alan was vaguely reminded of the screwdrivers he used to drink with James. For a moment, he felt an emotional drop, but he shook it off. He knew that James would have wanted the date to succeed, since he worked so hard to help Alan.

Alan drank four full gulps in the time it took Kyle to pop back up at their table with a small red basket of garlic sticks. Alan and Kaiya had to slide their glasses over to make room in front of them, despite the basket's size. The garlic sticks tickled Alan's nose with the aroma of cheeses and butter. Alan and Kaiya thanked Kyle and each grabbed one of the rectangles.

With the garlic stick in his hand, Alan's mouth started to water with anticipation. He took a large bite, and the taste overtook his mouth. It was such a simple flavor, but Alan's taste buds were in utter delight. He looked at Kaiya. Her eyes were rolling back into her head, eyelids flickering. She was experiencing the same pleasure as he.

*If the appetizers are this delicious, I wonder how amazing the calzone will be*, Alan pondered. Other than the occasional hum of satisfaction, they finished their two sticks apiece in complete silence. Once the last crumb was eaten from the basket, Alan broke the silence with, "This place has some pretty amazing food."

Kaiya smiled at him. "It sure does. Ever heard about this place before I mentioned it?"

"One of the people me and James worked with said it was good," Alan explained. His eyes grew distant at his own mention of James. Being with Kaiya now wasn't any sort of betrayal to James, and Alan certainly did not want to forget him entirely. However, Alan could not help but think he should be alone in mourning every time James came into his mind, and this made him want to forget, even if just for a day.

Kaiya did not seem to notice Alan's discomfort and asked, "How long have you known James?"

Alan tried to focus his mind on Kaiya. He hadn't yet told her what happened. But he also did not want to ruin the mood for the whole dinner, so he swallowed his own distress and began, "I've known James for about four years. After I finished college, I got a job working with him. He was my mentor until I got the hang of it all." Alan trailed off for a moment to reminisce.

Kaiya noticed this time. She urged, "You two seem to be really close."

Alan sighed, "We are." He wished she would not talk about James. "He's my best friend, and I love him." Searching for a subject change, he said, "What about you? He said you moved here a couple months ago."

Kaiya smirked. "I did. In August," she answered. "I actually just started college at metro this year. It was a little late, but my family wanted to go back to Sicily for a long vacation when I finished high school." She sipped on her straw for a second and continued, "Right after we moved here for my college, my nonna got sick. So everyone went back but me."

"So you're here all alone?" Alan inquired.

"That's right," she confirmed. "My family moved all over for a long time. Most of my young childhood was spent in Japan. But we lived for the longest time in southern Georgia. That's where I get my awful accent."

"I like your accent. It's cute," Alan blurted.

Kaiya giggled and covered her mouth. In the deepest southern accent Alan had heard in his life, she said, "I betcha don' thank it's cyoote naow." She laughed heartily, and Alan joined her. Actually, he thought it was more attractive than he wanted to admit.

"So your whole family is from Sicily. Is that why you love the Italian cooking so much?" Alan asked.

"That's right. My mama always cooked for our family, and Italian reminds me of home. I miss them a lot, ya know?" Her eyes grew slightly distant in the reminiscence of family and past experiences. Alan knew that look well. He was certain he had the same look often enough today.

"Why did you end up moving around so much?" Alan folded his hands under his chin.

"Oh, right," She explained. "Before I was born, my parents moved to America. My papa joined the Air Force to make a living for mama and me. That's why we jumped around a lot."

"Oh," Alan said and rubbed his chin. "That must have made having friends pretty hard."

"It really did, but I got used to being on my own. Even living in Georgia for a long time was hard. Every couple of years, my papa would be stationed at another base. There were only three, but we never spent long enough in one place for me to keep any friends." None of this fazed her. She kept her beautiful full smile the entire time.

"If you just started college, then you must be younger than I thought you were." He scratched his chin thoughtfully and sipped more of his drink. It was already more than half finished.

Kaiya snickered, lightly. "How old do you think I am?"

Alan's eyes narrowed with discomfort. *How am I even supposed to answer that?* Nervous thoughts crashed into each other in his mind. *Am I supposed to tell her or not? Isn't it frowned upon to guess a woman's age?* A lump started to form in Alan's throat, and he cleared it, which gave him just long enough to gather his thoughts. "Um. I don't really know," he started, cautiously. "I thought you were around my age, and I'm twenty six."

Kaiya smiled, cutely. Her eyes showed an understanding which refreshed Alan's confidence. She took a nice long drink and said firmly, "I'm actually twenty one. I just turned back in November." Kaiya's smile started to fade, and she adopted a more serious tone. "Most people judge me for it, but I was held back in high school and didn't finish until I was almost twenty."

Alan reassured her, "I don't think there is anything wrong with that. What happened to get you held back?"

Kaiya looked down and bit her lip, softly. She shuffled, uneasily, and admitted without looking at him, "I didn't do the best toward the end. When we moved for the last time, I found this group of friends, and I had known some of them from before. Well, I skipped school a lot to hang with these friends, but they were the wrong kind of friends. I got into trouble and couldn't go back for a while."

"That can't really be that bad. Why would people judge you?"

"It wasn't really the school part. It was the trouble part that people judge me on. Like I said, it was the wrong kind of friends, and they started doing some things that were illegal. Of course, I thought they were my friends, so I joined in." Kaiya's face dropped. "When things turned for the worse, I was the only one that got caught. My family pulled me out of school to get me away from those people. I didn't go back until they were all gone."

Alan looked at her and could only think about the emotional storm raging in his body. He felt bad for her. He really did. But he couldn't help but want so badly to tell her about James. He needed to tell someone, anyone, about how much he missed his best friend. Perhaps it was acceptable now that she had shared something so personal. Alan opened his mouth to speak, but before he could mention anything, Kyle reappeared.

"Would you like another Red Snap Punch, sir?" Kyle asked, politely.

Alan looked at the half full glass and shook his head. "No thank you, but could you bring me a Pepsi." He did not want to drink too much before driving, but the alcohol also hadn't started affecting him. Even so, he decided not to drink any more.

"Is a Coke alright for you, sir?" Kyle asked, pleasantly.

"That will be fine," Alan said. He turned to Kaiya, sipping eagerly from her still mostly full glass. "Would you like anything else to drink?" She shook her head and smiled.

Kyle nodded his head and said, "Alrighty. The calzones will be right out." He zipped away again.

"I'm sorry you had to go through that," Alan offered his hand to Kaiya. She took it and held tightly. They sat in relative silence until Kyle returned, both staring at one another, as if to take in every detail before a long time apart. Kyle brought with him a large platter beholding two absolutely massive calzones. Alan and Kaiya hurriedly shifted their glasses aside to make room in front of them for the two plates.

"Alright this one here is the one with chorizo, garlic, green chili strips, and tomatoes," Kyle set a plate in front of Alan. A small cup of aromatic marinara accompanied the calzone. "And this one is with mushrooms, Italian sausage, bacon, jalapeños, and cheddar cheese." This plate he lay in front of Kaiya. "Oh, and one Coke." Kyle grabbed the empty tray and the basket in which the sticks were brought and left.

Alan and Kaiya stabbed into their calzones and dug in. Alan was in flavor heaven. The calzone burned his mouth, but he didn't care. He and Kaiya only partook in small conversation for most of the meal. Both were completely immersed in the tastes. Occasionally, one or the other would hum in pleasure.

About halfway through his plate, Alan stopped and said, "That is a lot of Calzone." He put down his fork and looked at Kaiya. She had eaten almost every bit of food on her plate. All that remained was a single bite. She looked expectantly at him. He looked down at his plate and remembered their agreement to share a bite with each other. He smiled back at her, and a small shriek of excitement crossed her lips.

Alan cut a bite equivalent to the one she had saved for him out of his calzone and held it over his hand. Kaiya ate from his fork. "I don't see how you could have eaten all of that," Alan remarked, as Kaiya chewed, voraciously. "It's so much. I couldn't even finish." She merely shrugged and smiled warmly. She did the same for him, and he ate the final bite.

# Chapter 11

As Alan paid the check and left Kyle a generous tip, Kaiya rocked happily back and forth beside him. She reminded him of a child waiting on a toy. When they exited, Alan noticed the sky was now dark with twilight, and he realized they'd been in there much longer than he'd originally anticipated. They walked hand in hand to the car, and Alan opened her door for her. He sat in the front seat and pushed the ignition. In the center of the dash, the analog clock read half past seven, and Alan let out a small gasp.

"We aren't gonna make it to the movie," he croaked. He looked at Kaiya apologetically, but she was just smiling at him.

"It's alright," she reassured him. "We can go to a movie some other time." But Alan remained crestfallen. All he wanted was to impress her beyond anything else. He sighed and looked at the steering wheel. He wanted to find some idea, some reason to keep spending time with her. Kaiya lowered her head and looked into his face. "Why don't you let me meet your kitty?"

Alan did not expect her to suggest going back to his house. This was their first date. He may not know much about dates, but it felt unusual to take someone into his home after only one not-so-successful date. But his mind was torn. Here he had the girl of his dreams asking to go back to his house. How could he refuse? He racked his brain for what he thought James would have told him on the situation.

Kaiya sat back into her seat with an air of disappointment. Alan realized he had taken much too long to answer her. Mind still battling but without thinking any further, he blurted out, "Of course you can meet Kipsy."

"Yay!" Kaiya exclaimed. She shook her fists eagerly and wiggled her entire body. Alan smirked and shrugged. Without any further hesitation, he put the car into gear and started toward his house.

Kaiya found Alan's hand and held onto it firmly. A few moments went by before she spoke, "I really love cats. They are my favorite animal in the whole world." Her words sounded far off, as if not directed toward him or anyone else in particular. Her thumb caressed the back of his hand softly, and her voice became dreamy and slow as she rambled on, "Yes, one little kitty cat will do just fine." Alan gently squeezed her hand. Her eyes refocused and she cooed, "Hmm?"

"I love cats, too," Alan told her. "I've only ever had the one, and she's always been just fine to me. She is everything to me, actually." Kaiya awed. "Did you have any animals growing up?" Alan inquired.

"My family always had dogs," She responded. "We had six all together. One was a Great Dane, two were border collies, and the rest were mutts. We did have one cat, and he was all mine, but he died when I was still little" She paused for just a moment and continued, "One of the border collies was named Jack, and he was my favorite of all the dogs. He was the smartest out of all of 'em, too."

Alan nodded and said thoughtfully, "I've never been a fan of having dogs. They're always so much work." Alan had never owned dogs, himself, but he thought this was the easiest way to let her know he did not want any. Kaiya did not appear to be flustered by Alan's admission, whatsoever and just nodded.

"What about your parents?" she asked.

Alan was taken a bit off guard by the question. He had purposefully avoided talking about his parents, especially after Kaiya had cried. Finding no way out of the question at hand, he began his short recollection on his later teenage years. "Well, my parents worked a lot while I was a kid. I don't really know what their jobs were, but they worked together. They both went on a lot of business trips out of state because of their jobs, so I had to learn how to be self-sufficient. When I was seventeen, they went on a trip to Chicago to some really big meeting." At this, Alan took a deep breath to ready himself. "The day before they were supposed to come back, they were killed."

Kaiya gasped deeply, turned, and said, "I'm so sorry. I didn't know." Her soft hand tightened around his. He could feel his palms starting to sweat from unease, and he hoped she didn't notice.

"It's alright, now," Alan added, gently. "After they died, I finished high school and went to college with what small amount of money they had left me. Kipsy was the only one there to comfort me, until I met James." Alan stopped talking for a few minutes. Kaiya did not push conversation any further, but she continued to caress his hand.

The white street lines passed in Alan's vision in an almost hypnotic way, and the weight of sleepiness started to pull on his eyelids. He shook himself and asked, "What made you choose Denver?"

"The mountains, really," Kaiya said in a restrained voice. "Do you miss your parents?"

Alan looked at her and back at the road. "Of course I do." He wasn't surprised by the question as much as he felt it should have been obvious.

"I just ask because you said they were gone a lot," she clarified. "I didn't mean to sound rude at all."

Alan noticed a strange absence of her southern accent, which seemed prominent no more than a few minutes ago, but he just shook his head to himself. "Oh, you didn't," Alan defended. "I was just a little surprised is all."

Alan turned onto his street and pulled into the driveway. He did not see Kipsy in the window, but the night was dark for the moon was entirely covered by thick, low hanging clouds. As Alan stepped out of the vehicle, he turned on his phone's flashlight and walked around to open Kaiya's door. Together, they crossed the slightly overgrown front lawn to his door.

They entered, and Kipsy immediately greeted Alan by rubbing against his leg. Alan scooped up his most precious companion and scratched her belly. He flipped the light switch for the living room and turned to Kaiya. Her expression was one of overt elation. Her hands were over her open mouth, and the only noise she made was a virtually inaudible high pitched squeal.

In Alan's arms, Kipsy purred nonstop. She stared straight at Kaiya and chattered a meow. Kaiya let Kipsy smell of her hand and tenderly petted her belly. Kipsy nipped at Kaiya's fingers, and Alan said, "She doesn't really like letting strangers touch her belly." Kaiya nodded with understanding and instead scratched behind Kipsy's ears. Again, Kipsy would not let Kaiya touch her. "That doesn't usually happen, I swear." Alan put Kipsy down, and said, "Would you like the grand tour?"

Kaiya laughed, "Sure." She did not give Alan the impression of being upset by not having been able to pet Kipsy. With how she had reacted at dinner, Alan found this to be peculiar, but he put it out of his mind.

"Well," Alan started, "this is the living room. Shocking, I know." She giggled into her hand. He led her into the dining room area. "This is the dining room slash kitchen area. Occasionally, I will eat here, I swear." They walked down the hall to the bedroom area, and Alan pointed out along the way, "That is the bathroom, and this is my room. I don't go into the other room very often, so the door is closed." He shrugged and asked, "What do you think?"

"It's definitely a cleaner bachelor pad than I expected," she joked. "But it is very nice."

Alan looked around his room. It was unusually clean. There was no pile of clothes and no dishes. Alan was extremely proud of himself for his unintentional cleanliness. Kipsy, who'd been following the two around, sat on her rump atop the desk next to Alan's computer monitor, licking her paw. Her bright yellow eyes never left Alan.

Kaiya took Alan's hand and led him back out into the living room. "We were going to watch a movie, right?" she said, giving him a smile. "Why not watch one on Netflix or something?"

Watching a movie on a loveseat with a beautiful girl was not something he would ever turn down. "That sounds like a great idea," he said. They sat together on the loveseat and Alan turned on the television. Kaiya leaned into him as he switched to Netflix. "What sort of movie would you like to see?"

She nuzzled her cheek against his shoulder and said with glee, "Let's watch a horror movie. There are a few good ones." Alan could feel the warmth of her body against him. Her breast pushed into his arm, and his heart fluttered unsteadily. Alan had never been so close to a woman before in his life.

He found a horror movie on which they both agreed and settled back with his arm around Kaiya. Kaiya interlaced their fingers and moved Alan's hand to be positioned on her stomach. Alan could not really focus on the movie, as his mind was transfixed on the woman by his side. Her body radiated heat, but she shivered with cold.

Alan looked at Kaiya lying against his chest. From the angle Kaiya was positioned, Alan noticed he could see a good portion down the front of her dress. He snapped his eyes back to the television. It felt somehow wrong for him to look, to notice. He stared at the T.V. but did not see a single scene of the movie. His brain focused solely on Kaiya next to him.

Alan felt her body move with each breath and gasp which accompanied parts of the movie. At one point, a jump scare issued a reaction which shook Kaiya's entire body. She nestled closer to him and held his hand tighter. Kaiya moved her hand closer to her breasts, and Alan's went along with it. Her other hand grabbed onto his, and she clung to it.

Through his fingers, Alan could feel the consistent beating of Kaiya's heart. Its tha-bump-tha-bump echoed through his bones. Her fingers slid slowly and softly up and down his arm. He forced himself to resist the urge to move his hand anywhere else unless she did so.

The movie had another jump scare. This time, Kaiya gripped his hand between the two of hers and held it to her chest between her breasts. She let out a cry of astonishment and pushed his hand deeper into her bosom.

Her heart was racing. The steady tha-bump turned into a rapid bump-bump-bump-bump. Her reaction actually made Alan jump slightly from surprise. Unintentionally, his hand tensed and squeezed her breast ever so slightly. Her cry of astonishment ended in a moan of pleasure.

Alan was in shock. He blurted, "I didn't mean to. I swear."

"No. It's okay," she whispered. With her fingers, she gently rested Alan's hand on her bare chest just above the height of the dress. Her skin was soft and warm under Alan's clammy fingertips. His hand trembled, nervously. Now, his heart was the one racing. He was absolutely sure the pounding in his chest could be heard by the neighbors.

Kaiya pressed his hand firmly against her and slid it down. The hem of her dress caught against his palm, and she stopped moving his hand. She ran her fingers down his and pushed against his hand, preparing to guide him. "Wait." Alan blurted, before he could stop himself. Her hand dropped ever so slightly, and she looked at him, confused.

"Is something wrong?" She asked, southernism once again losing prominence. "I thought-" She trailed off, and her gaze dropped to the floor.

"Oh, no." He said, brushing his free hand against her arm and resting his head against the back of hers. Her fragrance consumed his thoughts, and he let it. He wanted to breathe her in, to let her essence fill him. Alan squeezed her gently and continued, "I've never done this before. And I want you to know that this isn't all I want from you."

Alan felt, rather than heard, Kaiya sigh, and he hoped it was from relief. Once again, she turned to face him. "This isn't all I want, either," she said, giving a half smile.

He returned the smile and said, "We don't have to stop." The hand on her chest moved so minutely that he could have sworn she hadn't noticed, but her smile widened.

"Let's do it, then." Her voice was cocky, and Alan was even more aroused by her tone than he'd been by her forwardness. She picked herself up off the loveseat and took his hand, leading him toward the bedroom. He followed and watched as her other hand found the zipper on her dress. It fell to the floor halfway to the room, and for a moment, the light from the bedroom outlined her figure in an almost angelic halo.

Alan's heart beat faster and faster with anticipation. His breathing became labored, and enough sweat was pouring from his hands to have filled the pacific. Before he knew it, she was lying on the bed before him, completely exposed. He didn't know what to do, so he let his first instinct take action and kissed her.

She clung to him wildly as they made love for the very first time. And a second time.

Now out of energy, head swimming furiously, Alan toppled heavily onto Kaiya and breathed out in exhaustion. She ran her fingers through his hair and whispered in his ear, "That was damned amazing." Alan agreed. He'd never felt so great in his life.

With the last ounce of his strength, he rolled to his side and lay next to her. She rested her head on his arm and ran her fingers slowly up and down his chest. It tickled him, but he enjoyed the feeling of her against him. Kaiya curled next to him, and he laid motionless spread eagle on the queen sized bed.

Alan breathed out one long sigh. His body was so exhausted he was left with only his thoughts. His only thoughts were of Kaiya next to him. He wanted her to be next to him for the rest of his life. At the current moment, that was everything he wanted. His mind circulated around the idea of her. They could be married and have children. He wondered if she was thinking about the same thing.

At that thought, he realized he had not used a condom. Alan smacked his forehead and groaned. Kaiya asked concernedly, "What's wrong?"

Through semi-gritted teeth, Alan said, "I didn't use a condom." He looked at her between his fingers. She did not look concerned at all. Alan became thoroughly confused. She should be upset. That was how everyone reacted when it came to not using protection. Why wasn't Kaiya upset at all?

After a few moments pause, she spoke, "I don't mind that ya didn't use a condom." She stared up into his eyes. Her accent had returned "All those times ya came into O'Barron's, I knew you were there to see me."

"It's true," He said. "I did usually go just to see if you were there."

She tittered and said, "I sort of stalked you a little bit, after I first noticed you."

Alan was a little taken aback by this. He had never been stalked before. And though he felt a bit off put, he was also slightly flattered. This beautiful woman had actually shown interest in him before he had made a fool of himself and ruined the whole thing.

"You're being quiet again," she demurred.

Alan glanced at the dim blue alarm clock on his bedside table. It showed almost midnight. "Sorry." He said. "I really don't mean to."

"It's alright." She continued, "I only found out where you worked. James told me. I was the one who came up to him and asked him about you." She rolled on top of him and held his arms down. "We talked about you quite a bit, you know. I hope you don't mind."

Alan could not help but notice the way eyed him. It was almost hungrily. She bounced up and down on his chest. She was extremely light and hardly made breathing difficult for him at all. Her bubbly demeanor didn't detract from his emotional distress. He still did not know when or how to bring up what had happened to James. His insides were knotted with uncertainty. He did not know if telling her now would change how she felt. At the same time, he knew he had to tell her, no matter how it made her feel.

Noticing Alan's distraction, she bounced harder and whined, "What's wrong?" She made sure to put on her best pouty face to keep up the façade.

"It's about James," he confessed.

"What about him?" she pressed his hands further into the bed, bringing her face close to his, lips almost touching.

With no way out now, Alan said, "James... Well, he... James, actually..." He paused. He couldn't think of how to phrase it. He looked away from Kaiya. "James... um... He died Monday afternoon..." Alan had no other words. His eyes could not meet hers. He swallowed hard, but his dry throat protested. She picked herself up off his chest, and he thought she was getting up to leave. Alan felt the warm caress of a soft hand on his cheek. He let the gentle force guide him to face Kaiya, who had lain down next to him.

"Everything is gonna be alright," she murmured. "Let's get some sleep." Alan did not object. His whole body was aflame with muscle pain. He had outdone himself. Kaiya released him and lay down close to him. Her figure pressed against him, and their legs intertwined. Kaiya's sweetly fragrant hair filled Alan with comfort, and he fell asleep almost immediately.

Alan's dream took him once again to the corridor filled with doors. The one to his left was still gone, and through the doorway, Alan could see the park in which he once stood. Outside, the sky blazed with color brighter than it had before. He wanted to go through, but his curiosity of the other doors overwhelmed him. His movements were not quite as hindered, this time.

Eagerly, Alan walked to the door on his right. He touched the handle, and the door disintegrated into nothing. Beyond the door was another gate of pure blackness. He stepped through, confidently, and he melted through the sheet to reveal a crisp mountaintop. He stood upon the very peak. The snow covered crags were a staggering sight. Below him, he could see rolls of snow drifts covering the mountainsides all around. The white snow glowed bright in the lustrous aurora above.

Alan looked skyward into the aurora which lit his dreams. Its ever increasing glow burned dancing images into his vision. Without thinking, he covered his face with one hand to ease the brightness. His transparent hand did not block any light, whatsoever. Through the haze of light, he could see another golden twinkling sphere. This one did not spin round. Instead, it floated gracefully closer to Alan until the sphere was inches away from Alan's outstretched arm.

The sphere's glow swelled and receded like waves on the ocean tide. The sphere tried to come closer to him, but it bounced back as though some barrier bound it a certain distance from him. Alan brought down his arm, and the sphere floated closer to his face. Alan had an overwhelming feeling that he knew what this sphere was, but he couldn't place it. This thing, this sphere was something important to him, and he would give anything for it to stay with him forever.

Alan mouthed the words "Who are you," but nothing came. His voice was empty, like his physical body. The sphere responded with a burst of rapid glows in some sequence Alan did not understand. "What?" He mouthed, hoping the being could understand him. Once again, the sphere glowed in the same sequence. Alan wanted to know. He wanted to understand. But he couldn't.

The sphere started to spin around and around in circles. Alan knew what was coming, but he willed it not to happen. He needed to know what this was, what was happening. As the little sphere ascended into the heavens, Alan silently cried, "No-o-o-o-o-o-o-o." It soon became a speck amongst the lights above, and disappeared in a flash toward some point in space amidst a cluster of stars.

Feeling disparaged, Alan walked back through the door into the long corridor. The brightness from outside each doorway did not carry through into the corridor, but the corridor was lit by some ambient sheen which covered the walls like a fine film. Alan walked forward to the next set of doors. Wanting to keep consistency, Alan walked to the door on the left. Alan reached for the door handle, but before his hand could make contact, an odd sensation caught his attention.

A dribble of something was landing on his chest, not his dream chest, but his actual chest. His dream mind quickly evaporated, and his consciousness reentered his body. His room was dark, except for the dim glow of his blue alarm clock. His mind did not come into focus right away. He blinked several times to wake himself up and became aware of his inability to move his arms, which were above his head. Alan stared blankly into the darkness and wriggled his arms. A searing pain shot through his wrists.

Alan looked around him for Kaiya. *Surely, she knows what's going on.* She was not on the bed next to him. Again, he felt something drip onto his chest. Looking down, he saw a small puddle of dark liquid which reflected the glow of his alarm clock. His mind started to panic, and he struggled to free himself.

From beyond the light, he heard a soft, low woman's voice, "Welcome back... Alan."

Finding his voice, Alan replied, "Kaiya, is that you?" The only response was a cold laugh. A piercing white light illuminated his vision above him. For several seconds, he was blinded. Tears welled in his eyes, and he blinked repeatedly until he was finally able to see. Above him, hanging from a rope, was Kipsy's limp body covered in blood.

## Chapter 12

The first scream that pierced through the cold quiet house echoed, hauntingly. For minutes, its resonance was the only noise Alan could hear. Every muscle in his body tensed and loosened repeatedly, teeth gritting uncontrollably. He writhed against his restraints, but the metal bed frame and solid ropes held fast against his effort. Again and again, he screamed, but none reached any audience, each growing shorter and more filled with dismay. Still he tore at his binds. His voice eventually broke from fatigue, and his body went limp with it.

The speaker in the darkness was talking again, but Alan didn't or couldn't understand. The long drawl of white noise that was ringing in his ears was all her could hear. He stared up at his once beloved cat. Her body turned slowly around in circles, as though some hidden hand spun her round and round. Alan caught a glimpse of Kipsy's once bright yellow eyes. They had turned grey and colorless, dead to all sight. Alan's chest quivered with anger and sadness, mostly sadness.

A solid, hard smack against his thigh brought his attention away from Kipsy. "Did you hear what I said?" the voice was now shrill with frustration. Alan did not want to reply. He was filled with enough rage to murder and enough sadness to break down crying, but he could not move and his emotional turmoil seethed out of him in the form of an air bubble caught between his stomach and throat. He grimaced toward the spot where the stranger stood and fought against his restraints once more. Another smack struck his leg. This one left a harsh tingling pain that became instantly red and warm.

"I said," the voice growled, "I've waited a long time to finally get this chance." Alan heard a dull tapping like a bare foot hitting pavement. The light in the room was conical, and its brightness made the darkness beyond even more impenetrable. No matter how much he strained his eyes, Alan could not see anything outside the sharp ray of light.

For the first time since he had screamed, Alan tried to speak. His voice was hoarse and almost a whisper. "What do you mean?" A rasping laugh responded. He heard a soft click, and the light diminished to nothing. Alan's eyes had a large white spot where the source had been. He blinked a few times, and the spot faded. He felt the tap of something cold against the inside of his leg. It ran up his thigh and came to a stop just before his manhood.

A small prick of pain made Alan jump slightly. He heard the footsteps of the stranger walk slowly away from him. The light in the room burst into life, and he had to close his eyes hard to keep from being blinded again. It took a long minute for his eyes to finally adjust to being able to open. The stinging light still made him squint, but he could see clearly, now. Standing next to the light switch with her back to him was a beautiful young woman with long strawberry blonde hair.

Alan was completely dumbstruck. His loss for words was only matched by his inability to comprehend the situation. Blood from Kipsy still trickled down and dripped onto his chest. His mouth moved, but no words formed. Kaiya turned to him. In her hand, she held the only knife Alan owned. It was completely covered in the red glisten of blood. She was still naked, and blood had been wiped across her chest and vagina as though she had masturbated in the blood of his beloved Kipsy.

"I've had my eye on you for months, now." Her voice didn't sound like the cheerful, bubbly one Alan had fallen in love with. Her eyes did not shine their brilliant blue. They had turned dull with the crazed hatred she expressed in her face. "I didn't lie when I said I stalked you." She flipped the knife over in her hands. "The bitch in here thought it was her." She tapped her temple and walked toward the bed, swinging her hips wide.

Alan stared at her, flabbergasted. "What are you talking about?"

Unconcerned, she bent over him and ran her finger down his cheek and flicked it off his chin. "Did you really think I was interested in such a fuck up? Seriously, the only day I followed you to work was the day you got fired." She laughed maliciously and smiled. "I actually had to talk to your friend in order to even get close to you because you're so intolerably antisocial." Alan still could not believe what he was hearing. How did sweet, loving Kaiya turn into the beast of a human in front of him? She no longer had the slight southern drawl or cute thoughtless way of speaking. Her words were cold, calculated.

Alan's hoarse voice coughed the words, "But why, Kaiya? I don't understand. I thought-"

Again, she laughed, cutting him off. She swung the knife carelessly through the air and spun in place. "Why?" she chuckled. "Because I can. I'm an amazing beauty that can get whatever I want." Her smile turned into a despicable frown. "And I want to kill you. Never mind if the bitch actually did love you." With one fluid motion, she grabbed the tip of Alan's penis and swung the knife across. Alan screamed a cry of unfathomable pain. Breathing hard, he continued to bawl in agony. Maniacal laughter rang out over his cries. Alan looked up at her, tears welling. His eyes grew wide when he saw what she held in her hand, and he screamed one last time. He shuttered and fainted.

Alan woke once more to a tap on his cheek. Kaiya stood over him and smacked him repeatedly with the flat part of the blade. "You know, I hate it when I have to wake people up. What a waste of time. It's just a little pain." She stepped back from him and shot him another malicious look. "You know what made me want to kill you? I thought you were weak. And it turns out I was right. I hate the weak. They should all be rid from this world."

Walking down the length of the bed, she scraped the tip of the knife against him. He cringed in pain as blood bubbled from his broken skin. "I had to stem the bleeding on your tiny pecker. But I have to hand it to you. You do know how to use it. I haven't had sex that good since my first victim."

Alan shivered from shock. He could feel a throbbing deep inside his stomach. He still didn't understand why this was happening to *him*. Of all people, why did he have to be the one to date a psychotic murderer? He watched, shakily, as Kaiya placed the part she had stripped from him onto his desk.

She turned back to him and paused. Her hand went to her head and she staggered. When she regained her footing, she looked back at him. Her eyes had reverted back to the deep blue Alan had come to know. "I'm sorry, Alan. She's in control, now." The southern drawl had also come back to her voice. "I can't-" Her voice broke, and her head drooped. She quivered and coughed.

"Right." She said, cold, emotionless voice chilling Alan to his bones. "I wish I could shut her up permanently. Now, what part am I going to take next? Everything else seems pretty insignificant in comparison. I think I'll cut off all your toes first. I want you to know what real pain feels like." She pulled up on three of his toes and started hacking away at them. The blade was neither sharp enough nor thick enough to cut straight through, so she had to saw the knife back and forth until each separate toe tore away from his foot.

Each saw from the blade left Alan agonized and breathless. He couldn't scream any more. Kaiya laughed as she tore his flesh away from itself. He felt horribly sick. In succession, she ripped through his skin and pulled off his toes with the dulling blade. Alan could not count how many times he passed out. He wanted to just die. He wanted her to end the torment through which she was putting him, and every cut sliced deep into his soul, furthering his will to die. He coughed and spat dribble, which caught in his throat making it hard to catch his breath.

An eternity passed between the first toe removal and the last. By the end, the blade blunted enough for Kaiya to have to chop numerous times before his bone would give way. Although he knew they were gone, he could still feel them on his feet. For some time, she paced the room honing the knife with a long metal rod Alan had had in the kitchen.

He tried to move, but his muscles were prostrated from blood loss. It felt to him that every ounce of his own blood was now pooling below him, unable to soak deeper into the mattress. Feebly, he managed to shift his waist to one side. The sticky blood made the sheet cling to his back and legs. His strength gave out after only a second, and he rolled back with a groan of pain. The exertion had completely wiped what energy he had left.

Alan loosened all of his muscles and gave in to his impending doom. *This is the way my life is supposed to end.* With his head propped on a pillow, he was able to follow Kaiya with his eyes. Even now as she walked around his room a crazed psychopath, he thought she was absolutely gorgeous. Her skin was covered in his blood, but he could see its flawlessness underneath. For a moment, he thought he saw a flash of those once brilliantly dark blue eyes he had come to love so dearly. It was enough to invigorate another small burst of energy.

His mind was foggy, and he could not think clearly on what he could say to her. His mouth opened and his lips formed the first thought to cross his mind, "I love you." His voice was a cracked almost inaudible whisper, but it was enough to make Kaiya stop in her tracks. Her face turned from a smile to a deep frown, and she looked at him from across the bed. Her eyes no longer contained hate or spite. Alan thought he saw confusion and pain.

Minutes passed as she stood staring at him, holding the knife to the hone. Finally, she spoke, "Why do you love me?" Her voice was toneless, but not the harsh voice she'd been using. It was the soft voice Alan had known before. Alan blinked ever so slowly. He could not answer her. All of his energy was completely gone. Each vanishing breath came in short rasps which grew farther and farther apart. He would give anything in the world to tell her she was beautiful one last time.

The last traces of air left Alan's body. He could draw breath no longer. His eyes began to fade off into the distance. With their last sight, he saw Kaiya run around the bed and scream something. What was it? He couldn't hear her. She beat on his chest hard, but he didn't feel anything. Alan's eyes closed, and the world was blackness.

Someone was saying his name. He could hear the distress in her voice as she repeated it over and over. "Alan. God damn it, Alan. Answer me." Alan could hear several hollow thuds. Alan tried to move, but nothing happened. The woman was screaming again, "Alan, you asshole. You aren't allowed to die on me. Not yet." For a second, he was befuddled. *Is that Kaiya yelling my name?* Alan's confusion did not last long, however. It was replaced by a sudden intense fiery pain that washed over his entire body. He tried to cry out, but he still could not move at all.

In his mind, he begged the pain to go away. It was worse than the torture he had just been put through. *Is this hell*? The fiery blaze consumed this thought with another wave of intense pain. Alan was surrounded by blackness. He could not see the source of his suffering. Suddenly a bright light filled half of his view. He could see his blood soaked room. Kaiya was holding his eye open and slapping his face. Another shot of fiery pain billowed outward from his depths, and he tried to wince. He still couldn't move. In between waves of pain, he noticed she was not the source of the pain he felt now.

She looked different, however. Alan tried to make out what it was, but he was struck once more by the fire which consumed his being; this time his eyes went hazy from the intensity. Once he was able to refocus, he could see Kaiya pounding on his chest again. Each hit was the same hollow thumps from before. She was crying. *But why*, he thought, *why would she cry when she was the one that killed me*? One particularly hard thump forced his eye closed to a slit, and Alan was shrouded in almost complete blackness once again.

The fire from before became a volley of constant throbs. Every one of them felt like a hit from a sledgehammer. The blows would have staggered Alan, had he been able to move at all. Kaiya had stopped speaking and he could hear her throwing things around the room. *Why is she upset*, he wondered. Another score of blows buffeted him. As the pain subsided again, he became aware that he was not breathing at all. In fact, he didn't even feel the need to do so, and this fact sat strangely with him.

He stared into the blackness around him and felt another sharp pain pierce his chest. Through the slit of light, he could see Kaiya stabbing him in the chest with the knife. Her face was different again. It had returned to the maniacal sneer. A small, weak spurt of blood issued from the spot in his chest. The waves of pain subsided and were replaced by a constant burning sensation which filled his thoughts. What was this pain from? He couldn't be alive. Kaiya had stabbed him through the chest. But if he wasn't alive, how could he see, now?

The burning was starting to drive Alan mad. He tried with all his might to move, thinking his inability was somehow linked to the pain he endured. No matter how much he squirmed, his body would not budge from its place. He could see Kaiya leave his bedroom from between his eyelids. He did not know how long she was gone, but she came back after a while with wet hair and no longer covered in blood. She gathered her things and left. Alan never saw her come back.

Alan was left, tortured by consistent painful throbs, for what felt like forever. His constant pain weakened his mind, and he frequently begged for some sort of higher power to free him from his prison of constant sorrow. He lost track of how many times he had asked 'why me.' Through his eye, he could see the thin outline of his blackout curtain brighten and dim as the days went by. How many, he could not tell.

Left with only his thoughts for company, he eventually began to focus solely on his pain. He tried counting how many times during any given day it would occur, trying to find a link between the pain and something, anything, constantly talking to himself to make sure his sanity did not lapse. However, each time he would lose count before the day was out due to one or several particularly long and terrible issues of pain during which he could hardly think. After what could have been eons for all he knew, he heard a loud knock on his door. For a moment, he thought it was James coming around to find out where he'd been. Hope filled his being to overcome the pain through which he had suffered for so long only to be replaced by the reminder of James' recent death. The pain reverberated more fiercely than ever.

The loud knock came again, and Alan waited. He heard the sound of shattering glass and splintering wood, and a few moments later two policemen entered the room. One covered his nose, and the other spoke into his radio. Alan was grateful they had finally come to find him, but his heart was still filled with sorrow.

# Chapter 13

As Alan's body was lifted and carted away, his still conscious mind moved with it. He could feel the hands of the EMT's pick him up and place him on the gurney to be taken away. One of the EMT's closed Alan's one window to the world, and he was once again surrounded by total darkness. He had tried to listen to the police officers and EMT's, but he did not understand any of the codes they used. As a result, he was only able to understand bits and pieces.

The consistent throbbing pain through which Alan had gone subsided to a dull constant feeling of being compressed, as if his body had come to find itself underneath the single most massive whale in existence. Though, he would still occasionally feel a sharp shooting pain at some point or another on his body. Without the ability to see, he wondered if each of these were from an EMT prodding his body or the other force which had been tormenting him.

Alan felt every bump on the road; every turn seemed to want to make his body careen from where it lay to one side or the other. The ambulance in which he assumed he was riding only slowed occasionally, but no siren was sounding, at least not any he could hear. It did not take long at all to finally arrive at the destination. Alan found this strange, however, because every hospital he knew was many miles away from his house. *They have to be taking me to the hospital, right? I must still be alive somehow.*

Alan heard the opening of the double doors on the ambulance, and a few voices uttered words he couldn't understand. The sounds coming from the people he could hear seemed foreign. Their words jumbled together into muffled squawks of incomprehensible nonsense. *What is even going on?* Alan's thoughts gave him solace in their consistency. So long as he still understood himself, he did not feel afraid.

The gurney on which he had been placed carried him somewhere new and unknown. He wondered if it could be the morgue, but he couldn't tell. More people were talking around him. He could make out at least three different voices, but even the tones had started to become similar. One of the voices reminded Alan of one of the EMT's who had come for him. He could also make out a dull whir of what he thought was a machine. The people around him had stopped talking, and he heard footfalls of two leaving.

An abnormally bright light penetrated Alan's eyelids, and he could see abstract shapes move across his tangerine colored stage curtain. A blinding burst of white filled Alan's vision as his eye was opened by a man in a white coat. He held a black instrument over Alan's eye and peered all around inside. *He must know I'm still alive.* The man closed his eye. Once again, Alan was forced to see only the shapes behind the tangerine veil.

After what seemed like only a few minutes, the light which allowed Alan to partially see faded, and a jerk of the gurney told Alan he was moving again. This journey was not as far. Only a few feet away, Alan's body was lifted and placed on a hard surface. The surface shifted under him, and he slid toward his feet. He stopped short and heard a great clang of metal, as though a door had closed.

Alan could tell the change in temperature. Although he, himself, was not cold, the air around him was near or below freezing. Alan waited. His being was still bombarded with pressure. Alan could not tell how long he remained in this tomb of ice. To pass time in some way, he started to contemplate where he might be. He ruled out any sort of hospital bed. They may not be the most inviting, but at least they were soft in some way. The surface on which he lay was definitely hard. How he knew it was hard was strange to him. He couldn't feel the surface, itself. But he could somehow tell by the way his body reacted to the surface that it resisted him much more than his body resisted it, as though the surface would prefer to push itself into him than to be pushed into by him.

Remembering the man in the white coat, Alan began to wonder if he was in some sort of examination which required cold temperatures. He had not had much experience with being in hospitals, so this explanation made sense. He knew he must be alive, so everyone else must also know. After all, how could he think if he weren't alive? *What was the saying? 'I think therefore I am,' right?* But this thought caused a confusion. Alan had no idea how that quote popped into his head. It had been so long since his college years and that single philosophy class he'd taken, and yet he could remember it perfectly, despite having failed to pay attention for the vast majority of time spent there. Now that he tried, he found he could recall every moment of his life almost perfectly, not simply what he saw, but every sound and smell. *Is this what they mean when they say you see your life flash before your eyes? If that's the case, I must be dying.* Just as his thoughts came to this conclusion, the clang came again with another sliding motion, and his mind was drawn back as the surface on top of which he lay also drew back.

Immediately, Alan could feel the warmth of the place he'd been previously. There was the sound of muffled voices, again. This time, they all had the same monotonous drawl to them. He strained to hear, but nothing changed. Every word blended together to form one long confusing hum as though his ears had been covered by sound dampening headphones. A few moments passed, and the voices stopped again. He was slid back into the cold place, and the clanging of what he now assumed was, in fact, a door sounded again.

Alan waited with only the presence of his unending pain and his memories. He thought of Kipsy. He was almost able to forget about the issuance of throbs with how happy her memory made him. From her first moments in his arms to her last, he walked through every moment of his life with her in the span of seconds. Or, at least, it felt like seconds. In this darkness, he couldn't tell how much time passed. Seeing Kipsy's face so clearly in his mind was heartwarming. He remembered how she used to nibble at his fingers and how it always made him wince without taking the smile off his face. Kipsy had been his most valued companion through life. He hoped Kaiya hadn't made her suffer. Kipsy was his everything before he met Kaiya. *How did I end up in this mess, anyway*?

His mind wandered lazily back to his last words to Kaiya. He wondered what, in those crucial minutes, caused him to admit his love to her after she had desecrated his body so violently. Even after all his suffering, he still wanted her to know he cared about her. For many minutes, Alan puzzled as to why he loved her so. His conscious mind did not know the answer to his perplexity, specifically why, even now, he couldn't find it in him to be angry at her. What was it about this woman that made him fall so helplessly in love with her, and further still, why had her actions against him not changed his love for him? Any other person would have been vindictive or vengeful, were they in a similar situation as he. Or would they? He hadn't the faintest idea.

As he lay isolated, his mind could not help but to wonder at his own life. What had he accomplished in his short lifespan? *Virtually nothing*, he answered himself. Aside from his parents dying when he was a teenager, his life had been comprised almost entirely of boring interactions which ultimately led him to meeting James. There it was. The memory of James popped into his mind involuntarily. Aside from Kipsy, James had been his only source of comfort in life. James' crazy antics and ability to overcome any obstacle had given Alan hope for his own future. But what future could he lead now? Could he possibly be dead? He couldn't tell. As far as he'd known, he had never been dead before. *Maybe this is what hell is*, he thought. *Perhaps, the afterlife is simply remaining in your own decaying body until you finally are driven mad by constant pain and the ability to remember your whole life from boring start to boring finish*, by the end, his mind was screaming at itself. If he could have, he would have let his head fall backward with dissatisfaction. Frustration. And his inability perturbed him further.

Alan did not know which part of his current existence would make him insane first: the incessant squeezing or the inability to move whatsoever. There was no way for him to tell how much time had passed, but the days in his house counted around 15. He could only guess by his memory of how many day cycles he remembered seeing through his curtains before the police broke into his home. But in this darkness, he couldn't tell night from day or even what time it could be. His internal clock had never been great before, but all of this was completely throwing it off. That's not even to mention how quickly those 15 days had passed for him. To Alan, it had been closer to 15 minutes, but he knew this couldn't be right. That wasn't how time worked.

The door opened again and out he slid. The same monotonous drone of voices met him on the way out. This time, his body was lifted from its platform and placed elsewhere. Not many words were spoken by those around him. His body lurched one way, and he was moved swiftly away. Three turns, two stops, and many hums later, Alan was lifted away from wherever he had been laid. But he wasn't placed anywhere, like before. He was thrown against something hard, and he heard the crack of two doors slamming. The familiar rumble of an engine vibrated his entirety.

The road on which they traveled was bumpy, or maybe the vehicle had horrible suspension. Alan could not tell which. They took corners tightly, and Alan rolled this way and that. It was at this moment he knew, there was no possibility anyone thought he was alive. There was no way doctors would treat a patient this way. But how could he tell someone he was alive. He was still unable to move whatsoever, and even if he could, he wouldn't be able to see anyone around him.

The vehicle came to an abrupt halt and the doors opened. Two strong hands grabbed him and lifted him out from the vehicle. Another short trip later, Alan was lying face down against a soft, spongy surface. He had a notion he would be here for a while, so he let himself be overtaken by his thoughts again.

*Why don't I feel tired*? He wondered. As far as he could tell, it could be a month or ten minutes since he last slept. He had heard before that going without sleep for an extended period of time could cause brain damage and hallucinations. Or maybe he was asleep, and this was all part of some elaborate dream his mind had concocted. He recalled back to the dream he had been having last. It seemed so vivid and clear in his mind, now. He began to wonder about the shining orb which had confronted him.

It had tried to tell him something, he knew it. But there was no way he could tell what the orb had wanted to say. He tried to remember back to his high school days, when he had been told about Morse code. His teacher had never gone into detail of what the lines or dots meant, but Alan had still received a handout with all the letters and their corresponding dots and lines. He tried to match each one to how the orb had pulsated, but no matter how much he concentrated, he couldn't find a pattern in the throbs.

The spongy surface on which he lay shifted, and he toppled down, interrupting his thoughts. Alan felt several thuds against his body, and he came to rest under a mountain of something. A loud voice yelled, and another, quieter voice responded. The objects on top of him were lifted away, slowly. When he was finally freed, strong hands gripped his shoulders and lifted him onto a hard surface. Some contraption under him groaned, and he started moving elsewhere.

There were only a few yards between where Alan began and where he stopped again. He heard a loud clunk of metal on metal, and a roar erupted just a few feet away. The platform on which Alan was resting lifted and moved toward the roaring sound. Alan suddenly became worried. *What are they going to do to me*? His thoughts rushed around in his head.

A burning sensation erupted on his toes. Quickly, his entire body was encased in boiling flames. He could feel his skin starting to bubble with second and third degree burns. He screamed, but the only noise he heard was in his mind and the terrible roar which ate through him with its growing intensity. Every nerve ending in his body was transmitting at once with immense stabbing pains. Around him, he could feel hot plastic melt into his skin and bond there only to be burned to dust by the waxing waves of heat.

The lids of his eyes burned into nothing, and Alan was able to finally see what was going on around him. He was inside a large compartment with nine massive holes on the top. The ceramic walls had started to glow red from the heat emitted by flames coming out of the holes. He could see his skin blister and pop as the heat intensified.

The blistered skin cracked and blackened as the top layer of his skin died and charred. Large flakes flew away from his body and floated against the ceiling with the rising air. His body was entirely overwhelmed by pain. The skin which had not been burned to a crisp was boiling off of his bones until all that remained of his hands and feet were skeletal.

The fleshy part of his thighs became gooey and jiggled with the force of the torches above. His internal organs began to froth through the gaping hole in his chest. They turned into mush and liquefied with the raging heat. The gurgling liquid steamed outward from his chest. Inside of him, he could feel the boiling organs roll throughout him.

His stomach, which had become thin from chipping skin, burst open, and his insides exploded outward.

As they covered the walls and ceiling, the remaining intact pieces shriveled and dissipated into dust. His now completely exposed inside burned and formed boils. Each layer of skin was now peeling apart and crumbling off of him into dust bombs which fragmented and burst upon impact with the floor. His thighs stopped jiggling and turned to a thick hard crust of black.

Still unable to move, Alan screamed out in pain again, still no sound came from him. The bones in his hands and feet became brittle and cracked. He watched as each knuckle quivered and fell to the floor. Every bit of his skin was scorched and started flaking and collapsed under the weight of itself. The unprotected bone hardened and cracked repeatedly. His knee caps fell from their perches and splintered into many pieces.

As the bones in his hands and feet turned to dust, he found he was no longer frozen in place. First, he was able to wiggle his fingers. Eventually, he was able to grasp with his whole hand. *What?* He thought, incredulously. *But my hands are gone. Why can I still feel and move them?* More and more of his skeleton fractured and fell into the growing pile of dust that was his own remains. The skull in his periphery fell, too, and Alan was able to tilt his head slightly. Many of his larger bones remained intact, and stood tall against the blast furnace.

Alan then realized he was no longer in pain. Neither the constant pressure nor the burning sensation ailed him any longer. The fires which burned above shut down unexpectedly, and the entire ceramic box in which he lay started to cool down immediately. A few moments or hours went by, and an end opened to reveal a large dark area beyond with a small light and what looked like a pile of elongated trash bags. Alan recognized these to be cadaver bags and very quickly deduced that he'd been taken to a crematorium. *I must have been dead, then.* The other end opened, and there stood a man in black garb with a push broom.

The man pushed out the dust and bone still in piles around Alan. The end of the broom came into contact with Alan's leg, and he noticed something. Although his leg was translucent, it had material, but could not be seen unless Alan focused on the edge of his outline. The broom moved partially into his leg, and the same immense, stabbing pain from before crippled his movement. He cried out and an audible wisp, like a breath of air, came from his lisps.

He tried to move from the spot where his body once lay, but his movements came in long slow bursts of effort. He tried to grab the edge of the box, but each pass of the broom sent shooting pains through his entirety. He cringed in pain and pulled with all of his might through the hole. It was as though the very air around him hindered his movements. He came over the edge and started to fall.

But his fall was not quick. Instead of tumbling to the ground, he floated as a feather would to the floor a mere foot from the edge. His body touched the ground, and Alan landed flat against it. His movements reminded him of those poorly done slow motion scenes he'd see in movies. Still confused by everything, he strained himself to stand.

## Chapter 14

All around him, Alan saw pipes and gizmos which he did not recognize. There were gurneys everywhere with cadaver bags lying on top. For the first time, he noticed a second man shuffling about in a long black apron and a sort of gas mask he did not recognize. Both men had a faint glow to them that throbbed rhythmically, as though their life energy emitted outward from them.

Confused, Alan tried to step forward to get a better look. His leg strained from the movement but slowly moved forward. With great effort, he was able to take his first actual step in this new and strange life. The man was already several more feet away from Alan by the time he could make another step. The two were not bustling whatsoever. In fact, it seemed to Alan they were moving rather slowly, yet he was outpaced significantly. Alan made one final step to place himself near the path of the man in the apron.

As he passed by, Alan could see the slight glow emanating from the man's skin. The only places Alan could see the glow was from the exposed parts of his body. Curiously, Alan reached out his hand to try to touch the man's arm when he stood still for a moment. Alan's hand could not move any closer than a few inches away. Try as he might, Alan's hand would not touch the man. The man walked away, and grabbed one of the large black bags. He heaved it into a coffin-like cardboard box atop an empty gurney and taped off the top.

The man in black finished sweeping out Alan's dusty remains into a large bin at the base of the crematory and carried it down the brightly lit hallway to Alan's right. Alan wanted to follow, but was still far too hindered as though walking through water. As fast as he could manage, Alan forced himself forward behind the man. The man went round a corner and out of sight before Alan could even take three steps. The opening and closing of a door behind him forced a rush of air to propel Alan forward into the hallway.

He half expected to slam straight into the wall directly in front of him, but the strong breeze whipped him around the corner where the man had disappeared. The air flow started to settle when met by a set of swinging double doors, and Alan was able to regain his footing. The two swinging plastic doors led to a small lobby on the right and on Alan's left was a staircase leading downward into a dark cavernous cellar. The sound of footsteps echoed up to him from below, and he decided down was the way to go to find out where this man was taking his remains.

Not only did Alan have to push hard to move, he had to wait for his buoyant body to float downward with every step. By the time he'd made it down a quarter of the stairs, the man was standing at the bottom and staring straight at him. Alan stopped in his tracks and waited for the man. The man peered through the darkness and squinted as if to have seen Alan or what trace of him there was to be seen. Shaking his head, the man ascended the staircase quickly. Alan sidestepped as quickly as his infirmity would allow just in time to let the man past him.

The man passed by Alan so swiftly the small gust of air left in the wake staggered him. Once out of sight, Alan continued down the flight to the bottom. The descent took ages. Occasionally, Alan would hear the roar of the crematory firing up to burn another cadaver. At the bottom of the stairs, there was hardly enough light from the top of the staircase to illuminate much around him. Alan could just make out the sharp edges of metal shelves which lay in incremental rows and along every wall he could make out.

The sound of the crematory faded as Alan forced his way through the air, his own subtlety still a hindrance to his motion. Along the shelves were boxes, like the one in which his remains had been placed. The man in black occasionally came down to place another box, so Alan watched where the man went each time. The boxes he brought down were stacked along a shelf close to the middle of the room. In the time it took Alan to come to the row of boxes, the man had placed six more.

The room was dim enough to make the labels on the boxes difficult to see, but Alan had no trouble seeing in this light. Every source of light was magnified to make everything in the darkness visible. Upon finding the box labeled 'Alan Jacob Po,' he put his hand against the side and stood for many minutes. Alan could not feel the box under his fingers, but he knew by its resistance that he pressed against it. He had reverence for himself. After everything he had been through in his life, he'd become some sort of ghost. But there were no others that he could see. Now that he thought about it, he hadn't looked for another.

He pried around the room, thinking for sure another would be here with him, if anywhere. He looked for that edge against which the light refracted slightly. Alan saw nothing and no one. He tried to call out and the same simple flittering wisp of air passed through his lips. It was nothing more than a whisper or an exhale. Once again, he tried. The susurration dissipated in the thick, dank air. For the first time since he had died, Alan felt alone.

Alan was clueless as to what he could do, now. He didn't even know where he was, much less how he could get out. He pushed on the box with every bit of his strength and could not budge it in the slightest. *I can't even move a tiny box. How could I open a door*? He pondered for a minute. The surrounding room vibrated with silence. He remembered the gust of wind pushing him forward. *Would I just blow away if I went outside*? Again, he pushed against the box. He took note of his inability to push himself into other things, as the broom had come to occupy the same space as he. This intrigued Alan, but only so much as to wonder why he was so definite upon his interaction with things when other things passed through him without resistance.

He made his way back toward the stairs and realized he had not seen the man come down with a box in a good while. Puzzled, he came to the stairs and saw the man in the apron take it off and hang it on a hook beside the double swinging doors. Alan climbed the stairs as quickly as he could, but only made it up two or three before the lights were all shut off. Left in complete blackness again, Alan waited a few minutes to see if the men came back.

After a time, Alan realized they'd gone for the day and climbed the rest of the flight and walked slowly back into the crematory area. It was vast and empty without the two men or all the cadavers. All of the gurneys had been stacked away in one of the corners for storage, and the lights which had once covered a side panel of the machine were completely out.

To the Grave

Although still sluggish, Alan's movements had begun to be easier as he walked around the building to find some place or hole through which he could exit. None revealed itself, however. He searched high and low, in every nook and cranny of which he could think. He even thought he might be able to escape through the crematory, itself. However, the vents at the top were entirely too small for his form.

Through the double doors to the lobby, Alan could see out another set of doors to the lit street outside. This was the only way he was able to tell the time of day, although it was simply whether or not the sky was dark. Each round he made through the building seemed to only take him a few minutes, but after only seven, the sun began to rise in the sky. The sun was high before any activity started. Alan was just barely able to catch it. His relative speed had increased, but walking still felt strained. He was sure running would be out of the question for a while, yet.

Alan strode toward the door as he heard a loud intermittent beeping from outside. He sped up as much as he could to see the commotion. A white box truck which spanned about 30 feet passed by the door and slowed to a halt just outside Alan's vision. After a second, a man in a blue coverall came to the door. He held up a large ring of keys, picked one among the dozens, and unlocked the door. A swift breeze swayed the doors in front of Alan. One of the two knocked into him, and he stumbled backward a few steps.

Alan watched as the man flipped a large switch in a fuse box on the wall. Every light in the building flickered on. The man walked lazily toward the double doors and picked up a clipboard on the end of the lobby desk. He checked off parts of the clipboard and opened the double doors. Right as he was about to step through, he stopped and blinked at the clipboard. Alan took the slim opportunity to slip past the man.

The lobby was bigger than he originally thought. Beyond the double doors and to the right was a sizeable area with three leather reclining chairs and a plush couch. They all looked to have been used extensively but were not in bad wear. To his left behind the desk was another open doorway with a unisex washroom sign next to it. Alan wondered what his reflection was like, now that he was ethereal and decided to find out. While making his way to the open doorway, the front door opened with another zephyr which pushed Alan. This time, he was not staggered. His airy physique merely swayed, and he was able to maintain his balance, which surprised him, altogether. His vitreous impression was beginning to become less affected by his surroundings, and he associated this to the same unknown reason for his ability to walk becoming easier over the course of the night.

Alan looked over to see the same two men from before. They both wore the same outfits as the previous day, and one was considerably scruffier. They marched briskly past the desk and through to the crematory area. *Thanks, guys*, Alan thought. Without them, he did not know how long he would have been imprisoned in his own decaying body. For another moment, Alan stood with respect to the two men and continued.

The light was not on in the washroom, but light trickled in enough for him to see into the mirror. Reflected there was a translucent humanoid form that only just bent the light around the edges. If Alan moved back and forth, he could barely make out the differences in the tile behind him. However, once still, his outline was virtually unnoticeable. He touched the glass of the mirror. The only mark was a tiny steamy outline of his hand. *So, I'm warm. That's interesting.* The instant his hand left the glass, the print faded to nothing.

An idea came to his mind. He was able to touch the mirror and other objects around him. Perhaps he was also able to interact with objects around him. He excitedly grabbed the knob on the sink and pulled with all of his might. It did not budge. He put one foot against the sink itself and used his leg strength to give a mighty heave. The knob still didn't move. *Weaker now than I was in person. What a disappointment.* Alan scoffed at his own disability. He pounded a fist against the mirror, but even the fragile glass did not break.

Disheartened, he turned to the switch on the wall. Instead of a regular flip switch, a paddle switch stood without a cover. Alan had used these before. Surely he would be able to press this and turn on the light. With every bit of strength he could muster, he slammed the bottom of his closed fist against the top portion of the paddle. For a split second, the light flickered on and then off again. Gaining courage, Alan punched the switch twice as fast as his fist would carry through the dense air. Nothing more than another flicker. Disheartened, he placed his hand over the switch. The light burst into life. Alan was taken aback. He had actually done it. He didn't fully understand how he could do it, but he could interact. Out of excitement, he whooped. Yet again, only a wisp came from his lips, and as soon as his hand left the switch, the light went off again. He looked at his hand and back to the switch. *What? How?* He placed his hand once more onto the light switch and watched the light spring to life again.

Alan left the washroom and looked at the desk. Aside from a few stacks of paper and a computer, it was barren. The computer was old and dusty. Alan recognized it as the same kind his dad used when he was a kid. *How old is this place?* The top of each stack of paper was a list of names. Some were in italics, others were scribbled out, but all had a small check next to it. The lists were small and far from alphabetical. Looking closer, he could make out faded dates starting from the early 1960's. *Well, that answers that question.*

The man in coveralls came through the double doors again with such force they crashed into the walls. Startled, Alan stepped back from the papers as though he had been doing something wrong. The man stormed out the door and down several of the steps before raising his hands into the air and bellowing profanities at all who would listen. Alan was immediately perplexed by the sudden outburst. But he shrugged and realized he hadn't needed to step back at all. He smacked his forehead with his palm. However, Alan did not feel any contact with his hand at all.

He brought down his hand and looked at the place where it should have been. It was there. He could see the paper thin outline as he turned his hand over. He touched his arm. Nothing. *Come to think of it, hitting the wall didn't hurt at all.* He considered this fact for a few moments, and the two other men came out of the double doors, too. The man, who wore the apron the day before, walked straight to the breaker box on the wall and flipped the switch for all the lights.

Alan recognized this as an opportunity to leave this building once and for all. He made his way around the desk and stood next to the second of the two men. The first exited and held the door for the other. Taking the chance, Alan walked out into the sunset lit parking lot.

## Chapter 15

The large industrial area outside was completely quiet. Alan found the eerie stillness discomforting. The box truck in which the coverall man came was nowhere to be seen. Alan assumed he had left in a rush to somewhere. He stood at the top of a small concrete staircase which led down into a completely empty lot. A soft wind blew across him, and he was unbothered. He had had plenty of time inside his body to think about what he would do after he was better. *Not really what I imagined would happen, though.*

He took each step, easily. He practiced the whole night specifically for this moment, and, although he still floated downward like a feather, his movements were swift and natural. No more was he hindered by the air itself. Tirelessly, he walked down the street. The remaining daylight burned by in seconds, and when the sun was hidden by the horizon, he realized he had walked all the way into the inner city.

He was greeted by the colorful lights of the Sixteenth Street Mall and a sparse bustle of people. He looked around at the small crowds here and there. A few couples were holding hands or walking arm in arm. He nodded to himself and continued his journey. During his time contemplating what he'd do once he got better, he consistently thought about returning to Kaiya and talking to her about what happened. He needed to understand why. Now was no different. Determinedly, he walked on in

To the Grave

the direction of Kaiya's apartment, his thoughts mapping out the entire journey in his head.

Alan was not afraid of walking down the alleyways in downtown, any more. As a person, he had always been an overly cautious man, but he didn't think he even *was* a person any more. The only people he saw were occasional vagrants who nestled into boxes or under covers. Alan was reminded of the money which James had left him. *Where will it all go*? He didn't know what he would have done during life with that kind of money.

His mind followed the trail of thought all the way back to Kaiya. He would have wanted two kids with her. They would have grown up without want and still have been the most well behaved children. He would have left every cent to her and them. They would not have lived in a big house with lavish items. He was sure they would all still live in his childhood home. There would be several renovations over the years to accommodate the children, but that would have been the easy part.

He wanted a boy and a girl, but the girl would be first. Her name would be Kayla and his James. Kayla would be just like her mother, a beauty beyond compare. James would be a rambunctious and active one, but he would also be sweet and a mother's boy. He could see this potential future play out in his mind as though it had happened, already. His emotions fluttered at the idea.

Before he knew it, Alan had found his way back to the apartment from which he had picked up Kaiya. By the time he had arrived at her door, it was already midday again. As he knew he would remain unseen while sitting still, he crouched and sat beside her door. There, he waited for her return or leave, whichever occurred first.

Alan remained by her door for three full days without any change. Time passed slowly at first, but gradually seemed to increase as he remained still. No one came or went from the building, at all. Alan didn't even see cars pull into or out of the parking lot. The only company he received was a stray tabby cat which wandered up to the third floor stairwell.

Upon turning around the banister, the tabby cat jumped high and scampered back down a ways. Alan watched carefully as the scraggily cat crept back up the stairs, keeping a close eye on where Alan sat. The cat did not have brilliant eyes, like Kipsy, but something about its demeanor reminded him of her. The cat paused at the top step to observe. Finding no danger, it slunk over to him and sat with eyes affixed.

Alan stared back at the cat. He wondered if this stray had some sort of home. He reached down to pet the cat, which he had named Arnold, and his hand would not get any closer than a few inches again. Arnold glared up at Alan with disapproval. Obviously, he wanted to be petted. Arnold turned around in place and curled up next to Alan's feet. The purr that emanated from Arnold was intense. Alan could hear the vibrations clearly from where he sat. Alan tried once more to touch his fur, but there seemed to be some unseen barrier.

Alan cursed with another tiny puff of air. Arnold stretched his belly and covered his eyes. Alan could definitely see a bit of Kipsy in this tiny new companion. The sky grew dim with the falling of the sun, and Alan was astounded to find the same faint golden glow from under Arnold's coat as the men had had on their bare skin. Alan pondered at this phenomenon but could not reach any firm conclusion. The only connection he could make was to

To the Grave

his dream. This color was exactly the same as that of the orb. *But that would be silly.*

Arnold slept by Alan's side until the call from some unseen bird awakened him from slumber. With the perk of his ears, he stretched, lengthily, and sidled off down the stairs. *Off on some official kitty business*, Alan chuckled at himself. Arnold did not come back the next day. Alan decided four days was more than enough to know Kaiya was not coming back to this place.

Alan picked himself up and climbed down the stairs for the final time. He stared up into the twilight filled sky and wondered at where he would try next. Dusk turned to starlight before Alan decided to search for her at O'Barron's. It was entirely possible her entire life he'd known was a lie, but Alan had to try. He had to know. There had been a time when he'd wanted to spend the rest of his life with her by his side. While Alan gazed into the night, a lone, bright star shot across the sky and disappeared from view.

The bar was not too far from him, but he knew the trek there would take him long enough for it to be closed by the time he arrived. Even so, he set out. Instead of his usual quick pace, he strolled, leisurely. The streets at night were nearly devoid of all traffic, which made crossing streets even easier. He thought getting hit by a car would probably not kill him, but after the intensity of other objects passing through his body, he didn't want to endure the same again.

The morning rush started fairly early the next morning. Alan figured the day must be a Monday. For whatever reason, drivers were always more frantic on Mondays. Now two blocks away from the bar, Alan stopped at a crosswalk with a group of college age people. A few of them were wearing packs or satchels. Nearly all were engrossed in their phones, playing games or sending messages. The light changed, and only one of the students started walking.

A medium height girl with long strawberry blonde hair set off at a brisk pace across the street. She wore a long white dress embroidered with different floral designs. The way her hips swung from side to side mesmerized him for a second. Shaking it off, he tried to catch up with her. Her long strides matched his and kept her several feet in front of him, despite her significant height difference. Across the street, she turned and headed west down the sidewalk on Evans. Alan was starting to struggle with keeping up. His body was not used to traveling this fast for longer than a few seconds, and he started to feel the strain.

At the next cross, she stopped and tapped her foot. Alan was finally able to catch up to her. He walked around her to look at her face. The once beautiful face was sunken and blotched. Her deep blue eyes had become grey with emotional discontent. Regardless, Alan still found her to be absolutely beautiful. The light turned, and off she went. Alan chased after her for twelve more blocks north. He almost lost sight of her through another thick crowd of people who surrounded them at an intersection.

Kaiya's destination was a large complex of nice looking apartments. Being so close to the center of town, Alan knew they had to be pricey. He followed her up each flight of stairs as quickly as he could all the way to the top of the six story building. Alan could not help but notice how much more well-kept this was compared to the apartment at which he had first picked her up. The outside wall was layered red brick, and he did not see any cracks in the mortar.

Kaiya opened her door to reveal a quaint entryway with white airbrushed walls. Straight through the door was a small tiled foyer. Only two pairs of shoes could be found on the floor. Both had looks of wear, and Alan could see they were the same size. Alan slipped in between her and the frame and walked down the hallway. She closed the door behind her and locked the deadbolt. The short hall led into a much bigger living area with a small dinette to one side.

The living area housed a large black leather sectional which stood in the middle of the room. Mounted to the wall in front of the sectional was the most massive television Alan had ever seen. On the opposite side was an open space with several lounging chairs, a small glass table, and several ferns Alan had never seen before. Several floor to ceiling windows lined the wall to provide a spectacular view of downtown Denver. Several more ferns filled the corners of the balcony, and a single metal rocking chair sat facing the edge.

The dining room lacked the spaciousness of the living area, but its elegance was extraordinary. A gold and silver diamond chandelier hung from the tall ceiling over a black walnut table with candles and a fruit basket laden with grapes, bananas, and other various fruits. The picturesque scene fell short only by the apparent lack of use. Dust clung to the surface of the table and the fruit appeared to be plastic. Three bar stools were aligned symmetrically under the mini bar which separated the kitchen from the dinette.

Kaiya sauntered toward him and slid off her dress. She was only wearing a black lace thong underneath. But what caught Alan's attention was the sizeable bump in her stomach. His jaw dropped. He realized now that her sunken face was from exhaustion. Kaiya continued past him and down the hallway between the living area and dinette. Alan followed, eager to ease the loneliness he'd endured thus far.

Four of the five doorways in the hall were closed. Kaiya shuffled through the only open door and collapsed onto the bed in the middle of the room. Her eyes closed, and she fell instantly to sleep. Seeing as Alan did not need sleep whatsoever, he stood as a sentry by the door and waited for her to wake until night fell. *She's slept for quite a while, now.* Somewhat concerned, he made his way to the end of the bed. He looked her up and down. She slept serenely and was certainly a work of beauty, despite looking almost completely different from the woman he once knew.

On either side of the bed were nightstands, each with a lamp. One of the lamps was glowing brightly and lit up the room. Alan soundlessly made his way to the lamp and looked it over. The switch was a small flip on the base of the lamp. Alan wanted to try turning off the lamp, but he was unsure if the noise would wake her. He was also unsure he'd even be able to flip the switch after his failed attempt in the crematory. He had a sensation of being stronger, now. He couldn't explain why or how he knew, but something inside him was ever intensifying. He wanted to try again.

Alan pushed his finger against the switch, firmly. It did not move, but the light flickered. Unlike the open switch in the crematory, this lamp had no exposed circuitry. Alan pondered at how he could have made the light flicker simply by touching the switch. Once again, he pushed against the switch and saw the light flicker. The intensity inside him was growing with each flicker, and an idea culminated out of his physical inability. He began to focus on the power inside him. He gripped it in his mind and forced it into the tip of the finger with which he was pushing into the switch. The light shut off.

Alan looked sideways at this strange phenomenon and stepped back from the light. Instantaneously, the light flickered back to life. The flickering light roused Kaiya momentarily, and she drowsily rolled over to reach the off switch. She flipped it, rolled back into the center of the bed, and fell back to sleep. The only remaining light in the room was a dim blue glow from a digital clock on the opposite side of her bed.

Alan hadn't noticed the clock until now. Perplexed, he ventured over to the opposing table. Peering closely into the face of the clock, he noticed it had the same numbering and positioning as the one he'd had at home. It was even on the side of the bed his had been. He looked elsewhere in the room. Although he'd have been perfectly capable of seeing through the darkness with the light of the city outside, the blue from the clock saturated the room. He noticed a wingback chair in the corner. Behind the chair was a small group of photos. In this light, he could not make out who was in them from his position, but they were the only group of photos he had seen anywhere in the house.

Opposite the wingback chair was an ornate armoire whose finish reflected the blue throughout the room. Directly adjacent to the armoire, a door was left open. Alan walked into the open door to find a master bathroom with a small collection of bottles and brushes he assumed were for makeup stacked neatly around the sink counter. A newspaper had been left beside the many bottles. He had to squint to read the letters on the page.

The date read February 14. Alan thought about Kaiya. *Why would she have a paper from Valentine's Day?* Squinting harder, he studied the front page until he found an article which caught his eye. About halfway down, a bold title read 'Man Found Brutally Murdered in Home: No Known Suspects.' He stood up, unable to continue reading the fine print. His spirit sank.

*I was found on Valentine's Day? It took that long?* His mind spun this bit of information over and over. He could not believe so much time had passed between his last day alive and the day he was found. It had felt like only a few hours had passed. He exited the bathroom and noticed day had broken. Kaiya had moved into the fetal position. He hadn't seen her move but heard a small sound came from her, like a shuddering sob. He looked a little closer at the girl. Tears fell from her eyes onto her bed spread, and she curled tighter into a ball.

Feeling utterly helpless, Alan walked around the bed, sat beside her, and tried to put his weightless hand on her shoulder. A few inches from the skin, his hand stopped and shivered. He wanted to move closer. Giving all thought and force into putting his hand onto her, he pushed. His hand did not move, but his body convulsed with concentration. Alan gave up the attempt after his body unwillingly lost its strength. Defeated, he sat next to her until she fell asleep again.

## Chapter 16

Kaiya slept well into the next evening. Alan had just started to worry about her wellbeing when she stirred from slumber with a groan. He remained seated while she got up from the king sized bed and dropped her panties to the floor. The bulge on her stomach was even more prominent now that he was able to get a good look than it had been the previous day. Her long strawberry blonde hair was showing her auburn hair at the roots. Her face was no longer gaunt, and Alan supposed she hadn't slept in ages when he'd first seen her yesterday.

She trudged to the master bathroom while wiping the sleep from her eyes. Not wanting to soil her privacy, he stayed seated and waited the few minutes it took for her to return. She reentered the bedroom washed and prepped with a face full of makeup done exquisitely. Kaiya opened the armoire to reveal an assortment of long dresses hanging close together. Every one of the dresses was vibrantly colored, and she picked one from the middle which was sky blue and speckled with little pink flowers. She bundled it up, slipped each arm and her head through their individual holes and let it flow down the rest of her body.

She pulled the entirety of her voluptuous locks out of the dress. Still damp, a few strands clung to her skin. She shook her hair with vigor to match a sizeable earthquake. Curls erupted everywhere. Kaiya grabbed a paddle brush from the top of the armoire and ran it through her hair until it straightened itself into brilliantly tidy tresses which covered her shoulders and most of her back.

The tummy bump was hardly visible under the loose fitting dress, though the looseness did not take away from its exquisite beauty. As she walked from the armoire to the wingback chair, she took out a set of small diamond and gold stud earrings and replaced them with silver and turquoise crescent moons. Each one hung slightly below her jaw line and accented her lipstick perfectly. Alan had the overwhelming urge to hold her tightly. He wanted to hug her and make her feel safe in his arms the way he would have if she had not bled him to death.

She stood in front of the chair and contemplated for a moment whether or not to sit. Alan decided to get up from the bed and move in a bit closer. He took a spot just behind the wingback chair. Kaiya stretched and sat, heavily, and the spring in the chair groaned. "Oh, shut up," she exclaimed to the chair. Alan, forgetting himself momentarily, said, "You're not even that big. Don't worry." The same small puff of air crossed his lips as he spoke. Although it was virtually inaudible, the room had gone completely silent, allowing Kaiya to hear the faint issuance. Kaiya turned her head to face where he stood, and Alan stepped back from the chair. Now against the wall, he was completely motionless and hopeful she hadn't also noticed his shimmering outline.

She turned entirely around and gazed backward at where he had once stood. Her face was screwed up with puzzlement. She stood on her knees in the chair and looked over the back. Noticing nothing in particular, she raised an eyebrow, shrugged, and sat back down. Alan relaxed against the wall and walked around the chair to sit on the bed again. *It's probably best to keep my distance.*

To the Grave

He leaned against the headboard and watched her. She glanced at the dim blue clock and sighed in disappointment.

Getting up from the wingback chair, she strode, briskly, across the room and out the door. Alan did not have the time to rise and follow her before he heard the front door open and close. For the first time since he had awoken in his own body, he closed his eyes. Despite the afternoon sun glaring, harshly, off the whitewashed walls, Alan was encased in total blackness. Closing his eyes was considerably more relieving than he thought it would be. Before now, his eyes were not dry and did not hurt whatsoever. However, a slight numbing burn stung his eyes for some amount of time before disappearing.

When he did open his eyes, night had fallen. *How did that happen*? He'd only closed his eyes for a few moments, not hours. He looked at the clock next to the bed and saw 2:04 a.m. Had he been asleep? *Definitely not.* There was no way he could have been asleep. He hadn't even dreamt whatsoever. He also specifically remembered every moment of his eyes being closed. And surely he would have remembered his dream in this state. He remembered every other dream. He shook his head and got up. He was still perplexed by how much time had passed when he walked into the hallway.

Kaiya had not yet returned, so he went out into the dinette area and tried to pick up one of the strangely shiny plastic fruit from the basket. It did not budge. *Just like everything else*, he thought. The light filled city poured its illumination into the apartment through the floor to ceiling windows in the living area. Running his fingers across the overly smooth surface, he wondered if he ever needed to eat. If Alan was to believe the date on the newspaper, he had been dead for at least two months. The plastic fruit was covered in dust, and the place where Alan had tried to pick one up had no indication of interaction. *How strange.* He turned toward the kitchen. A thin film of dust covered every surface in there, too. He went in and tried the handle for the faucet. He was still too weak to turn it.

He did not try to turn too hard for fear he would not be able to turn it back once it was on. The limit of the city lights was just past the kitchen sink, and his vision changed when he crossed the threshold of light. There were no decorations on the refrigerator, and the majority of cabinets were closed, save one, inside which there were exactly two plates and one glass. *Not really one for entertaining, I guess.* He went into the living area and sat on the part of the sectional facing the balcony. He looked out over the balcony toward the city. The traffic was antlike from where he sat. The flash of moving headlights on main streets sparkled between one another in the fast and slow moving traffic. In the distance, he was able to make out the occasional blue and white flashes of police lights in pursuit.

Alan leaned back onto the sectional and closed his eyes again. This time, he was not surrounded by blackness. Instead, visions of a long, narrow hallway filled his view. He tried to open his eyes at once but was plunged into a dream not unlike those he had in his final days.

A long hallway manifested itself in front of Alan. On his left and right were the open doorways leading to the park and mountain. He could see the vast dancing glow of the aurora emblazoned night sky through each of them. The hallway, itself, still retained its ambient luminescent glow which allowed him to see down its complete length without difficulty. He wanted to break his trend of opening each door in succession, so he walked halfway down the hallway.

He passed three sets of doors and turned to the left. The door in front of him was different from the ones he had opened before. The first two were each etched markings. Alan could make out the same kind of markings on this door, but they were more defined and intricate, almost like letters to form words. For some time, Alan studied these markings and could almost make out a pattern between them.

Around the edge of the door were about thirty different symbols which worked their way around the door from the top right corner to the top left corner. At the top of the door, an impression of each symbol was laid out in vertical lines. Alan looked a little closer, comparing the ones on the frame to the ones on the door. The vertical lines were not all written downward. Every other one was written upward. Curious about this style of writing, Alan touched the door. A bang shot out across the hallway.

Alan looked around. Two more bangs echoed from down the hall, where he had begun. Slowly, Alan tiptoed toward the sounds. With each step, he became tenser and focused on what could be making the noise. This was, after all, only a dream. His mind circled this thought repeatedly. Another loud, crashing bang from the door next to him gave him a frightened start. He was standing next to the third door. Realization dawned across him. He had to progress down the hallway in this fashion.

He took a deep breath and turned the handle. The door swung open of its own accord and cracked down the middle. The force of the swing pushed Alan backward several steps. Its two pieces fell to the floor in the hallway, and each dissolved into the black and white checkered tiles. Once again, he was face to face with an abyssal blackness which appeared to push outward against the very air.

Cautiously, Alan stepped forward, hand outstretched. His fingers touched the veil, and it resisted him. He pushed harder against it and felt it give way. He stumbled forward and through. On the other side, he was met with a massive moss covered staircase leading straight down the side of a mountain. His body continued to propel forward, and he nearly did not catch himself before the first drop. His arms swayed, frivolously, to keep his balance.

Once stable, Alan looked around him to see a temple behind the doorway through which he'd come. On the both sides of the temple stood grey stone statues covered with green moss. He could not see the entrance to the temple, for the doorway blocked his view. Toward the steps of the temple, he could see great valleys and a stone city on the peak of another mountain. He had seen pictures of this sort of place in geography and history books. A place he'd always wanted to go was Machu Picchu in Peru. Ever since he was a kid and learned about the Mayan civilization, he had dreamt of coming to finally see the city atop a mountain. This wasn't Machu Picchu, though. Alan wondered where it could be, since he'd never seen a place quite like this in his life.

Alan looked up. The sky was different here. Across the other two doors was a bright, shimmering aurora. The sky here was full of thousands upon thousands of pulsating star-like lights which swirled in rhythm with each other. Every few minutes, one or two would begin to spin faster. Alan recalled the star-like orbs from his previous dreams which would shoot up toward the stars.

# To the Grave

Alan watched, intrigued, as more and more lights spun faster and faster. Then the first of them shot straight toward a single point in the sky. Alan was unable to see where through the other lights clouding his vision. The moment one or more lights vanished into space another would take its place. Alan remained captivated by the swirling lights and their rhythmic movement.

After a while, he noticed a peculiar occurrence. He waited a few more minutes to see it happen again. He squinted up into the sky and scanned every square inch to find it again. Finally, he was able to spot it. Two of the lights were growing closer together. Other than spinning, every other light he could see was static in its position. But these two had stopped spinning entirely. Steadily, they inched toward each other until so close they appeared to touch.

Alan could not make them out quite as well from this distance, but they appeared to pulsate the same way the orb had for him. Amongst all of the other spinning lights, the two seemed to disappear, traveling together across the sky. Alan wanted to follow them. As though his wish became an instant reality, the Earth jolted to the side, and he soared upward toward the lights. He cried out, and his voice came out clearly. He shook his head in disbelief of his own voice, and he started to fall.

Although his descent was quicker than he had experienced outside of his dream, he could not hear air rushing by his ears. His held his hands out at his sides to keep from tumbling, and his body stayed upright. He fell past the tops of mountains and into a deep serpentine valley covered in thick trees and brush. Alan's feet landed on the ground hard, but he felt no impact, whatsoever.

In his own thoughtlessness, he had forgotten to keep an eye on the two lights, and he didn't know how to get back to the doorway to the long hall. He looked skyward for some semblance of direction but only saw the canopy of the thicket in which he'd landed. Cursing himself for getting into this sort of mess, he walked in the direction of one of the inclines around him.

Alan's ethereal body could not push the firm bushes out of his way. Crawling or manipulating his body to fit between or under the underbrush, he worked his way slowly up the mountainside. As he moved higher, the vegetation became thinner, and he did not have to contort himself as much. He hiked faster once unhindered and quickly made it to the top of the peak.

He looked around. The lights in the sky did not form any shape he could use to guide himself. The other mountain peaks only appeared to be green with no defining features. *How far did I go*? Alan could not tell where he had ended up, but he focused all of his thoughts on going back to the door to the hallway. Once again, the Earth gave a lurch to one side, and he was lifted into the air.

This time, he did not cry out. He kept his focus on the destination and watched as the mountain range zoomed by under him. The green and grey peaks were a blur of movement, and Alan closed his eyes to keep from feeling motion sickness. Suddenly, his body slowed, and he fell straight toward the ground once more. He looked and could see the temple below him get bigger as he drew closer.

His feet touched ground, and the familiar temple and doorway surrounded him. He looked around one last time and passed through the door into the long hallway. He walked across to the next door and put his hand against the etchings. These were considerably less detailed than the one halfway down the hall, but Alan thought he knew for what they were used. He tried to turn the handle, but it wouldn't budge.

At once, a deafening whirring sound filled his ears. He clamped his hands around his head to try to drown out the noise, but nothing would work. The hallway began to evaporate around him, and he turned around and around to remove this horrid, torturous echo. His eyes opened. He was still in Kaiya's apartment on the sectional, and the whirring still surrounded him. Looking around, he saw Kaiya completely naked pushing a vacuum over the carpet between the couch and the television. He now understood and jumped to his feet to escape.

He moved as quickly as he could to the master bathroom and sat on the side of the bathtub. The horrible sound still echoed in his thoughts and jumbled his ability to think. Alan shuddered and held his head in his hands. How could such a simple everyday thing cause him so much pain? Still holding his head, he waited for Kaiya to finish. The roar echoed through him.

# Chapter 17

Alan remained in the bathroom for several hours after Kaiya finished vacuuming. He dare not close his eyes again, for fear he might waste another block of time. His mind went over and over the dream from which he'd been awakened. Particularly, he pondered the swirling lights in the sky. How oddly they had spun round and shot into the air. There were hundreds if not thousands this time, when every other time there had only been one or none. What could they have been? More importantly, why had those two not stayed in place like the others?

As he sat quizzically on the edge of the tub pondering the dream he'd had, his mind jumped to many different points, including how he lacked the ability to interact with objects and people. *At least I can touch things.* A thought came to him. He looked at the toilet to his right and tilted his head. He'd never had an encounter with water in this body. It hadn't even rained or snowed since he'd been outside. This was not unusual for Denver weather, however.

Alan stood up and looked into the bowl. It was sparkling clean. Despite its cleanliness, he still had several reservations about sticking his hand in a toilet. As confident as he was nothing would happen to him, his mind still retained some anxiety when it came to unsanitary actions. Gathering as much courage as he could muster, Alan shoved his hand straight into the toilet and cringed at what might happen. When his hand contacted the water, he felt resistance, but not remotely as much as he'd had from other objects in the world. He pushed harder.

It felt as though he was sticking his hand into a can of thickened paint or glue, instead of water. The water clung to his infirmity. Alan tried to bring his hand out, but the suction was too much for his lack of physical strength. Alan pushed against the seat and with his legs hard, but the water would not let his hand free. He started to panic at the thought of being stuck in a toilet forever. Once again, he tried to pull himself out, but he was once again trumped by the force of the water.

Alan stopped trying to pull himself out after the third failed attempt. However, he did not want to let his hand go any deeper into the toilet, so he pulled up on it constantly. He waited there for what felt like ages. Suddenly, an idea struck him. If he could flush the toilet, perhaps he would no longer be prisoner to the suction of the water. He put his hand on the handle and pulled with all his might. It did not budge. He sighed in disappointment. *Just another terrible thing about being whatever it is that I am.*

Out of the corner of his eye, he saw Kaiya enter her bedroom. She was headed straight toward the bathroom. Again, Alan began to struggle. He pulled harder and harder, but each pull seemed to drag him deeper into the pool. Thrashing, he fought against the water which cuffed him. Kaiya walked into the bathroom and looked at herself in the mirror for a moment. She stroked under her eye to remove a lash and yawned wide. She stretched, and Alan could not help but stare at the way her breasts perked. For a few seconds, he forgot what he was trying to do.

Kaiya turned and looked straight at where he stood. He saw the intent in her eyes. As she drew closer to him, he squirmed. He didn't know what would happen. He could not touch her, but what would happen if she touched him? He was helpless. She walked straight through him. Stabbing pains pierced his body and mind where her body made contact with him. Not wanting to alert her again, he kept his mouth shut in a grimace of pain.

The way she sat, Alan's arm was paralyzed inside her leg. He had been able to move slightly out of the way to avoid being impaled by her, but even this small amount of contact sent him reeling in waves of agony. He could feel warmth trickle down his arm and into the bowl. Shivering in disgust, he shuffled his feet and held his head with his free hand.

Kaiya wrapped her arms around herself and slouched. It was not long before she finished, but to Alan, time slowed to a crawl. His entire arm was shaking with the intensity of the throbs which shot up it and through his body. He dared not close his eyes. Even through the pain, he knew he needed to stay aware of Kaiya and work fast once she stood.

The stream down his arm stopped, but she did not prepare to rise. Resting her elbows on her knees, she cradled her head in her hands. From where he sat, he was able to see the side of her face between her hands. Tears fell steadily from between her fingers. She was whispering something under her breath, but he could not make out her words.

Kaiya promptly tore her hands from her face, wiped herself, stood, and flushed. Alan was still slightly dazed by her tears and was not prepared to pull his hand out. The torrent of water yanked his arm further into the toilet, and reality seized him. Quickly, he grabbed the seat and pulled against the current. The flow of water tried to drag him down. With all of his strength, he held onto his position and waited for the pale yellow water to finally flush.

The bowl emptied with a gurgle. Alan's arm flung outward and upward. His body careened backward, and he hit the wall behind him, hard. Despite the impact, only a soft knock came from the spot where he landed. He looked concernedly at Kaiya, but the sound of the rushing tap masked the noise. She left and collapsed onto her bed, still unclothed. He let out a sigh of relief and stood.

Water still dripped from his fingertips, so he decided to wipe what remained onto the towel which was racked by the doorway. *Now I know to stay away from water, in general.* The mental note was not how he thought the experiment would go. He decided to be much more careful with testing his own limits from then on.

Hand dry, Alan fell onto the plush bed beside Kaiya. Her sobs were muffled by the body pillow on which her head lay. He wanted to stroke her shoulder and comfort her. He also knew to try would be frivolous. Instead, he did the only thing he knew he could do in this form. He stayed beside her until she cried herself into a restful slumber. During the night, she curled up into a ball and shivered. If Alan could have thrown a blanket over her, he would have in an instant. But his ghostly body was not yet strong enough to interact properly with his surroundings. Unlike her waking state, she was peaceful during sleep. Her eyes were no longer tense or welled with tears. Though her cheeks did not curl with a smile, no trace of a frown could be seen, either. As he watched, Kaiya's eyes would move back and forth to the scenes of some dream she saw.

Alan studied her face. When he'd first known her, she had voluptuous lips, cheeks which were lined perfectly with a smile, and her eyes. Alan would never forget her eyes. They're sapphire iris was encompassed by a small ring of darker, almost violet color. Lines of lighter blue incremented from the outside in and stopped just short of her pupils. He remembered how her eyelashes were light in color and appeared blonde. Although light, they were prominent and long. The happiness in her smile was accentuated by their almond shape.

For a moment, he lost himself in reminiscence. Snapping back to the present, Alan realized the sun had risen well above the horizon, but dark clouds blemished the beautiful sky with a haze of light halting anger. A furious storm had moved in overnight. He had been distracted by Kaiya for so long; he hadn't noticed the rolls of thunder and parabolic strikes of lightning which seemed to forget the ground, entirely, reentering the clouds to disappear in a flash of indignation.

A particularly close bolt ignited a building a few streets over with a jet of sparks. Alan raised himself into a crouching position and watched as flames shot in all directions, spewing from an improperly connected rod. The rain which had accompanied the storm was much further north. The quickness with which the fire spread atop the roof fazed him, greatly. The dryness from the last week or more allowed the licks of fire to web out.

Soon, the entire roof was consumed by an inferno which rose high into the sky like a pillar. The room around Alan flickered in the light. Each dancing wave pirouetted across the walls and furniture. Alan was frozen with shock. He could do nothing but stare as the blaze jumped from building to building. A streak of lightning flashed once more but was only barely visible in front of the burning buildings. The bolt struck a transformer near the first building, and it burst into another sea of sparks which ignited treetops nearby.

Alan could see pedestrians in the surrounding streets running away from the bright glow of destruction. The sound of a fire engine grew nearer. One by one, he watched four trucks stop on every side of the street around the buildings, now charred by the raging heat. Momentarily, he was reminded of the way his own body had shriveled and blackened in the crematory. His body shook with anxiety.

The first of the fire trucks shot out an arch of water toward the first building. The jet of water made the fire explode outward with a force that rocked the truck. The firemen all covered their eyes and shut off the flow of water, immediately. Alan had heard of this happening. A fire too hot could split the water molecules into oxygen and hydrogen, both of which are superb fuel for a fire. Another column of flame erupted outward from the entrance of the first building.

Two bodies shambled out. The bigger of the two carried what looked like a child a few steps and fell onto the sidewalk just outside. Fire had consumed them, and Alan could see the clothing they wore was still ablaze as several firefighters rushed to their aid. An ambulance siren whirred loudly and the vehicle appeared around the corner of Alan's vision. It stopped away from the heat emitted from the building. Two firefighters carried the people to the gurneys which awaited them.

Alan wanted to get a closer look at the situation. He had never seen a blaze so magnificent before. Suddenly, the ground shifted below him. His body was lifted through the roof and into the air Alan was surprised, but he didn't move at all. He recalled his dream. *This can't be real. I must still be in the dream*. As though a hand gripped him, his body was flung in a high arch, and he landed right next to the paramedics pushing the gurneys back to the ambulance.

The scene was much louder than it had been in Kaiya's apartment. The sirens of more ambulances could be heard in the distance, but they were almost drowned out by the deafening roar from the inferno. He could hardly hear the shouts of the paramedics next to him, and the firemen were virtually inaudible.

Something caught Alan's attention. The child which lay still on the gurney was still glowing. *Surely they put out the flames, first*. He walked closer. The child was glowing, alright. But the emanation was pulsating, like the faint glow on the bare skin of every person he had seen thus far. This, however, was much brighter. Intrigued, he followed them back to the ambulance and watched over the child as care was administered to the best of the paramedic's ability.

The child was still, but Alan could make out the rise and fall of fleeting breaths. Each one became slower and shorter. After only minutes, the child became entirely motionless. The glow which shone through the child's skin became ever brighter. Alan assumed he was the only one to see the strange phenomenon, since he'd never experienced anything similar during his life.

All at once, the glow disappeared. He tilted his head in confusion. A spark of brilliant light rose through the child's chest in the shape of a familiar scintillating orb. Alan stepped backward. What was he seeing? Dreams were not real, right? They were purely figments of his imagination. The orb throbbed with light, and began to rise slowly into the sky. He reached out and called to the orb. It did not respond to his plea and continued upward.

The orb began to spin in loops as it flew higher. Alan merely stared at it. Faster and faster it spun until a burst of radiance emitted from another orb, this time from the adult. The child's orb slowed and waited in the sky for the other to accompany it. When the adult orb found itself next to the other, they both began to spin more and more rapidly. He was almost unable to make out anything but two bright circling streaks, and spontaneously, both orbs shot into the sky toward the same point in the stars.

Several minutes passed while Alan stood and contemplated what he had just witnessed. Around him, the bustle of activity blurred into a smear of similarity. After a time, the buildings burned into an ashen heap of scorched remains. On one, only the metal skeleton remained standing amongst a pile of rubble. But Alan did not pay any mind to these occurrences. His only thoughts were with the two orbs whose destination he did not know.

Alan willed himself to follow, as he had done before, but nothing happened. No lurch of the Earth. No spring in distance. He thought long and hard about where they might have gone. Perhaps some distant planet. Night fell once more before Alan moved from his spot of contemplation. When he finally decided to walk back to Kaiya's apartment, he noticed traffic had been diverted to other streets in the vicinity to avoid the potential collapse of the building. Alan willed himself to be in the apartment, and he sprung through the air and down to the very spot he'd been lying next to her.

## Chapter 18

For many days, Alan stayed mesmerized by the movement of orbs from all around the city. He sat on the balcony outside Kaiya's apartment amongst the few ferns in the lone rocking chair which filled most of the empty space. Alan could not move the chair in any fashion, as his own weightlessness proved once again to be a sort of hindrance. But he did not care whether or not the bulky thing would submit to his will. The regular human impulse to rock back and forth no longer held its grip over him. Added to that, every fragment of his attention was undivided and focused on the occasional light which rose up somewhere in front of him, spun quickly, and flew into the sky.

From his position under the overhanging roof, Alan could not determine where the orbs went once they set off. However, each one would disappear so quickly he dared not blink for to miss it. Over time, he became curious as to whether these orbs all came from those who had died. Once or twice, he had thought about jumping to where one had come from, but his ability to move from destination to destination instantaneously had started to take its toll on his physical resilience.

He'd actually noticed the change after his fourth jump, during which he had decided to follow Kaiya to work and watch the orbs rise from there. In the middle of the jump, he had been buffeted by an intense pain in his chest unlike any other he had experienced. Upon landing, his legs had given way proving his delicacy, which Alan had found disconcerting. From then, he had decided to only use this newfound power sparingly.

Despite his inability to find the source of each orb, he speculated that, since the only two he had seen were, indeed, from two people who had died, it followed that every other one was likely to be from those that died. Taking this as the only possible drawn conclusion, Alan decided to call the orbs the only word which came to mind when describing them to himself: 'souls.' Although this particular term was fairly more religious than he had tended to be in his life, he could not find any other suiting word without some sort of religious connotation.

Alan attempted to count each soul which rose into the air and shot into the sky on multiple occasions, but he was unable to continue after several thousand. His count had been broken by Kaiya's entrance into the apartment. The sound of the sliding glass door gave him a start, and he turned to look behind him.

Kaiya came out onto the balcony for the first time since he had found her after his body burned. In her hands, she held a pale green watering can. It was only then Alan realized the ferns around him had started to wilt, considerably. His eyes followed her as she went from fern to fern and poured a fair amount of blue tinted water into each terra cotta pot in which they had been planted. Alan could see life beginning to come back into the wilted leaves as each one perked up with the promise of relief from their impending death by dehydration. The plants' stems gorged themselves, thirstily, and became full.

Kaiya finished her watering, and leaned against the railing on the balcony. Her chin dropped to her chest, and she started whispering to herself under her breath. Alan got up from his seat out of curiosity and approached her.

As he drew nearer, he could make out a few of the words she spoke. "... Sorry... Shouldn't have... I was wrong..." Her body convulsed into an overpowering shudder of emotional discourse. Without being able to control the volume of her own voice any longer, Alan was able to hear her more clearly.

"I'm so sorry, Alan." The mention of his name made him recoil, slightly. He didn't know what in her mind made him come up. She was, after all, the one who had said she hated him for being weak. Now she was apologizing to the air? Alan took a step closer, wanting to listen in on this most unusual soliloquy. A single tear slid down her cheek and rested on the tip of her chin as if rebelling against gravity. "I am going to turn myself in tomorrow," it was as if Kaiya spoke to the wind or knew he was there and listening. "I don't want to hurt anyone else."

Her final words struck a chord of emotion in Alan's being. His body seemed to find more physical impression. He could feel himself gaining firmness as he stepped forward and tried to place a hand on her shoulder. Inches from touching her again, his body stopped, but this was not like the other times. Every time before, he'd felt a sort of force which disallowed his further progress, but now his body just would not continue forward, resisting his wishes like a stubborn child.

Alan sat back in the chair and clamped his mouth closed. The sky grew dark and Kaiya continued to shiver in distress for quite some time. Waiting patiently for night to fall, he crossed his arms and watched the now countless souls rise into the sky and zoom out of sight. They no longer piqued his interest, but his effort to take his mind off of what she'd just said forced his attentions on them. He tried to keep count, but his mind still wandered to

Kaiya's recent statements. *She's going to turn herself in? And what does she mean by 'anyone else?'*

His mind circled these two thoughts until well after Kaiya retired to the comfort of the apartment and eventually the bedroom. Alan decided to follow her everywhere tomorrow to see if she truly would confess her crime against him. He didn't think any less of her. The love for her around which his actions had previously revolved had begun to sway more toward compassion. However, his love had ended with his final words to her, as though he had realized upon their utterance that he couldn't possibly love a person such as her.

He pondered through the night until the sun peeked its nose brightly over the horizon, illuminating vast dark clouds forming just over the mountains. Rising from the chair, he looked through the glass to see if Kaiya had roused from her slumber. She still lay on the bed, unclothed, but her eyes were wide and puffy. Alan assumed she cried the majority of the night. He watched from the balcony as her chest rose and fell, steadily. The bump in her stomach had started to become more prominent in the time he had been here. How long was it? He couldn't even manage an accurate guess.

Time was slipping further and further past his level of comprehension. He vaguely recalled the concept of time completely consuming his life at one point, but as he stood, staring with eyes wiser than he would have believed possible in his short life, he knew that time had become, to him at least, a construct by which he could no longer be bound. He could go seconds or days, and each would feel the same length. In fact, even the memories of his experiences during his life were recallable at his vaguest whim. No longer were his memories fleeting and indiscernible. He needed only concentrate slightly before familiar faces, friendly places, and convivial gatherings would flash before his eyes. Although only echoes of experiences once had, he could clearly remember James and his beloved Kipsy. If his form was able to smile, he imagined it would have at their memory.

Kaiya sat up on the bed and rubbed her eyes, feverishly. Her entire form shook from the enthusiasm with which she attacked the sleep that had built up there. Alan pressed his hand against the glass and watched her finish and walk into the bathroom to shower. She left the door open, but the balcony did not have enough room for him to watch. At the thought of watching her shower without her knowledge, he looked away with embarrassment. Alan had not been a peeper in his human life, and he did not intend to become one, now.

Carefully, he leaned backward against the rails and crossed his arms to wait for her to finish bathing. While he waited, the dark clouds which now covered the purple to orange sky began to trickle a light shower of rain. The drizzle soon turned torrential, and thunder clapped after bolts of far off lightning. Recalling the last issuance of weather like this, Alan turned to observe. Water from the rain was starting to flood the streets, already. *Kaiya doesn't own a car. How does she plan of going anywhere with the weather like this?*

He pressed his finger into his temple in thought, and the rain suddenly left his mind. He could feel his finger against himself. To be sure it was not some trick of his own mind; he tapped his finger against his temple. Tap tap tap. Sure enough, he could feel his own touch. He ran his finger around his head out of curiosity. Right above his left eyebrow, he stopped being feeling the sensation of touch. Alan furled his brow.

Starting from the top of his head, he poked the rest of his body, systematically. He found three different spots on his body with some sort of feeling. Each was about the size of an orange, and one was much more sensitive than the others. He wondered at how long each had been there. It had not ever occured to him to touch his body, especially after initially finding himself unable to feel. Alan made a mental note to continue searching for more every once in a while. *No telling how long that could take.* He chuckled to himself, and a small puff of white gas filled his vision.

*It must be cold.* He turned back around to find the foggy thin outline of a hand still on the glass pane he had touched. He tilted his head. The one on the mirror before had gone away almost instantly, but this one remained. *Why? It can't be that cold, can it?* He looked back around at the rain to which he had not paid much attention, wondering if it had turned from rain to snow. What he saw instead was more wondrous than he could have imagined. The droplets were now suspended in the air around him. Alan could not believe his eyes. Just to be sure, he blinked hard. Upon reopening his eyes, the rain around him had completely changed. Only a few drops remained in the air, and crepuscular rays now loomed through the clouds in vast patches, lighting up different parts of the previously darkened city. Alan reached out a hand to touch a nearby droplet. When his hand came into contact with the water, it burst into hundreds of almost microscopic fragments, but none of these moved from their spot.

Across the parking lot, he saw a car splashing a deep puddle high into the air. The car looked to be moving at a fairly high speed and was not at a standstill, like the rain was. It moved through the puddle at an almost imperceptible crawl, and the taillight he could see left a short streak of reddish light behind it. Alan gaped. *What the fuck is going on*? Even after his own comprehension of time affecting him differently, his mind could not wrap itself around time actually standing still. His legs wobbled, and he realized he felt dizzy. Gripping the railing tight between his fingers, a surge of distress washed over his body, starting from his chest.

All around him was complete silence. No noise whatsoever found his ears or filled his senses. He started to hear ringing in its stead and put his hands around his ears to muffle the roar. The ringing did not subside, and Alan lowered his hands. This sensation was the most terrifyingly strange experience he had ever encountered. His legs gave way, and he dropped to his knees and let go of the rail.

This was too much for him to handle. Staying in his decaying body after being tortured to death? Sure why not. Souls coming up at random points in the city and flying into the sky? No problem there. Being completely unable to interact with the world around him? What else would someone expect from a ghost? Jumping from place to place without regard to distance in a split second didn't make much sense, but he was willing to accept it. But now, he was standing in the middle of everything with time basically stopped.

He had noticed how easy it was to lose track of how fast time appeared to fly around him, without him, but this was entirely new. Before he'd realized time was different for him, he figured time slipping by was just a result of boredom or inattentiveness. With his current understanding of time, he was still not entirely able to grasp fully the passage of time in his state. His once noticeably more organized mind was now racing with thoughts, jumbling and crashing together into formless, seamless garbage. Unable to concentrate on even any one fragment, his head began to swim, and the dizziness became unbearably worse.

He couldn't look at it any longer. Turning away from the scene, he crawled his way toward a corner of the balcony. His entire body was too weak to carry him much farther than a few feet before he collapsed from exhaustion. His mind fought itself to keep order, and he was finally able to formulate a complete thought. *Make it stop.*

The roaring sound of silence faded into the light pitter-patter of the few raindrops which had still hovered in the air. The splash of the puddle was overtaken by the rev of the engine which had created it. Almost as if it never had been enervated, Alan's body revitalized itself. His head stopped swimming in a sea of broken thoughts and became the efficient organized machine he had found it to be since his death.

Slowly, he rose from the concrete on which he had lain. Through the glass, Kaiya was just exiting the shower with a towel around her strawberry blonde hair. Alan sighed in relief and straightened himself into a standing position. The hand print had evaporated. Everything in the world was as it should have been once again. He closed his eyes.

# Chapter 19

By the time Alan opened his eyes, the sun had dipped low behind the mountains bringing a mock nautical twilight to the sky. The clouds in the sky were bright with the sun's rays, but the peaks of the Rockies were tipping the flat cumulus bottoms with jagged lines of deep shadow, giving them an unnatural look of greys and reds. The penumbral dark beyond the clouds gave an eerily rueful accent to the feeling now welling up inside of him.

Kaiya was gone from the apartment, and Alan had absolutely no way of knowing how long it had been since she left. He was still wary of using his ability to jump from place to place, but it seemed to be his only choice at the moment. He didn't know how the jump would make him feel after the exhaustion he'd suffered through time slowing down around him. Even now, his movements were sluggish and cumbersome, as they had been in his early days as an apparition.

Alan focused what little energy he felt in his body and thought about Kaiya. Nothing happened. His body did not jump into the air, like before. The energy he had focused diffused through him, and he relaxed into a slumped sitting position. Wondering what he had done wrong, he hugged his knees. Every other time was simple: think about where he wanted to go and jump through the air to wherever he wanted. For a while, he contemplated what could possibly be the issue which kept him from jumping to Kaiya. It seemed odd, but at the same time, he had been almost completely debilitated just a short time ago.

The largest problem Alan could think of was how to rejuvenate himself in any way. As far as he could tell, there was no need for him to eat or consume any sort of sustenance. His body did grow weary as he performed tasks which were in some way unnatural to him. Alan only had a rudimentary understanding of physics, but the concept of time slowing to a crawl was something he only knew to exist in sci-fi movies. *I didn't think anything like that was even remotely possible*. Then again, he figured the same about being able to jump instantly from one place to another. His own limited understanding motivated him to learn more on this subject, but in his current state, doing so would be virtually impossible. Therefore, he put the idea out of his mind until further notice.

Alan's first line of business was to find Kaiya, again. Having said she would denounce herself, he assumed she would be going to some police station. But how could he know to which police station she would go? Determining exactly how precarious trying to find her could be, he thought hard about his situation. As far as he knew, there were six districts in Denver. Knowing how long it would take for him to walk to each one individually, he reckoned she would probably be processed and jailed by the time he arrived to the one she picked. And he had absolutely no knowledge of where the majority of them were much less any of the jails or prisons to which she might be sent.

To Alan, there were not many other choices to contemplate. He had to find a way to jump to her. He stood from his slouched position and walked across the balcony to the rocking chair. Sitting down, Alan leaned back into the chair and weighed his options again to be absolutely certain. Again, he came to the same conclusion, but the troublesome part was how. Of course, he would need to revitalize himself. He went over in his mind all of the things he might be able to do to regain a bit of energy.

Then the obvious hit him. He had been able to sleep in this state before. There was no telling how much time had passed between when he had closed his eyes and when he'd been awakened, but he was almost completely certain it would allow him some rest. He also knew, no matter how long he slept, he would be able to jump to exactly where Kaiya was, which meant time was almost completely not against him. He wondered for a moment if this was the right decision. Just closing his eyes could leave him hours or days in the future. Every day blended together like a bowl of swirl ice cream stirred until the vanilla and chocolate combined into an indistinguishably light brown liquid. He needed a way to tell the date. At least then he would have some clue as to how long each rest could potentially last.

In his mind, he laid out the details of what he would do. Find out the date, sleep, find the date again, jump to Kaiya, and then he could worry about his discovery further into the parts of his existence which he did not understand. Luckily enough for him, he didn't have to find a way out of the apartment. His inability to do so would have completely hindered the first step. He figured a fall from this distance would not hurt him, given how jumping from place to place seemed to work. Without a second thought, he jumped.

His descent was quick compared to how he had fallen after exiting his body, but it still was not as fast as he expected. When he landed, he felt no impact or shudder from the forces of gravity. Immediately, he started running. There was no time to waste. Running was still fairly difficult, but the strenuousness did not impede him as much as it had when he'd first tried. His plan was to find the nearest newspaper stand. He hadn't the slightest idea where he might come across one. Still, there had to be one nearby.

Alan raced three full blocks before slowing to a quick jog. He wasn't too tired, but the force he had been exerting had become too difficult to maintain. Glancing around, he saw two stands and stopped. Two blocks ahead and across the street were green and blue boxes he recognized from when, during his life, he'd stopped every once in a while to grab the day's newspaper. Jumping into another full run, he dashed across the street and looked for oncoming traffic. He had to stop on the median for a bumbling old pickup truck to pass by. Once on the sidewalk, he jogged the rest of the way to the boxes and slowed to a halt. What he saw inside the box made him gasp and take a few steps back with a confused grimace.

The date on the newspaper inside the box read July 3, 2018. Alan covered his mouth and stepped back another pace. How had he been dead for almost 8 months, already? Had that much time really passed? Surely the date had to be wrong. Kaiya's pregnancy was not even showing that much. Still moving backward, he tripped over his own feet and fell against the building behind him. The crowds of people which passed him on the street blended together as if time were fast forwarding in slow motion. Scenes of people interacting with one another or completely ignoring their surroundings filled his vision, and he began to feel dizzy again. Against the stone wall in the middle of the excited droves of sightless onlookers, Alan curled his legs into a ball and fell asleep.

Alan was looking down the long hallway again. He found the three doors through which he'd already passed still open, but the scenery beyond each was slightly different than it had been before. Light from daybreak was spilling over the edges of all thresholds, causing sheen across the already faintly luminous tile floor. Each landscape, despite apparently being from entirely different locations on the Earth, was being lit by the same sunrise. The park in which the first soul span and zipped out of sight was lit as if by fire with rays of bright orange upon the green blades of grass. The blue and purple flowers were indistinguishable from one another in the red and orange tendrils of sunlight.

The snowy mountain shone brightest, as the rose gold light reflected off the melting banks of pure white. In the distance, Alan could see the glimmer of an ocean or sea which mirrored the sun and sky almost perfectly from this far. The waves which he knew had to be there were so indistinct as to appear completely flat. Through the third door, the green grassy mountains hid the sun from view, making the morning haze glow in the shadowy shapes of their peaks. The temple steps which led down were now more noticeably cracked. Alan had not before been able to see exactly how ancient it had looked.

Alan wanted to explore every door more, now that dawn had peeked over the far off horizons and illuminated the worlds through them. For several minutes, he stood and contemplated how long it might take to traverse every outcropping and every valley in even the last door he'd opened. *Probably hundreds of years, at least*. Taking one last look through the doors in turn, he stepped up close to the fourth door. The etchings were similar to that of door three, but he could see the minute changes in each figure. They all seemed to become more defined the longer he stared at the door. Alan reached out a hand to touch the marks, but thought better of it. *They might disappear*, he thought. He took in every detail he could see about the door, and the differences became more and more evident.

Having his fill of door focused observations, he grabbed the handle, turned, and pulled. The door floated away from its place in the wall through Alan and faded in opacity until it was no more. The familiar black veil met his eyes with a shimmering wisp of movement like ripples on an otherwise completely smooth water surface which looked to only be a trick on his eye. Confidently, he pushed his hand through. No resistance met his fingertips, as he had not strayed from the unspoken rules which defined his existence here. The blackness melted away, like it had before.

On the other side, Alan was met by a grand white sandy beach. Waves lapped happily at the shoreline, and the relatively calm waters pulsed inward and outward as if the entire ocean moved at once. The sun had not yet risen enough above the horizon to light the sky here with more than a gradient of violet to powdery blue before becoming thoroughly masked by the thick palms which covered the island behind the door. A single mountain peak, covered almost entirely in green foliage, showed its grey, craggy tip just above the crowded treetops. The crest was outlined by a halo of pale pink sunlight the brightness of which was dimmer than that of any sun he had seen through the other doors. The brightest stars still shone in the fading night sky.

Above him, Alan noticed only one spinning soul orb. This one spun so slowly, however, it was almost insignificant. It crept along at a speed slower than the sun that lightened the sky. Alan wondered if he could call it down to talk to him, but at the exact moment his mind mulled this thought into existence, another slowly rising orb appeared just above the trees and met the first in the air. Together, the orbs moved toward the end of the anticrepuscular and into the dark part of the world. Alan did not want to lose this opportunity to follow the orbs.

Willing himself to follow, his body rose into the sky, notably slower than he'd been used to up until now. The force which lifted his body felt as a hug to the middle would, but no arms wrapped around him, or none he could see. Once away from the ground, the red-orange sun blinded his vision and forced him to look away from the two orbs, but the force continued to move him through the air and toward the orbs until he found himself a certain distance away. He maintained only 100 or so feet from the orbs while they strode through the dawn light round the island. Their pulsations became more and more prominent the longer his eyes remained transfixed upon them.

They could have been a couple taking a much needed relaxing stroll through the park, hand in hand. The way they swayed in the nonexistent wind gave the orbs the look of two actual people enjoying each other's company one last time before death took one permanently. Circling the tiny island could have taken hours upon hours, but the sun did not climb any farther into the sky, which gave the entire scene a romantic and warm lightheartedness.

After countless revolutions, the pair stopped in the grand shadow of the lone mountain peak, pulsated to each other quickly, and began spinning, slowly at first and then quickly. Alan willed himself to get closer to them and see precisely where the two would fire into the sky. Now he knew how long he'd been ethereal, he could tell the wonderings of where exactly these souls went had been crowding his mind for months. His body drew nearer and lower compared to the souls to give himself a perfect angle with which to view their final moments on Earth, or even in the air above the Earth. Faster and faster the souls spun round until finally becoming a blur of light which left streaks in his vision. Alan wanted time to go slower as to have the ability to see their motion and destination with as much accuracy as possible. However, time had already come to an almost complete standstill, the souls remaining unaffected; Alan had not the knowledge whether this was the dream's doing or his own.

Even in the dream, the notion of time moving this slowly around him was nauseating. Wiping the thought from his consciousness, he focused entirely on both spheres, not knowing if one or both would go off first. As suddenly as they'd begun to spin, the left one shot right into the middle of its own circle and straight into the air toward a distant and dim star. Alan made note of where this star was located and eyed the other sphere. It, too, sprang into the middle of its circle and shot directly into the sky toward the exact same star.

For many minutes perhaps even hours, Alan studied the sky above him to make absolute certain to which star they had gone. The dense sunlight had not quite masked the stars enough to make the task difficult whatsoever. The star and its neighbors burned themselves into Alan's mind, and he did not look away until he could close his eyes and find them exactly in his thoughts. Once he knew he would be able to find their exact location again, he turned midair, floated down to the place where he knew the door still lay open and secure, landed, and sat contemplatively upon the sand below him.

The fine grains below him sifted through his immaterial fingers as though he had form. Their gritty nature did not cling to him, however. His body did not have wrinkles in which the sand could become stuck. The ocean behind him no longer roared with tide or movement against the sand, and he looked straight out into the dark ring opposite the sun. None of the waves moved on the water, and each reflected the complete ghostly blackness which emanated from the ring. He shifted his body in the sand and stood up. His time on this island was coming to an end. He turned on the spot and walked through the doorway into the long hall.

The next two doorways were just around halfway, and he walked to the one adjacent to that which he'd just entered. Looking at the markings for a second time, he remembered those which had covered tonight's door. These were similar in shape and form but entirely more complex. He knew the door would not open at all, so he reached his hand up and touched the symbols. Running his fingers down the length of the first line, he felt each sharp edge and dull, smooth curve which made up the letters. His fingers reached the end of the line, and the hallway began to disappear into nothing.

## Chapter 20

Alan's eyes opened slowly. His other senses began to return to him, and the soft patter of a light afternoon rain surrounded him. The sun was bright in the sky above and shone through a hole in the sparse crying clouds to create an uncharacteristic brilliance which glistened off the scattered wet spots left behind on the asphalt and concrete by the rain. A breeze tickled the trees that lined the streets and swayed their leaves. He was not able to hear the rustle over the sound of the rain and passersby.

Eyes glancing around, Alan noticed that not much had changed since he had fallen asleep. Several cars which were parked along the sidewalk were the same ones which he vaguely recalled from before his slumber. The newspaper in the stand in front of him had a different cover, though. Making sure there were no pedestrians into whom he could collide, he stood up and covered the distance in three steps. He knelt down to get a better view and furled his eyebrow. The date read July 6, 2018. Somehow, three days had gone by in the time he was asleep. He muttered to himself and was reminded of his own inability to speak or make sound, not even the usual whisper of breath had come forth.

Alan stood in place, dodged a person walking by, and prepared himself to jump. His mind went to Kaiya, and he hoped this jump would work. His hands formed fists. *I want to see her*. His body moved so suddenly and quickly that he tensed up from astonishment. He was flying through the air faster than his eyes could comprehend the scenery under him. Blurs of greens, greys, yellows, and blues flashed by in an instant. As swiftly as he had left the ground, he was back upon it. The crisp drizzling streets of Denver were ages away. However, the place where he now stood seemed familiar to some far off memory.

Alan found himself in a fluorescently lit large room with an empty row of benched seats to one side and a reception area on the other. A few uniformed people stood behind the reception area. Off to the side of the reception desk was a line of six people against the wall all chained together. On either side of the line, there stood an armed guard. The guard opposite him motioned for the line to move, and they all turned around. In the group, he caught the glimpse of long strawberry blonde hair. He felt a light skip in his step and followed the line through the long hallway beside the reception desk and to a barred, cell-like door which had a keypad beside it. The buttons on the pad emanated a dim blue light.

The line halted, and the guard toward the front nodded to another which was out of Alan's sight behind a large glass pane. The barred door clanked and slid with a shuddering screech to the side. He saw several of the inmates wince with the sound, but he and the guards remained unaffected. Steadily, the front guard led them through the door and into a larger hallway with metal staircase leading up to each side. The prisoners around him were not dressed in the fashion he had expected. Most were wearing white cotton pants and shirt and sitting at tables scattered around the main corridor. Upon the tables were various games or puzzles, most of which went unnoticed by the inmates.

Alan approached several of the people in white only to be met by a cathartic faces and catatonic stares. A dawn of horrifying realization set itself over him. *This is a mental hospital.* He couldn't believe his eyes. The door behind him closed with another screech, and many of the patients looked round but did not speak. The guards unshackled the group of people, and all six rubbed their wrists and looked around. The only one which did not move from the spot was Kaiya. Instead, she stared straight at the ground. As if from nowhere, a nurse, sporting similar white shirt and pants as the patients, walked up to her and led her to an empty table with an incomplete puzzle. The only noticeable difference between the nurse and any patient was a little blue patch on her shoulder and a matching name patch. Kaiya did not go unwillingly, but there was a hesitation that Alan had read as rather apprehensive. Reluctantly, it seemed, she sat at the table. He drew close to her and noticed that her face was not like the others he'd seen. She was aware, and her eyes darted around, like a hawk.

Alan noticed how much more pronounced her baby bump was now than it had been while he had seen her in the apartment. Unbothered, he found a seat beside her into which he could fit between it and the table. Someone behind him muttered something about killing someone in their bed, and he turned around. The man who spoke quietly was a guard, and he was whispering to one of the nurses, only discernable by the patches. Alan strained his ears to hear a little better and tuned out the incessant tap tap tapping of games or puzzles around him.

"Right in his own bed," The guard breathed. "And the kicker is, she's pregnant with his child." The nurse raised her eyebrows at this part and rested her hand on her hip, as if unable to believe what he'd said.

"You can't be serious," her voice was low, but much more easily heard than the guard's.

"I am. She claimed insanity with proof from two different psychiatrists," the guard seemed to be impressed that whoever they were talking about was in this particular hospital. Alan rose from where he stood and went closer to the two. "Apparently, she has violent dissociative identity disorder. Super unusual."

The nurse nodded in the direction of Kaiya and said, "That's her?"

"Uh huh," the guard glanced around for any prying ears.

Alan looked from Kaiya to the security guard and back. What were they talking about? He didn't recognize the term 'dissociative identity disorder' right off, but it sounded to him like something he heard about in a psychology class back in college. He thought for a moment and remembered something about people becoming someone else at times. Kaiya had not immediately struck him as someone with a mental disorder. He decided to listen in a bit more to learn as much as he could about what had happened with her.

"- what do you expect?" The nurse was now leaning close to the guard who spoke in an even more hushed tone. "Her sentence wasn't conditional, like most people who come in from criminal cases. They are so rare, anyway."

"I don't think we should continue this conversation here. I'm on break in a half hour. Meet me in the usual spot?" The nurse flashed him a look of debauched deviousness.

The guard raised one eyebrow and smirked. His voice cracked as he said, "Abso-fuckin'-lutely." His voice was slightly louder than he had intended and carried well to several other attendants who looked round with looks of concern or disapproval. Embarrassed, the guard tipped his hat to the smiling nurse and set off to the other end of the room.

Alan needed to know more, so he stayed beside the nurse until it was her time to go on break. Kaiya remained seated and stared at the 100 piece puzzle which lay in front of her, so he figured she would be fine until his return. After the thirty minutes had passed, the nurse shot a look at the guard who met her gaze and walked quickly through the keypad door whose creak rang out through the room. Her pace was brisk for a woman of such short stature, but Alan was able to keep up with her. All the time he had spent traveling had reanimated his ability to move in the world.

The nurse turned down a long, musty corridor which looked to lead to an unused wing of the hospital. She looked behind her to assure herself of no followers and hastened onward. The only rooms along the corridor were on the right. The entire left wall was filled with small barred windows through which a barren, shabby courtyard could be seen. Many doors to the rooms were standing open, and Alan could see dust covered metal tables and beds without liners, some without mattresses. As they trotted on to the end of the corridor, the nurse brought out a single odd-looking key. The last door in the corridor was a large metal gate set into the wall by several inches. Sliding the key into the large hole on the door, she turned it with some difficulty. A loud clunk came from within the mechanism, and the door swung inward as if on some unseen age worn spring.

Into the passage they went. This particular way was nearly completely desolate. There were no doors open, nor clutter in the hallway. A strange feeling started to overcome Alan's essence. He hadn't the faintest clue as to its origin, but it wasn't one he had ever felt before. It was almost as if the minutest of tugs were pulling his form away from this hallway. Curiosity held a stronger draw on him, though. As he followed the nurse down the corridor, the pull to come away from this place grew stronger and stronger. Alan found himself to be troubled by keeping up with the nurse, as though the pull he was experiencing was physical as well as conscious.

The loud clang of metal behind him made Alan turn to look. As he turned, the scene changed from a desolate hallway to a rank graveyard of mold, grime, and matter covered walls. What had been an empty hallway was now full of overturned and broken gurneys, ripped mattresses, loose hanging lights, and grotesquely shaped bodies. Through all of this, the guard walked, seemingly not noticing a single detail. Alan drew back from the horror and turned back around to get away from the terrible things he was witnessing. Even as he turned, the scene reverted back to its regular self. The pull he had experienced before was virtually nonexistent, now.

He hurried his pace to catch up to the nurse. She turned at a set of two differently colored doors and inserted a key to open the one on the right. Inside were several amenities usual to the typical employee break room. A miniature refrigerator sat in one corner next to a couch made of several mattresses and a metal stand, similar to a futon. Across from the couch were two beds pushed together to form a makeshift full sized bed. In between the bed and couch stood a metal folding table with two folding chairs on top of a terribly brown rug.

Alan stepped through the door to follow the nurse. She untied her bun of hair, and a mass of long, curly brown hair fell to below her waistline. He took a seat along the wall beside the door and waited. The nurse took a bottle of beer from the mini fridge and popped the top with a church key attached to the side of the fridge. Taking a long swig from the bottle, she sat on the makeshift couch and leaned her head back. Mere seconds passed before the guard came in and shut the door behind him. For all intents and purposes, Alan was locked in. Not that it mattered much. He absolutely did not want to go back into that hallway, and he needed to find out what happened to Kaiya.

"Well, it's about time, Ron. I don't have that long." The nurse eyed Ron, who'd started to laugh sarcastically.

"I know, Jan. I know." He threw his cap to the floor and revealed a dark blond crew cut that looked freshly done.

Jan looked him up and down with a vicious smile. "Lose the clothes." With puppy-like excitement, Ron tore off his clothes until he was only in boxers and socks, revealing a rather robust and chiseled build. *Damn, that man has some muscles.* The ends of her lips curled, and she rose from the couch. Seductively, she moved her hips with lithe and untied the front of her trousers. They slid to the floor, and Alan saw Ron become almost instantly erect. This was not what he had expected when he followed Jan. She unbuttoned her blouse, and it, too, dropped to the floor. Her nude bra and panties conformed to her youthful body and made her look younger than she appeared in the face. They approached each other and started kissing, messily.

Zakary Darnell

Alan didn't want to watch the two have sex, so he looked away. The noise she made was horrendous. He knew covering his ears would accomplish nothing, so he attempted to block out the sound to no avail. Her cries were as loud as a banshee and made Alan cringe. Thankfully, Ron was disappointingly quick to finish. A sloppy grunt came from him, and Alan looked back. Jan had the most despondent face Alan had ever seen from someone who just had intercourse.

"Alright, now let's talk about this girl you were so impressed by." Jan rolled out from under Ron and put on her shirt. Ashamed of his performance, Ron stood and pulled on his pants. They sat on the couch together, and Ron popped the tops of two more beers. He handed one to her and took a deep breath.

"Well, she apparently turned herself in a few months ago. It was such an open-and-shut case because she'd been diagnosed with dissociative identity disorder by two separate psychiatrists."

Jan was listening intently, occasionally saying, "Okay" or "Mhmm."

"The judge ruled her to be criminally insane after only three weeks of trial. Her verdict was found on the grounds of having a violent identity. But here's the real kicker. She has apparently killed seven other men. And she always fucked them before she killed them. And she kept a collection of their dicks."

Jan raised an eyebrow. She either was not entirely listening to the story, or she was only mildly interested. Alan found himself compulsively staring at her, both in awe at the fact that Kaiya had killed eight me, including himself, and bewilderment at Jan's apparent detachment to the whole situation.

"The most interesting part, I think, is that she turned herself in because she fell in love with the last guy she killed. The news says that's why she kept the pregnancy. She's a true crazy, that one."

Alan had heard enough at this point. He wanted to be with Kaiya, but he also didn't want to waste one of his jumps. He'd only had four, previously. He also wanted to spend time thinking about what had just been said. They continued with odd conversations concerning the hospital staff and all sorts of drama, none of which interested Alan in the slightest. Eventually, the pair dressed themselves and left the room. Alan's mind was distracted enough by the happenings with Kaiya to completely forget about what he'd seen in the hallway and that he did, in fact, need to follow the pair down said hallway as to not be closed in behind them.

## Chapter 21

Alan moseyed along the desolate hall in the direction of the large metal door still going over everything Jan and Ron had said about Kaiya. All this time, he had wondered why she had treated him so heinously. Another thought process he followed was her distinct and sudden change in behavior that he'd witnessed several times. At the time, he had been confused but didn't put any effort into discovering what might have been causing them. Everything was beginning to make sense, now. He passed by racks of unused hospital supplies and I.V. poles strewn across the hallway haphazardly. As though a tornado had gone through and destroyed everything, the once organized, though mostly empty, ward was once again in disarray, unlike the ward in which Kaiya had been placed. The ceiling tiles and walls were covered in mildew and grime, again. In the matter of seconds, the hallway had somehow aged decades, but Alan took no notice of these things, now. His mind was focused on her, and his body moved around the detritus automatically.

*She has mental issues*, he thought to himself. *It seems like the sort that comes and goes at random. So that must be why she changed from the loving, tender woman into a crazed psycho.* He stopped sauntering forward and folded his arms to recall all of the events pertaining to Kaiya which led up to his death. When they'd first met, she had been happy, but broke down into tears when he merely stopped some random guy from touching her impermissibly. Now that he thought about it, she seemed to cry on multiple occasions, despite having mentioned it to be an unusual occurrence. *Dissociative Identity Disorder.* The words repeated themselves in his head. There was some knowledge in the recesses of his brain that had to do with something like that.

Alan inaudibly tapped his foot on the residue covered tile floor and rubbed his temple to think. It was only then that he noticed three things. One, the door at the end of the hallway was shut tight. Two, the hallway was in the state he had briefly seen on his way in. Three, the pull which he had experienced was back again. It was no longer in one particular direction. Instead, it pulled at him from every direction. He turned around, rapidly, hoping the hallway would revert back the way it had done before. To his dismay, the hallway did not change.

Alan turned back around to see the doorway was hanging off its hinges, rusted and dilapidated. The sounds of buzzing flies filled his ears. A blinding static in the otherwise audible silence. He tried to run down the hallway, but the pull debilitated him to the slowest of crawls, zapping his energy. Despite his situation, he moved on toward the metal door. The static of buzzing flies grew louder and louder in his ears until it became a painful, deafening roar. Alan clenched his fists as a substitute for strength, and a crack shattered its way across his vision. The pull dissolved, and a flash of light appeared from the crack as it grew wider. He closed his eyes to avoid the flash. In the instant he did, the buzzing completely stopped. He opened his eyes to see the hallway back in its original state.

Alan sat on the floor underneath a barred window to gather his thoughts. Similar to after his ordeal with time slowing, he felt drained of energy. But he could not begin to believe he had been in control of it. Time slowing down or speeding up was nothing compared to this. The best way he could describe what had happened was to assume the place he had seen was another dimension. During his life, He had been a fairly big fan of science fiction and fantasy. This was straight from a horror movie. Based on all his observations and previous knowledge, the only conclusion Alan could draw from these happenings was that he was not supposed to be here. He didn't know if what he had just experienced had been a dream or not. He certainly had not been asleep. The sound he'd heard was the main justification for this conclusion. The only times he had gone through something similar was in his dreams. Once, when he'd touched the wrong door, and again when Kaiya had started a vacuum. Whether it was the cause of some greater power or a guide he was being forced to follow, he decided to get out of the hallway as quickly as possible.

His mind went to the large gate at the end of the hallway through which he and Jan had come. *It's probably locked.* He marched forward to the barred gate and examined the mechanism which hid the lock. A small bar jutted out of the door and into a solid metal box on the frame. *Definitely locked.* There was no way he could ever make the door move or even jar it open with all his might. A small part of him wanted to jump immediately to Kaiya and be done with everything, but he knew doing so would leave him with fewer jumps in the future. Since sleeping seemed to be the only surefire way to reenergize himself, he was constantly dissuaded from doing so as to not miss several days of events once again.

Alan twisted around and peered down the hallway. The end was quite a distance, but he could see a turn to the right at the far side. *Maybe that goes back to the entrance.* Wanting to make good time, he set off on a jogging pace. His own incapacity for time meant he could not accurately guess how long he'd already spent in contemplation in the disarrayed corridor and then sitting trying to recover. He traversed the length of the passage. Doorway after doorway crowded his right periphery. Windows passed by in flashes of barred light on his left.

Alan slowed once he came to the end of the passage and rounded the corner. It veered sharply to the right into an even grimmer and disturbing sight than he'd seen before. A windowless hallway stretched out in front of him. What appeared to be blood soaked the floors and mattresses strewn about. Vomit lined the wall skirting. A door hung on only one of its hinges with splintered frame pieces everywhere as if blown outward by an explosive force. Although the hall was not long, the scene was completely horrific. He gulped a breath and faltered when a light flickered on in one of the doorways on his left. Inside the room, a desiccated corpse lay on the ground with flies and other flying insects buzzing about the scrawled body. Alan covered his mouth and continued down the hallway in hopes of its disappearance.

Without looking in any other doorways, Alan ran the rest of the way down the short hallway and found himself next to a similar gate through which he'd come. This one, however, stood somewhat ajar. There was just enough space for him to squeeze through, and so he did, eagerly. He wanted to spend as little time in this place as possible. Once beyond the doorway, a vast gathering hall opened on his right with a narrow flight of stairs that led down to his left. Alan could hear the sounds off clattering game pieces from across the gathering hall. Taking this as a sign of respite, he walked quickly across the gathering hall. The one time he looked back, he saw the hallway through which he'd come to be pleasantly lit and orderly. Still, he hurried.

On the other side of the gathering hall, Alan found himself looking through another barred door. On the other side was the main hall in which Kaiya still sat amongst the other patients. The bars here were thinner and much less robust. Looking it over, he still could not find a way through the bars. The mechanism was smaller than the other one, but it was still sturdy enough to hold back the occasional crazed patient. He groped the bar and shook it with every bit of effort he could. The door didn't even clang against itself. Slumping his shoulders in hopelessness, his eyes came upon an opening at the top. It was hardly wide enough for a person. *But*, he thought, *I'm not really a person any more, am I?*

This concept pierced him deeper than he could have imagined. He wasn't a person. He looked down at his transparent 'body'. The word didn't fit in his mind any more. His entirety was phantasmal. There was no matter, no countenance. He even lacked enough of a profile to make himself out without knowing exactly where he was already. For all intents and purposes, his existence had been obliterated from history. The only people who would remember him would be gone soon, and where would he be? Would he remain in this spectral state of pseudo existence for the rest of eternity? As a man, Alan had never been distracted by the thought of his own mortality, nor had he given much thought of the hereafter. But now, he was living in the hereafter. *What was it James always said? 'I think therefore I am?'* He held his hand up to the light to try to catch the refraction of light in the bright fluorescents above. *I do think. That much I know.* Even in the light far above him, he could catch the light on his outline. *Is that all I am, though? The outline of someone that used to be?*

Hand still outstretched, he grabbed hold of the bars in front of him. He started to climb up them without much success. His hands were not strong enough to grip the bars, and his feet slipped down as he tried to jump up and catch himself. The crossbar overhead was not far out of reach for him, though. It took a couple of tries to jump high enough to grab it, and Alan's lack of normal gravity felt like a complete waste of time during both unsuccessful attempts. When his hand closed around the crossbar, he gripped tightly and pulled himself up. He was surprised by how easy it was to lift himself into the air once he'd caught a reliable grip. Climbing on the last trip he'd been on with James had been remarkably more strenuous than right now. Holding himself strangely sideways, he pushed one of his legs through the gap between the crossbar and the cinderblock ceiling. The other was much more difficult, as his knee did not want to cooperate with him, but he was able to finally get it through. One forceful tug with his arms later, he found himself stuck.

The apparent curvature of his buttocks and size of his waist kept him from moving any farther through the hole. Alan immediately became confused by his inability to force himself into other objects in the world. *Why can a broom go through my knee but I can't go into a metal bar?* Perhaps it had something to do with his inability to touch any living thing, or perhaps it was his own lack of strength by comparison to objects with substance. He did not know, either way. Struggling to coerce himself through the hole, he wiggled his legs and pulled harder. *Damn it all.* Several more fruitless attempts left him dispirited and frustrated. Once again, his mind went back to his current state of being.

If he truly was alive, then he was going to spend the rest of his life trying to find out what in the world he had become, and why, precisely, he had become stuck in this door. *I can't very well do that if I'm stuck in a door, can I?* If what Jan and Ron had said was true, she carried his child, and he wanted to be with her and the baby as long as he could, not because he was in love with her but because he felt a responsibility to do so. That could also possibly mean she really hadn't meant to kill him. For a moment, his memories went back to her screams right after he had died. *'You're not allowed to die on me. Not yet.'* It came back to him as clearly as when it had happened. Her voice had been filled with remorse, almost anguish. Alan felt the weight of great sadness in his chest, and suddenly, he was in a different place. In his mind's eye, he was back in the classroom in college.

His old psychology professor was talking in his slightly squeaky voice, "Dissociative Identity Disorder has been known as multiple personality disorder for quite some time. Only recently has that terminology been thrown out because of the connotation of one having multiple disorders associated with personality, since there are so many. However, Dissociative Identity Disorder is when one's own mind sort of has separate compartments which house a different person. Each one is disjoint, which leads to some common symptoms, like memory loss, loss of time, and rapid mood swings." In Alan's memory, he sat beside himself and watched as he picked at the eraser on the end of his pencil. *That's probably why I never could remember any of this stuff.* The professor continued, "With this disorder, the patient is oftentimes completely unaware of their actions when controlled by the separate entity in their mind. For all intents and purposes, the patient is a completely different person when each identity is active."

Alan popped back from his recollection. *What the actual hell is going on today?* He didn't truly have the time to contemplate what might have happened just now. The bars still surrounded him, and his body bowed backward farther than he thought possible. But this was not the difference which distressed him. All around him was in a state of darkness. *Oh, no,* he thought. *I've skipped forward again.* There was no telling how far he'd gone ahead, and, being stuck in these bars, he could not know where Kaiya had gone or in which room she had been placed. Feeling utterly powerless, he decided against all his better judgment to jump. It would be one less until his next sleep, but there seemed to be no other option, now. His mind went to her, and he was off. His body made its way through every level of the building, up high into the sky, and coursed through the cold night air as swift as an airplane. The scenery under him scrolled by slower than it had on his last jump. With as far as he was traveling, it was apparent to him that she was no longer in the mental hospital. As quickly as he'd gone up, he plummeted to the ground and was encompassed by a surge of dazzling white light.

Alan waited impatiently through the flash to be able to see again. Around him, the personnel were wearing a strange color to him, but he did recognize the dress. He had landed in the middle of a hospital waiting room. Confused, he looked around for clues to Kaiya's possible whereabouts, hoping to find some reason as to why she would have found herself in such a place as this. He started to wonder if his ability had actually worked, or if he'd been transported to somewhere entirely different from where he had intended.

Just as he turned back to face the reception desk, the sliding glass doors opened and caused his attention to divert. Through the door rushed two EMT looking people pushing a gurney, accompanied by two officers who walked purposefully a few feet behind the gurney. They all moved too quickly for Alan to catch a decent view of the person being carted, but his interest had been piqued, and he quickly jogged behind them.

Through several long hallways and mechanical doors they went until coming into a room with a hanging sign labeled 'Surgery.' Alan's heart sank deep into his chest. How had he found himself in this situation again?

## Chapter 22

Alan slowed his pace to shambling speed as the EMTs rounded a corner just past the automatic doorway. A strand of long strawberry blonde hair fell beside the gurney as it moved along, and he stopped dead. Arms dangling limply at his sides, he shuffled forward. But he was too late. The doors shuttered and started closing with a low hiss of decompressed air from the door closer. He had completely locked himself out by his own hesitation. Feeling utterly useless and hopeless, he slumped his shoulders and prepared himself for yet another jump. Never before had he done two so close together, but there was no other way without waiting for the next person to open the double doors. He couldn't wait, and Alan knew he could not press the heavy button himself. *Hell, I couldn't even push the light switch.*

In frustration, he slammed his hand into the wall next to him. The faintest of thuds came from the spot he'd hit. The fury which was flowing through him stood still for a fraction of a second. He had never heard a sound from hitting anything before, not even when he'd hit the wall in Kaiya's apartment. It only took Alan that fraction of a second to conclude he needed to hit the button and let loose his rage into it. There was no logical reasoning behind his decision; he just knew he had to do it. With every ounce of might in his feeble, indistinct body, he hit the button. It clicked. Beside him, the heavy wooden mechanical doors shuddered again and opened with a jerk.

Alan did not want to waste time wondering at how it could have worked this time. He ran through the hallway and to the right, following the group. Every door passed by without luck. None of them housed Kaiya. He came to a tee in the hallway and glanced around. There was no sign that he could see, so where had they gone? He bounced on the balls of his feet with nervous anticipation and ran left. There were fewer doors this way, but he figured fewer doors also meant less time checking each one. However, every door was completely empty this way, too. The closer he came to the end, the more he began to doubt his initial decision of turning left. Just as he approached the last door in this corridor, he heard a deafening scream come from the other way. In his heart, he knew it had to have been Kaiya.

Alan tried to sprint. His joints protested, and the air around him pushed against his infirmity. But he could not stop, now. His own frailty a hindrance, he was forced to slow after only several yards, but still he ran as fast as his legs permitted. Each stride brought him closer to the one he once loved. Another scream echoed through the hall, and he knew he was going the right way. There was a turn ahead of him with a sign labeled 'Maternity,' The edge of relief tickled his mind as he pressed on at a slower speed. *She is probably alright. No need to worry, Alan.* His own name reverberated in his mind. It was almost alien to him. He shook his head. There was no need to concentrate on insignificant things like the sound of his own name. The hall veered left, and he was met by another door.

Through the window on the door, Alan could see the gurney slow and enter a room just behind the nurse's station in the middle of the ward. He no longer was overcome by anger, but nevertheless, he slammed his fist against the metal button. To his surprise, it gave way just as easily as the one before. Awestruck, he stepped back to allow the door to open fully. As the mechanical door swung, he saw the door to the room in which Kaiya had been taken start to close. His hand shot out, and he tried to yell, "No." The imperceptible wisp of air his voice used to be had now become a more prominent but still indistinct growling sound. The moment Alan had spoken, time slowed to almost a standstill.

Immediately, he started to feel the strain on his body from before. He knew that he had to move now or lose his chance. His intentions on moving quickly never came to fruition, however. He lurched forward, and the effort made him nauseous from agony all over his body. Through all the pain and nausea, he trudged forward. Step after agonizing step he grew more and more weary. Two more. One more. He came into the room and collapsed onto the floor next to a chair beside the door. Time reverted back to normal, and out of the corner of his eye Alan watched the EMTs roll the gurney up beside a maternity bed. They transferred the panting Kaiya to the bed, and she huffed in and cried out in passionate misery.

Alan was powerless to help her. He watched in vain as her screams became louder and closer together. The doctors around her appeared to be doing absolutely nothing for her. At times, she would pass out for several minutes and come back to consciousness with another tormented cry. He shuddered with every sound she made, knowing how it must feel to have her entire body convulse with anguish. Upon the third instance of her fainting, he picked himself up off the floor, arms writhing in protest and stomach wrung in knots. Something was not right. He didn't know what it could be or specifically how giving birth was supposed to go, but this did not sit well in his mind. Slowly, he crawled his way to her bedside between her heart monitor and a nurse who was standing still beside her holding a clipboard but not taking notes. Using the bed as support, he lifted himself onto his feet and leaned as close to Kaiya as he could.

Kaiya let out another blood curdling wale and collapsed into her pillows. Her arm, which had been upright in support of her body, fell into Alan's hand. The heart monitor went from a rapid yet consistent intermittent beep to a constant flat tone. Alan looked into her face and saw the glow on her skin diminish to nothing. Desperately, his eyes darted around to the faces surrounding her. The nurse next to him glanced at the heart monitor and to the overseeing doctor. From the middle of Kaiya's chest, a glowing golden yellow orb rose and hovered steadily over her. Alan's heart dropped into his stomach. *No. Please, no.* Around him, doctors and nurses fell into a rush of activity. Their jumbled words made no sense to him, but the sudden scurry made Alan have to move away from Kaiya.

He found himself shaking with nervousness and anxiety in a corner and watching while the nurses and doctors tried to save the child in Kaiya's womb. There was no telling how long he stood in that corner. Before the doctors were able to perform an emergency C-section, Alan saw another glowing golden yellow orb rise from Kaiya. This time, the orb rose from her stomach and spun restfully next to the other. Alan's entire body relaxed and crumpled to the floor. He let out a woeful howl which manifested itself in the form of a rasping puff. No one around him noticed his sorrow. He was now completely alone.

Alan held his legs to his chest and stared at the ground. The doctors and nurses around him blurred into a flow of speedy activity which appeared to him like a movie on constant fast forward. He did not want to watch as they pronounced Kaiya's death or as they pushed her out of the room. His heart had sunken so low in his chest that he could feel himself trembling from its absence. Cradling himself and rocking aimlessly, he thought nothing would be better than to skip through all this pain and find himself at some point in the future. Kaiya was gone. If he could have, he would have cried long and hard. This bodily form disallowed tears. Still shaking, he couldn't tell now if it was from anger at himself for not being able to express his despair or from the loss of the woman he knew had loved him upon her death just as much as he'd loved her upon his own. He knew she loved him because he could clearly remember the remorse in her voice when she had whispered to herself as well as when she had screamed his name upon his death. Without any other thing to do and only a wish to move forward, he closed his eyes and fell asleep.

The long hallway materialized in front of his eyes. Down the hall were five different bright white and gold thick strips of sunlight which streamed through the five open doorways as though from five different suns. This was the first time Alan truly noticed how strange it was to have five completely different locations all with the same time of day. He thought, however, that the locations could not have been on any other planet but Earth. They were all familiar to him, and he felt the strong urge to go back through every door just to visit each again. They had all been beautiful in their own right. The mountain ranges which had been both snowy white and grey with green vegetation had been his favorites. Having grown up in Colorado, he absolutely loved the mountains. But he knew that now was not the time to revisit anywhere. First and foremost in this dream, he had to go through the sixth door. By this dream, he had come to realize these dreams were more than just a hallway filled with doors that led to random places on Earth. Something was happening to him each time he entered this place. Whether benevolent or malicious, Alan did not know. It was no matter to him, though.

His legs no longer trembled as they had in the hospital. With sure feet, he stepped forward, passing in and out of the beams of light filling the hallway. His feet brought him straight to the sixth door without fault. The letters on the doorway were becoming more distinct. Alan was now able to make out each individual mark, but he still had no comprehension of their meaning. Instead of grasping the handle to turn as usual, he peered around at the open doors. He reminisced what had happened in each one. The first was simple enough. He'd stood in the park and watched as the sky was blazoned by an aurora of dancing lights. There had been one spinning orb in the sky there. For a second, Alan wondered if this could have been the soul of James. *I did have that dream right after he died, after all.* The second was a high mountain filled with snow. Another soul had been there, but this one was much closer than the other. It seemed to have known him, but he didn't know why.

These two stuck out in his mind. These were the only two he'd had while alive. Those were the only times he had personally experienced death. They'd also been the only ones in which he had only seen one of the glowing golden orbs. To call them souls was crude, at best. He had no definitive information on whether or not they truly were. For all he knew, they could have been a manifestation of the human mind passing on into another dimension. There was not much Alan knew about anything which could begin to explain what was going on around him. Turning to the sixth door, he decided that this door was a stepping stone for him which needed to be crossed in order to find out more, no matter what there was in store for him in this life now. Definitively, he grabbed the door handle, which turned easily downward. The wooden material splintered and crumbled into hundreds of pieces straight downward through the floor and disappeared without a trace.

Without any hesitation, Alan drove himself headfirst into the black veil. Like a thin layer of goo, the veil hugged his body until he burst through the other side as a hand would go through silly putty. On the other side was the crisp, dry air of clean yellow-sanded desert. No wind blew that he could see, and the sand felt warm under his feet. *Strange,* he thought, *I'm not used to feeling heat any more.* The warm sand tickled between his toes and shifted under his weight. *That's not usual, either.* The sensation made him look down at his feet. His body was no longer completely absent from view. Instead of transparency, Alan saw for the first time a ghostly shaded presence where his body was supposed to be. "What in the..." He gasped and covered his mouth. His voice had made a sound. It was a mere whisper but distinguishable. He'd actually heard his voice for the first time in almost a year. A shudder ran down his body from his head to his toes. *What is going on?*

Alan wiggled his toes in the sand. The movement made toe prints in the soft, warm sand, and he bent over to touch with his hand. He scooped up a handful and let the dry grains trickle through his fingers. The warmth of the sand in his palm resonated through his body. For the first time in what seemed like forever, Alan smiled. He had almost completely forgotten what it was like to touch and feel things and sensations around him. He let the rest of the sand fall out of his hand and stood. Around him was a vast desert with absolutely nothing but sand. The dunes rolled into the distance with crests that wisped in far off breezes. Serenity surrounded him, and he was in complete bliss. He looked out over the dunes and watched the sands shift. He sat down in the sand and, for the first time in his memory, he closed his eyes during his dream.

It was only then that he noticed the breeze in his ears. It was just slow enough to not feel it against his face or body. The meager wind whistled low in his ears. Though the sand was warm against his legs and buttocks, he did not feel the sun's hot rays. It had been eerie how they pierced his phantasmal body in the beginning, but Alan was used to that, now. What caught his attention was how he was sinking slowly into the sand around him. The spot where he sat was filling with sands from neighboring dunes, and the specks of hot dust pelted him in the wind that started to pick up to a gust. He furled his eyebrows. The supposed serenity had started to falter, and he opened his eyes. The winds were coming from the other side of the door by which Alan had sat. He found that, if he leaned back just a bit, he could see around the door. But what he saw was not at all what he'd expected.

On the other side of the door, there was a dark mass headed swiftly toward him. Alan blinked several times and stood hastily. *Is this normal?* He'd never actually been to a desert before, and his Hollywood influenced idea of sandstorms was not at all what he had seen. Again, he looked beyond the door. Sure enough, an almost black mass of swirling sand was moving in a harsh gale toward where he stood. The only thing he could think to do was go back through the door, but he was second guessing his instincts. He'd never been hurt in this form. Not even an inferno had hurt him. For the first time in his existence, Alan felt absolutely no fear of what might happen. Instead of running like a coward back into the hallway, he stood his ground and waited for the incoming storm. But nothing ever came. The breeze died once more to a whisper. Alan was not necessarily disappointed by the anticlimactic turn of events, but he wondered about them, all the same. Around the door, the blackness was completely gone. As quickly as it had appeared, the storm had gone away without so much as a trace.

The tiniest of nudges pushed against his shoulder. He turned to see two of the golden spinning orbs. One was pulsating with the same sort of rhythmic flashes that he'd seen in his second dream. Alan had the overwhelming sensation that he needed to touch the orb. Tentatively, he reached out, fingers outstretched. The barrier which had been there before was gone. His fingers touched the small orb, and he gasped.

"Hello, Alan." Kaiya's lovingly sweet voice echoed though his head.

## Chapter 23

Alan almost did not recognize her voice at first. But the way she had said his name made his body tremble with excitement and elation. The sound of her was completely different than it had been during her life. It had a tinge of what Alan could only describe as brightness to it. She no longer sounded human, but preternaturally emphatic in tone. Her orb vibrated in his hand with a light, pleasant hum that brought him comfort. His smile, which had been on his face from the serenity he'd felt before, widened, though it remained virtually unseen. The orb next to Kaiya flashed and caused him to look over, curiously.

"Who might this be?" He asked with a light heart.

Kaiya's orb now flashed, and Alan heard her voice in his head again. "This is your daughter, Alan. She never was able to meet you, but I thought I was able to feel you with me the whole way through." He felt the pleasant hum shudder and an understanding entered him. Kaiya was sad. He could feel her emotion emanate from the orb. He didn't know how it worked, but he did know that, if she had been able to, she would have cried just then.

"Don't be sad." He consoled her. For him, there was nothing over which to be sad, much less now that he could finally talk to her and touch her. But Kaiya's orb shuddered again. It flashed quickly this time as an explanation streamed out of her and into his mind faster than he would have been able to understand, had she actually been speaking.

"I'm so sorry, Alan. I should have told you about my condition much sooner. I thought you were an amazing guy. That date was the best thing that ever happened to me, but for some reason the other part of me wanted to hurt you. I am so so sorry..." Her voice trailed off in his head, and he smiled knowingly.

"It's alright." He said. His whisper of a voice was becoming clearer with each time he spoke. "I already know that you had a mental issue. I don't know how had I come to love you so much, but that did change after I died. I'm not who I was, any more. I'm so much more, and I've been able to think for so long that I came to a realization." He paused for a moment to bring up his other hand to cradle her orb. "I can't even begin to tell you everything that has happened to me. At first, I wanted to find you and be around you, but as time progressed, I learned that it was not out of love. It was out of compassion. I wanted to know that you were able to find peace with what you had done to me."

Kaiya's voice once again entered his mind, somber and sullen. "Do you remember the last words you said to me, Alan? You said that you loved me. I can't begin to imagine how you could have loved me after what I had done to you, and that stuck with me through all of these last eight months. All I could think about was how sorry I was to have hurt you the way I did. Over time, I decided that what would be best for me would be to give up our child and live out the rest of my life alone." She paused, seemingly for a response. When none came, she continued, "But how did you already know I had an issue?" Her sadness waned into appreciation and inquisitiveness. "The only people I ever told were my therapists. They were the ones that told the courts. How did you find out?"

Alan had the overwhelming urge to hug her tight to him and never let go. "Oh, Kaiya. I'll have to start from the beginning to tell you how I know. I don't know if we have time for that." He knew she and their daughter would have to leave soon. To where, he still did not know, but nevertheless, he smiled warmly and understood. "But I will tell you that I was with you for a long time, and I was with you in the end. You were never truly alone."

Once again, his daughter's orb flashed, and Alan could tell she was becoming impatient. He put one of his hands on her orb and his head was filled with an angelically high toned voice which rang out in his head and filled him immediately with joy. "Mommy says you're my dad. Are... Are you?" There was a childlike innocence to the voice, but Alan could also sense a certain maturity, as though death had aged this newborn to an point of understanding.

He was brimming with excitement. He almost couldn't contain himself when he said, "Yes. I am. And you are my lovely, wonderful daughter." He turned his head to Kaiya again. "Have you given her a name, yet?"

"I haven't. I didn't know which name would have been best." Kaiya's voice said in his mind.

Alan nodded and said, "I have the perfect name. Kayla."

Kayla's orb hummed with excitement and her soothingly high voice squealed in his head, "Ya-a-ay. I love that name. Thank you, daddy." Kayla's orb moved close to his chest, and nuzzled against him. "I've wanted to meet you for so long. Mommy talked to me all the time, but never told me why you never did. Did you not want to meet me?" The sweet voice became filled with sorrow, and Alan's heart became heavy, instantly. He couldn't bring himself to tell her what had happened to him.

With love filled apprehension, he told her, "No, of course not. I just had to go away for a while. That's all. You are so special to me, and I wanted to meet you with all my heart. You're my Kayla, and I love you so much." Alan had never known before how much one could love another without ever having met before, but he knew now that he indeed did love Kayla. Despite not feeling the same love for Kaiya as he once had, he wanted to spend the rest of eternity with both her and Kaiya, but time was starting to run short. Kaiya's orb started to pull against him in his hand.

"I don't know what's going on," Kaiya exclaimed. "I don't want to leave yet."

"I know, Kaiya." Alan held her firmly in his grasp, but he couldn't maintain the grip forever. "You're going to somewhere in the stars. I know it must be beautiful there. You and Kayla will be happy, but I can't come with you. That's not how it has ever worked before." He didn't want to let either go, but with a parting, "I will find you both, some day." He let them both go.

As soon as he had, they began to spin and rise into the sky. He could still hear Kayla's voice in his head calling, "No, daddy. Please don't let us go. Please!" But as her orb rose into the air, her voice became more and more distant until he could no longer hear her pleas. His heart became heavily laden with dejection. His whole body shivered from it. They were high in the sky, now, but he didn't have to worry about their departure. Alan was going to follow them upward. His body shot into the sky to meet them. By now, each had begun to spin rapidly, and he knew there wasn't much time left. Faster and faster they spun, and his will would only make him accelerate so much. He heard them both say in the faintest of voices, "I love you." But just as he started to hear their voices in his head again, each shot off far into space. Struck by the need to follow, his heart and mind plunged further into want, and his body obeyed. He rocketed into the stratosphere just in time to see their orbs twinkle out of sight into a tight cluster of stars he had seen before.

Alan knew he couldn't follow his beloved family any farther. They had already gone completely out of view and were travelling swiftly toward... He didn't know where. The constellation into the middle of which they had flown was etched into his memory forever, but he couldn't look away. One by one, he watched other orbs, which he now knew to be the representation of a person's soul, disappear into the same tiny, hazy dipper shaped cluster. He hadn't the slightest clue what it was called, but he would find out.

He floated far above the ground so high the atmosphere around him was thin and only marginally shadowed the sun's rays. But he didn't look anywhere but the constellation. Eons could have passed in the time he spent staring up into the stars. He longed for them to come back to him, but there was no way they could have. He had no idea why, but he knew their parting was final from this planet. He needed to see them again. *No matter how far away you are,* he thought, *I will always come back to you. I may be crazy, but the only thing I know for certain is how much I care for you.* Alan knew that he sounded insane for having fallen in love with a woman that had come to kill him, and even now, he was insane for caring about her as much as he did without the same love he'd had. But the reason for his concern did not matter to him. At this point, he only truly felt love for that bright little girl he had helped father, and he owed her a responsibility.

Alan descended back onto the warm desert sands, but found his body once again completely unaffected by their temperature. He didn't feel the warmth of the grains under his feet, nor did the sand shift from his movement. The storm which had cleared almost instantly began to rage once more. Its heavy black form blew sand like bullets into him. Despite their velocity, he didn't feel their impact any more than one would feel a leaf fall on a clothed shoulder. Even so, he did not want to remain in this place any more, but he didn't want to leave the dream, either. He looked to the sky one more time to see the cloud of glowing souls fade into the growing abyss of sands around him. *Good luck, my friends.* There was nothing else he could find appropriate to say, and, with that, he stepped back through the door.

The doorways, which had allowed rays of light through at the start of this dream, had reverted back to their original state. No light came from any, regardless of the picture contained within them. Each was no longer lit by bright sunlight. In its place was the original swirling, luminous aurora in the otherwise dark night sky. In the long hallway, the same ambient light he knew so well once again filled the hallway and almost completely disallowed any light from crossing the invisible barriers between that world and this crossroads of sorts. Alan looked around the hall, and his eyes came to rest on the part he had yet to open. There were only six doors left. *I've come halfway, already.* He was incredulous. Had he really been having this dream that long? *It has been at least eight months since my death,* he reasoned with himself. That time had passed so quickly; it was almost unreal.

He found himself wondering what may lie beyond the remaining doors. Were all of the doors hiding an earthly landscape? Alan decided to take a bit of a chance and go on to the next door. Still filled with hesitation from his previous experience, he approached the door. The etchings were the same as he remembered them, but this time he partially understood what they meant. The symbols did not represent words, at least not the way that would translate normally. He wasn't even able to read them. Each group portrayed an entire idea which was explained entirely in his mind. But just like his only partial understanding of the symbols, the explanation in his head was incomplete. *Maybe, I have to see the finished marks.* Though he was tempted to continue down the hallway and look at the final door, he held himself at bay. There was no reason to go, yet.

Instead, Alan went back to the first door. The park was remarkably greener than it had been. The vibrant colors of flowers that had spread out over its vastness were replaced by green blades of grass with wheat like heads sprouting from the taller stalks. The moon shone bright at a low angle in the sky, but the aurora was so dazzling that the moon was almost completely unnoticeable by comparison. He stepped through the doorway for a short minute and looked into the sky toward where he thought the first orb had gone. The same tiny cluster was nearby. He nodded to himself and crossed back into the hall and through to the white snow covered mountain top. There, at a point in the sky close to where he thought the soul had shot, was the same constellation. *It's everywhere.* He smiled and sat down on one of the many snow drifts at the top of the mountain. The aurora here was not only in the upper part of the sky. It completely surrounded him and the mountain, or appeared to. Alan allowed the aurora's essence to consume him, and he closed his eyes.

## To the Grave

The wind at this altitude was different than the one in the desert. It did not whistle in his ears. The wind blew across the mountain below him and filled his ears with a low hum. His mind was able to think on his current ability, or his lack thereof. He was not sure if his body would allow him to follow Kaiya and Kayla into the stars. In actuality, he was certain it wouldn't. In spite of this knowledge, he had no feeling of trepidation. A cool, calm collection of ideas and thoughts entered his mind. *I still don't know where those stars are. I might as well make the most of this body, and what it can do.* A new plan began to formulate in his mind. All his previous plans had included Kaiya in at least one way. Now, he had no reason to plan around her. After he found the stars, Alan was going to travel the world and see everything that had brought him wonder during his life, all while mapping out from different locations where the constellation was in relation to the time of year or his own latitude and longitude. For the first time in a long time, he was thrilled.

His eyes opened to see the doorway in front of him. It was suspended in midair like a portal to another dimension. The snow around him blew pleasantly off the ridges made by overhanging cliffs. Flakes swirled like dust in the wind and curled into themselves. Alan knew he was finished here. All the time that he had needed to pass outside of his dream had gone by with ease. He stood, crossed the doorway, and watched while the dream world faded to black.

## Chapter 24

The hospital staff which had filled the room before were all gone when Alan woke. Kaiya's bed had been cleaned and fitted with new sheets. The cardiograph was tucked neatly behind the bed, and the privacy curtain was drawn round halfway to give the illusion of room separation. The door to the hall was completely open, and a group of people passed speaking in dialog and medical terminology he didn't understand completely. In the distance, he could hear beeps and bells of machines monitoring patients' vital signs. As the sounds of the group disappeared, he rose from his comfortable corner. The room looked as if Kaiya had never even been there. Alan wondered how long he had been asleep this time. *Days? Weeks?* Truthfully, he didn't care how long it had been. There was absolutely nothing keeping him here, except, of course, himself.

Alan left the room. Several nurses and a few doctors surrounded the station in the middle of the large room through which he had come. Many were looking at charts or pads without speaking to one another; one or two groups spoke in hushed voices. None of this interested him, and he thought on where the best place to find information on the constellation would be. The first place that popped into his head was a computer, but, of course, he would not be entirely able to do his own searching. Or, he hadn't been able to up to this point. Yet, in his dream, he had been able to interact with the sand underneath him. *Maybe I'm stronger, now.* Alan circled the desk to find an entrance to the middle, where three computers were viewable. Only one nurse sat behind the desk facing away from him by two monitors, each with programs on the screen that Alan assumed to have patient information on them. Another set of monitors sat atop the desk beside him, and he took to them. Sitting down in the computer chair, he touched the keyboard. The screen flashed white, and the hospital name appeared on the wallpaper behind only three icons. *At least I know I can poke around a bit.*

Alan looked around at the small group of people encircling the desk. No one seemed to have noticed the screen suddenly light up, so he went on with his business. He touched the mouse, and the cursor jumped wildly around the screen. He jerked his hand away with surprise. *Well, looks like I can't use the mouse.* Luckily for him, it came to rest on an icon whose symbol he recognized as an internet browser. He touched his finger to the left mouse button, and the cursor shot off to the other side of the screen again. A small circle appeared next to it, and Alan knew he had at least opened the browser. Fourteen separate windows opened to the same home page, and the topmost one came to the front with a flashing black cursor in the address bar at the top. It came as a bit of a surprise how well he could use the computer, but he also knew that he could interact with electronics, though how was still a mystery to him. Even so, this was working quite well for how spasmodically the cursor shot around. *Now, what am I going to look for?*

It hadn't occurred to him how he would search for the name of the constellation. He had at one point been quite skillful with a computer and searching the internet. As such, he tried to search as he would have done, then. The group had looked like a tiny dipper, so he decided to search for that and see what came up. He started to type out 'stars tiny dipper,' and about a hundred s's appeared in the address bar. *Well, that's not useful at all.* He touched the backspace button to make them all disappear and started over. As carefully as he could, he lowered his finger into the S button. About half an inch away, several dozen appeared in the bar. *Alright. A little faster this time.* Again, he pushed his finger into the backspace. This time, he flicked his finger into the S, and a solitary letter showed up in the bar. Alan smiled. It may be slightly more effort than he wanted, but there was no hurry, as far as he could tell.

He made a few errors and had to start over every time, but he eventually was able to type out his search. The browser brought up a google search which presented a number of results. The top result read 'Pleiades Star Cluster, aka Seven Sisters'. Alan had to sound it out in his head. *Pl-ee-ah-des... Pl-ay-uh-dis... Screw that. Seven sisters.* He wished he could click on the article, but there was no telling how frantically the mouse would fly across the screen or if it would even land on the link. But just then, someone made an exclamation that made Alan look up from the screen. Someone had noticed the screen changing apparently by itself and drawn attention to it. Several faces were now staring at the screen and waiting for another change. Without hesitation, he got up from the seat, but it bumped against his hip in his haste. The chair twisted around and caused a gasp from the onlookers. One nurse brought out his phone to make a recording.

Alan thought it better if he jumped somewhere, instead of waiting to see what happened. His limited ability to do so no longer played its part in his decision, since he didn't have any time limitations any more. The first place that popped into his head was the island which he had seen in his dream. In a split second, the Earth lurched below him, and he was off at remarkable speed. Forests, lakes, and mountains passed by below him in a blur of greens, blues, whites, and greys. In almost an instant, deep blue ocean filled his view, and he slowed. His feet touched the familiar white sandy beach, but the doorway was not in its place. The mountain was much more magnificent in the broad daylight. The sky was speckled with small fluffy clouds and was almost as blue as the ocean behind him. Palm trees along the edge of the beach swayed easily in the light ocean breeze. It was completely different compared to the pink sunrise he had seen the last time he had come here.

Alan traipsed along the beach to his right, leaving the faintest footprints behind him. He never noticed his own tracks. The scenery entranced him. Though he did not feel anything, he could imagine the ocean mist against his face and skin. The beach was not long, so he was forced to continue into the line of palms and through the short, grassy underbrush toward the center of the island, where the mountain rose. The incline was negligible, at first. Before he'd walked too far, he saw a small community show itself through the trees. Several thatch covered huts and gazebos lay on the outskirts of the village, but a couple modern buildings were amongst them. Men in flowered button-up shirts and swim shorts and women in bikinis congregated toward one of the huts. Alan assumed this was the bar hut.

The motion of people and the relaxed nature of the locality gave him the notion that there were many places he would have wanted to visit like this during his life. And yet, he never had the time during his life to take a vacation anywhere. Every string of days off he'd gathered were always spent drinking with James or sitting at home with Kipsy playing video games or watching television. Looking back, Alan was torn into wanting to have changed that and appreciating how all of his life experiences had led him to the person he was. There was no telling how many vacations he could have been on, had his life worked out the way he'd wanted it to back then or if he wouldn't have had the time. Now, he had nothing but time. So, what kept him from taking a vacation, now? Was there anything at all keeping him from going anywhere he wanted in the world? From every experience he'd had so far, there was absolutely no distance on Earth which he could not travel in an instant. As much as this island intrigued him in its beauty, he was more inclined to test the waters of his jumping ability.

· There was one particular place that stuck out in his mind. He had no idea why. He thought about it, and at once his body was springing through clouds and over more blurs of color. Two masses of land passed under him before he slowed, but they were almost as one in the quickness with which they passed. He slowed, and his body came to rest at the top platform of the Eiffel Tower. The sky was dark across the city of Paris, but the lights of residences and businesses illuminated his entire view. Despite how active the city appeared from the numerous windows lighted throughout the districts, the streets, boulevards, and parks were tranquil at this height. The combination of partial cloud cover and light pollution gave the illusion of a night sky with virtually no visible stars.

Few people were scattered around the park under the tower. A couple stared into each other's eyes several hundred feet away in a garden under the lights mounted throughout the tower. *This is such a magnificent view.* For no reason at all, Alan decided to fall. He wanted to feel the wind in his face as he spiraled to the ground. Climbing onto the banister which surrounded the platform, he leapt. His body did not fall as slowly as he'd expected. Gravity had its full effect on him, and he plunged into the thin air. It no longer was dense against his form. As he plummeted toward the ground, concern bubbled its way into his mind. *What if I actually can get hurt? What happens?* Closer and closer the ground came into his vision until all he saw was the light bathed, yellow tinged blades of grass below him. Alan began to think his buoyancy would not return, but he beat it from his mind. He didn't care if he died or not. If he died, maybe he would be reunited with his daughter and Kaiya.

In less than a second, his body would hit the ground, and in that time, his mind ballooned all of the thoughts he'd ever had about Kaiya, about starting a family, about the happiness he wanted to experience throughout life, and more. He thought about how Kaiya had stolen his life from him, how he was all too willing to let it deplete into nothing at the time for something as frivolous as a simplistic infatuation. He did not hate her. He did, however, regret having loved her. And in this split second of thought, he decided that he had absolutely no intention of dying right now. He wanted to see Kaiya and Kayla, but even more importantly, he wanted to visit the whole world. More, if he could. The whole universe was his to explore, if he had the ability. As if his thoughts had manifested themselves, his body contacted the grass and immediately stopped before touching the ground. Suspended with arms stuck mid-flail, he looked around him. Time hadn't stopped. He could see the couple chatting away nearby. Flitters of smiles and nudges of affection were being exchanged.

Alan's body remained where it was while he lowered his legs and arms into a kneeling position and hoisted himself onto his knees. He lifted himself to his feet. If he could have raised an eyebrow, he would have done so. In the moment he came to stand, he realized how far away the couple had been from the tower and that they were now only about twenty feet away from him. He turned around, slowly. Behind him, the Eiffel Tower raised high into the sky and gloriously shone light in all directions. He had leapt farther than he could have ever anticipated. *Can I actually fly like in my dream?* He wanted to test it, so he prepared for another leap. With his legs tensed, Alan sprang as hard as he could muster. His only movement was a hop which would have disappointed a ten year old at hopscotch. How was he able to jump from one location on the planet to a completely different one but could only barely manage to hop farther than a foot or so? Again, he attempted, and, again, he failed to make any further progress. He stroked his chin for several moments to contemplate how he might practice this again.

Of course, he could climb to the top of the tower again and jump off, but he would have to wait for someone to go up to the top. However, he hadn't seen anyone up there before he jumped. *It must be pretty late at night*. The few people who had gathered around were becoming fewer and even the couple nearby were showing signs of exhaustion. Each one had yawned at least twice since he had come down. Knowing he would be alone soon, Alan decided to take a stroll to the bottom of the tower to wait out the night. *Hopefully, it's not closed tomorrow.* The walk to the bottom was actually much longer than he had thought. The tree lined streets were nearly barren of activity, which made the trip much easier.

Upon arrival at the foot of the great tower, he stopped. Seeing no one, whatsoever, he sat beside one of the massive four supportive legs and closed his eyes. He opened them again, but all around was still darkness. *What?* This method was one that passed time often enough. It had always worked. He closed his eyes once more and opened them. Still darkness. Around him, every detail was the same. Nothing was making sense to him. One last time, he closed his eyes. This time, he kept them closed for a good amount of time before opening them again. The twinge of dry pain from keeping your eyes open too long struck him. He opened his eyes.

## Chapter 25

A score or more people were surrounding Alan. Several of them were simply staring straight at him. Others were holding up cameras or phones to take pictures. Confused, he looked around him. He was completely and totally surrounded by cats. Dozens upon dozens of all shapes and sizes were curled up or stretched out in a five foot circle. Some were even lying on top of others. *That must be why people are staring,* he thought. No matter what the reason, he did not see a point in staying there any longer. But when he began to rise from his spot, he noticed his outline was much more prominent. He also became aware of the feeling of the concrete beneath his fingertips.

Instinctively, he put his hand up to his temple. The motion made several of the cats look at him, intently. Alan pressed his finger into his temple and stroked firmly all the way around his face. The two spots from where he had been able to feel before had grown in size. He now had sensation around his entire face and down his neck to his shoulders. Parts of his legs and arms tickled with his touch. He hadn't actually perceived his own touch in so long that it was almost an entirely new experience. Alan sat gazing in wonderment at his own ability to finally sense himself, even if it wasn't entirely. He was almost completely oblivious of the now restless crowd shuffling around. The cats, however, were not unaware. The clowder of cats started shifting uneasily with the crowd.

## To the Grave

Alan looked up from himself and saw again the growing crowd of people. Some were starting to show horrified looks on their faces. Unsettled by the sudden change of mood, he slowly, tentatively rose from his spot. Whispers and gasps came from every mouth, almost at once. The clowder in one synchronous motion sprang to their feet together, tails fluffed and hair raised with vexation. He wasn't sure if his own action or that of the crowd around him caused the commotion, but he didn't really want to find out. He tried to step out of the gathering, carefully. Too late. At once, the hoard scattered in all directions, finding their way between legs, over bars, and through gaps to hide somewhere away from this mess.

Though some had watched as the clowder of cats dispersed, the majority of onlookers were still absorbed in watching Alan. A camera flashed, and he heard a woman yell, "I got it on camera!" In the moment, he didn't even realize he had understood her spoken words, even though she'd spoken French. A shuffle in the crowd told him from whence the shout had originated. Amid the crowd but only a few feet back, a woman was being surrounded on all sides by people who wanted to see her picture. A surge of excitement roared through them, and faces on all sides turned away from him to get their own look. He didn't want to wait around for the outcome of this affair. Without thinking of a place to go, his will to jump took him. He sprang upward and away from the crowd of people. But this jump was not expeditious as all others before had been. The Earth didn't lurch under him. His launch was slow enough to see the eyes of the crowd turn toward him in awe. Flashes of cameras followed him upward into the sky, while he flew toward wherever his mind might take him.

223

Even his relatively slow movement was quick enough for him to only catch a glimpse of his witnesses. Soon, he was soaring into and out of clouds. Rain pelted his face, and excitement overtook him. The rain soothed his skin like crisp, parched desert crust in the first rain of a season. Alan hadn't noticed how lifeless his body had been until he found himself cleansed by the warm Mediterranean cloudburst he passed through. Far below him, the shape of Italy showed through the clouds and he could tell which way he was heading. Every jump before had been so quick that he hadn't the ability to sense the direction. The Mediterranean Sea passed underneath him in a course of sparkling blue. He was far enough in the sky that intricate details were beyond his view, but specks of black, which he figured to be boats, drew across the water, leaving trails of white froth behind them. From up here, the world was full of bliss.

Alan had become completely lost in the landscape below when he started to descend. He didn't even notice how much closer he had come to the ground until a bird passed by him, squawking with displeasure. The surprise made him jerk and tumble to the side, and he was in flight no longer. Similar to the dream in which he had first found his ability to jump, his body went straight downward to the ground. He no longer knew exactly where he was, nor which direction he was going. Unlike before in the park in front of the Eiffel Tower, he landed with a thud on the ground near the sea. He gathered himself and got up. Alan stood on top of a crag which overlooked a terraced cityscape of colorful stone buildings. Waves lapped against low rock faced ridgelines that surrounded plazas and stone piers. Hand laid stone streets over which people interweaved through slow moving vehicle traffic, as if it were a shared space for all sorts of travel. It was one of the most remarkable sights he had ever witnessed. Incredibly, Alan knew he was in Greece without having any previous knowledge of it. As far as his geographical knowledge went, he had only seen pictures of this place in travel catalogues. The only things missing were monuments of ancient architecture for which Greece was most well-known.

After his experience in Paris, he wanted to avoid the streets, whenever possible. He didn't know if the crowd had specifically gathered for him, or if it was simply a gathering for the cats around him. *But what did that lady mean 'I got it on camera'?* He had, of course, noticed being able to see himself more prominently, but did that mean others could see him, too? His mind drew him back to the moment in the crematory when the man in black had seemed to stare straight at him. At the time, Alan had shrugged it off as nothing too important, perhaps the man taking a moment of rest. Now, the action was much more peculiar. It had happened again when Kaiya had heard him gasp in her apartment. *Maybe I'm not invisible.* If he were, he would not have been noticed while his body was its least prominent. It was, after all, much more difficult to see him when he was still. Some small part of him wanted to be able to interact with people, but that small part was almost entirely masked by an overwhelming sense that he absolutely should never do that. Alan couldn't explain it. He just somehow knew interaction with people would end badly.

Avoiding people would definitely be difficult at this time of day. The roads in view of his spot atop the crag were busy with marketers selling, pedestrians roaming, and children laughing and playing. For a moment, he pondered the possibilities. *I could wait until nightfall. No, that wouldn't work. But avoiding people altogether is only possible where there are no people.* Then it hit him. The one detail that he overlooked without meaning to. How he had come to be here was completely unlike the previous jumps. He had actually been flying, rather than jumping from one place to another. And just before that, he had glided at least a hundred feet beyond where he could have fallen. Is it possible he hadn't jumped at all? *Maybe, just maybe, every jump was just me flying where I wanted to go.* Alan's mind had settled. He was certain flight was his best option for moving around, especially if he wanted to avoid people. All he had to do was try.

He looked down the sloped side of the crag. It certainly was high up off the water. There was no beach below him, but he stood on one outer point of a cove encompassed almost entirely by the town in front of which he stood. Given his previous experience with water, taking a chance with a dive here would likely find him permanently at the bottom of the bay before him. As much as he wanted to learn flight, was he really willing to risk the water here? *If I can jump off the Eiffel Tower and glide, maybe I can jump up and down.* He jumped in place as high as he could, but he came back down on the rocks wrong and stumbled. His shoulder banged hard against the ragged surface. Though it did not hurt whatsoever, the force made him roll down the sloped side.

Eyes wide, Alan desperately tried to grab something to latch onto. His leg struck a large outlying stone, and he tumbled away from the rock face and out of its reach. *Fuck*. In his spinning vision, Alan could see the surface of the water below getting closer. The only thing he could do now was focus his mind, and he knew it. He closed his eyes to try, but gusts of wind blew past his ears as he fell and spun faster, making it difficult to focus on anything but his descent. Tingles spread over his body like he was a limb that had fallen asleep for far too long. He clenched his fists so tightly his entire body shivered. Concentrating as much as the distractions would allow, Alan thought hard about flight. The spray of crashing waves beneath him splattered against him. He knew he was too close, now. Much too close. Eyes still closed, he expected to hit the water at any moment. The moment never came.

Alan's eyes opened to see the waves below lapping benevolently against the rocks. He was floating a few feet above them mid-tumble. This wasn't quite the flight he had expected, but he was, nevertheless, not at all disappointed. Unlike in Paris, he did not fall shortly after coming to a stop in midair. Tentatively, Alan straightened himself to lie flat in the air. *Now, I just have to start moving.* He waved his arms about, much like a child first learning to swim. As far as he could tell, it didn't work. He tried kicking his legs, too. *I feel goofy.* Unsuccessful, he stopped moving about and thought, *I'd like to move forward.* Almost immediately, he jolted forward. He was shooting forward so quickly he couldn't see where he was going. *Stop stop stop stop!* In an instant, he jerked to a halt. He looked behind him. The shoreline on which he'd started was miles away.

Excitement shot through him from his toes to his ears. *I can... I can fly.* He didn't fully comprehend this idea, yet. Alan started to wonder how but stopped himself in the middle of a thought. He didn't care how. He could fly. *Up.* Alan soared skyward and into a large pillow-like cloud which swirled around from his passing. Tufts of vapor clung to him when he broke through. Ecstatic at his newfound ability, Alan wheeled round and propelled himself toward the town at an incredible speed. In less than a second, he'd arrived. He slowed to a creeping pace and gazed down at the now twilit town. Lights in windows brightened the cobblestone streets. Groups of people traveled the darkening streets in packs, typically avoiding stragglers.

Alan was suddenly reminded of Kaiya. He hadn't truly known her that long. In fact, he was finding it difficult to tell why he had loved her in the first. He absolutely did not love her, now. His reflection made him wonder why he kept coming back to thinking about her. She was only relevant any more as the mother of a child with which he could no longer interact. And then he recognized his own obsession with Kaiya had been simply about beauty. She definitely was the most gorgeous woman he'd ever seen, but he'd known nothing about her before thinking he'd fallen in love with her. There was no dread or despondency which often associates itself with a realization of lackluster infatuation. Alan felt nothing for her. Still, he hoped she was somewhere decent. That was the last thought he had of Kaiya. The changing Mediterranean air currents pushed themselves around and through him. *What a strange sensation,* he thought. He was aware of the wind, but it was a perceptive awareness. He could not feel it, whatsoever. In fact, he experienced nothing. No touch of the breeze. No taste of the cool, crisp evening air. He looked at his hands and turned toward the setting sun. There was no outline at all. He had become completely blank. Alan groped his entire body, searching for the spots which at one point harbored his last grip on his own dying humanity. They were all gone.

# Chapter 26

Alan drifted aimlessly through the sky for so long he'd lost track of the days. It could have been years or decades. Time was no longer relevant to him. He only avoided thunderstorms and cloudbursts. His geographic knowledge had grown to the extent of being able to tell precisely where he was at any given moment, but it didn't matter. As far as he could tell, his existence was purposeless and nonsensical. Other than believing this was some form of afterlife, he had no inclination of why he might have continued on after death. After Kaiya's death, his only drive had been to map the stars, and so he had done. He'd stared up at them every night for what could be a lifetime. He knew exactly where they were in the sky compared to his position on Earth at any time. There was no reason to find any more information on them. He'd then been compelled to travel across the world and see all there was to see, eventually losing sight of his want to go to the stars. Thus, he drifted, like a lone feather caught in the unending breeze of eternity.

Alan had roamed long enough to have an intricate knowledge of the earth. He knew with certainty above which continents or oceans he flew, where his favorite places were, and how long it would take to get there from any given location. Sometimes, he would decide on a direction and just go until he was no longer captivated by the apparent newness of his bearing. Other times, he would choose a specific direction to revisit his favorite places. One such place was the northern polar icecap, especially at night. There was something about the dazzling lights dancing through the sky in graceful pirouettes that made him reminisce. It brought him peace knowing he could see it in person. Alan hadn't had a dream since Kaiya's death and had begun to miss them. When he came to watch the aurora, transient visions from the past and new visions of dreams yet undreamt bubbled up from deep inside his mind. Every time he visited, he recalled the first dream with Kipsy, following her, watching her die, and waking up in a cold sweat.

If Alan had had the capability to be sad, his memories would have seen him filled with an unshakable morosity, and he knew it. But he could not find the ability within himself to feel much of any emotion at all. Without the ability to grieve or be happy, ennui overtook his life. In fact, he strove to find new experiences to drive out his own dissatisfaction with himself. Ages, perhaps even eons, had passed since he'd gone down to earth and been around people, however. Even so, there were only so many places he'd gone around Earth. Alan had been just about everywhere that didn't involve descending into human populated areas. He'd seen some truly marvelous sights. Why, then, was none of it enough to satiate his apathy?

Weary and frustrated, Alan found a nesting place atop a snowy peaked mountain somewhere in the north of Europe. He could not tell how long it had been since he last slept, but his natural clock was no longer natural. A day could pass instantly or at an abnormally leisurely pace. Time no longer appeared to matter to him. The nausea he'd felt when time first stood still ceased affecting him quite some time ago. Alan had set aside the mindset of himself still being constrained by time as he'd known it.

# To the Grave

Instead of being stuck going with the flow of time, as he had done during his life, he was able to move fairly freely through it. Going backwards through time hadn't happened, though he hadn't tried, either. To Alan, reliving the past was unnecessary and frivolous. That, and he acquired too many reservations about contorting past events from sci-fi novels and movies.

The soft snowy drift on which he lay was comfortable enough, but he didn't need comfort to know how tired he was. His fatigue was not from traveling. Instead, he had exhausted himself by drawing out his time around the aurora. Controlling the flow of time around him drained his energy quickly, even if it did take decades or centuries to feel its effects. Alan stared into the vast night sky. The stars and nebulae which made up the Milky Way shone brightly. From this altitude, he was close enough to them to see almost every detail. He could even make out Andromeda. He reached his hand toward the sky and thought for a moment. *I'd love to touch the stars.* For several minutes, he stared up at the sky. *That's it,* completely forgetting his promise to one day find Kayla. *I'm going to the stars.* Arm still outstretched, Alan closed his eyes and slipped quickly into a deep slumber.

The shadowy but inviting long hallway welcomed him once more. Familiar open doorways glowed with bright sun or were dark from starry nights. A thunderstorm flashed beyond the fourth door, but, unlike the abnormal sandstorm from his previous visit, the thunderstorm did not rage with his own emotions. Alan noticed the skies of each door were accurate by their relation to each other on Earth. He even knew where each one was. As he passed by each one, he thought about visiting them all once more outside of his dream after wakening, but as he stepped up to the seventh doorway and glanced over the writing, he realized that his place must not be on Earth. The symbols, which formerly resembled scribbles, made more sense to him. He'd thought they were individual markings which were written left to right in alternating up and down lines, but as he looked closer, now, the differing rows and columns blended together in a way that formed a single shaped symbol with jagged lines etched deep into the wooden door.

Alan drew himself closer to the door without touching it. He could not quite tell what shape the markings made. Shrugging, he accepted the futility of trying to comprehend them completely. He recalled the last time he tried to go out of order with the doors. It hadn't ended poorly, but he didn't want to test the abstruse, almost arcane, quality of this hallway. *Only six doors left. Five after this one*. Alan grabbed the handle. The door atomized and fell as dust into the blackness beyond. The darkness on the other side of this door was blacker and deeper than the others had been before it. The pitch of the veil was more absolute. It invoked a longing in him. He wanted to cross into it. Alan could not disobey. He pushed his hand as far into the veil as he could and fell past as it swallowed him, hungrily.

The shroud split down the middle and separated into individual droplets like a bubble had been blown from the hallway and grew too big to sustain itself. Alan watched as the droplets dissipated into nothing in the patches of sunlight strong enough to penetrate the canopy of the jungle in which he now stood. An ant colony marched diligently through the underbrush, over fallen tree limbs, and around various types of fungi sprouting from the obtrusive decomposition. Swarms of flying insects hovered in balls of furious motion, as a crowd would surround a furious quarrel. The lively animation of the ecosystem remained completely unaffected by Alan's entrance. Through the hums and buzzes which filled the air, he could make out a faint whisper of noise that seemed to call to him. It wasn't calling his name. Instead, he was being drawn to it by some external force. Following his instincts, Alan dodged the clouds of insects and strode soundlessly over broken limbs, shrubs striving desperately for light, and ferns which cluttered the damp forest floor.

He drilled through the underbrush as quickly as he could, ducking under the occasional low hanging branch and climbing over fallen trees, until he found his way to a small glade. The canopy above broke just enough to see a few stars and sparse flocks of souls spinning in the sky. The force which pulled him wanted him to go into the sky. Alan supposed it knew he would not have been able to move through the treetops. With a jump, he rose above the trees to see a hundred or so souls spinning and waiting for transit to the group of stars called Pleiades. Alan wondered why so few souls were in the night sky this time. Compared to the masses of souls he had seen in other dreams, this clutch of golden orbs was surprisingly small. As he grew closer to the souls in the sky, the whispering became louder, but it was incomprehensible, as though there were too many voices at once for him to hear properly. He knew the voices came from the souls. Alan focused on a single voice and could make out words of atonement. Prayers and apologies for sins once committed and a life spent in vain. *But is there really a god to listen to you?* The voices stopped. Every soul turned to him.

Alan was surprised by the reaction. *Did I say that out loud? I can't imagine I did.* The soul onto which he'd been focusing flashed and spoke, "Who are you? Are you here to lead the way?" Alan could hear the stress in the frail voice. It didn't appear to be distinctly male or female from the quality or pitch. "Why won't you answer me? I have so many questions." Alan noticed the desperation. He had to say something, but what could he say that wouldn't exasperate the situation or this poor soul's lament? "Am I going to heaven? I swear I've been pious. I attended mass. I was christened at just two weeks old." Alan had no answers. During his many travels around this world, he'd often wondered about what happens to the souls after they leave here. *I don't know anything about where you're going.* The tormented soul let out a hideous wail of sorrow and turned away from Alan to continue praying. Alan felt for the powerless soul before him. He may not be willing to go out amongst the people any more, but he had still committed a good portion of the time spent wandering to gazing up at the cluster of stars, Pleiades, to which all souls traveled. Alan had also spent many hours pondering whether the souls actually went to that constellation or beyond it, farther out into the reaches of the universe.

Most other souls surrounding him clamored to themselves in their own way, wondering or crying, praying or cursing, yet others were in silent contemplation or astonishment. Only two souls had left the Earth since his arrival above the treetops, but three new souls were gathered round. There was a great distance between him and the souls on the outskirts of his vision. Alan imagined there were probably many more around the Earth than the hundred or so here. He knew that in this dream state he'd be unable to follow a soul beyond a certain point. He had no idea how that knowledge came to him, but it was innate, almost as if he'd always known but only just come to realize. Outside of the dream, however, he knew no bounds. Alan had spent ages looking at the sky and mapping out the position of Pleiades over the course of years, perhaps centuries. He knew Pleiades called to him, but his heart wanted to see the other stars, visit other places.

Alan went back to the doorway and passed through. He'd grown unenthused by the world through which he had rambled. This hallway, however, still held secrets waiting to be discovered. The symbols still intrigued him. The way the hallway illuminated itself in a bath of ambient light that came from... Where? Shadows did not exist in this place. Columns that protruded from the walls left no indication of a light source. How was it the air itself appeared to be the cause? Alan had visited this place too many times to assume it was merely a figment of his own overactive imagination. Seeing no point in continuing on to the end of the dream, he walked slowly to the eighth door in the hallway.

The single shape was more prominent here but still indistinct enough to have no definable quality. One end was more bulbous than the other, almost like a portrayal of a ball drawn only with vertical lines and scribbles. The other side was still a jumble of nonsense, as far as Alan could tell. He progressed to the ninth door to see the same etchings. The tenth and eleventh saw no change, as well. But upon his arrival at the twelfth and final door, Alan found something peculiar. There were no markings anywhere on this one. The plain monotony of this door was unnerving. Every other one at least had an edge, as far as Alan could recall. In his distraction by the lack of marks, he had failed to notice the missing door handle, too. He wanted to reach out to touch this anomalous door, but his instincts held him back. *No markings. No handle. Is this even a door to open?* Alan guessed that he would find out after having opened the other four doors.

His attention was drawn back to the shape carved into the other doors, and he noticed another detail. Around the edges of the etchings were hardly noticeable notches made into a figure he recognized. It looked like part of the same small dipper shape of Pleiades, except the single point in the middle was missing. *Then what is the ball on the left?* He thought for a moment the indistinguishable portion on the right could be more stars that lay beyond the perceivable constellation, but that didn't seem to fit. There wouldn't be such a large bare spot on the left, were that the case. Alan stood pondering for such a time that the dream world began to fade away. Desperately, he tried to cling to it, to make it stay longer. He wanted to figure out what the shape could actually be. But the harder he tried, the faster the hallway dissolved to blackness. Tiny far off lights glistened into being and filled his vision. The night sky covered his entire field of view. He despised being awake.

## Chapter 27

The moon was at its fullest and brightest. It lit the entire mountain range on which Alan had decided to rest enough to see far off wisps of dusty snow being caught by the upward flow of wind. Recalling his last thought before slumber, he rubbed his chin on his decision to go to the stars. *Can I even go into space?* His supposition was yes. After all, he didn't need to breathe. As far as he could tell, his body wasn't composed of the same kind of material one could find on Earth. He was aeriform but held together by some force. To his knowledge, there was nothing else like him. But would he still be held together in space or dissipate to nothingness in the unending expanse of empty space? There was only one real way to find out, and that was to go. Alan thought it would be a better idea to start slow and go to the moon, first. He looked up at the great glowing mass above and wondered what it could possibly be like there. Alan wanted to know.

But the thought of going was still rather daunting to him. As unenthused as he was by the Earth after all this time, the prospect of travel outside of the Earth gave him a feeling in the back of his mind that was unshakable. Something told him this would be the worst possible idea. Worse than staying around people. Worse than anything he'd ever encountered. This something tugged at him, like it had done in the mental hospital. But Alan wanted to go. He wanted to explore. He wanted to finally go to see the place where souls go. Pleiades. Most of all, he wanted to see the stars up close. He wanted to know what it was like to be on another planet, in another solar system, in a different galaxy. The idea cycled and recycled in his mind until he was almost mad with anticipation. He didn't think there was anything else holding him back from going, but there was something he wanted to do before blazing a trail into oblivion. He wanted to go back to where he'd lived. It had been so long since his death that his old house could be a scrap heap by now.

Alan took a last look at the moon before blasting off the mountain top toward Denver, Colorado. Several days passed before he was finally able to find the place he'd lived. The once semi-peaceful suburban area had been replaced by city expansion. Houses that had lined the streets were replaced by multistory parking garages and businesslike establishments. It looked completely different than memories Alan held so dear. *Has it really been that long?* Alan dared not walk on street level. He stayed well above the heights of the buildings and simply looked on at the incredible and awful destruction of the place he called home so many years ago. Disappointed, he turned away from this unfamiliar urban wasteland to find the industrial area he'd been taken to be cremated.

Most of the older parts of Denver, which had been used mainly as manufacturing zones, remained untouched by development, but the city center and many of its suburbs had been overtaken by superstructures. In turn, land which was once used for wheat, corn, and various other crops was replaced by paved, gridline roads leading to the expansive new residential areas. Denver and the surrounding areas had grown by three or four times since the time of his death and departure. Despite the complete change that overtook the city, Alan was able to find the crematorium quickly by comparison to his old home. When he came to hover over the building, it was midday, so he decided to wait until nightfall. *There shouldn't be anyone there at night. I wonder if my remains are still there.*

The city was much less tranquil at night than he remembered. Masses of car lights crawled along the superhighways as though it were constantly rush hour long after the sun set and the moon once again greeted Alan. He glided slowly down to the rooftop of the building where he had last seen his body. The previous time he was here, he was unable to escape until someone had opened the door for him. But since then, he'd come to realize that he could occupy the same space as an object, so long as he was willing to endure a bit of pain. That was nothing compared to the loss he'd suffered. But he didn't know why that loss had hurt so much, any more. Emotions were outside his cognitive ability, now. Alan floated down to the doorway of the facility and looked into the lobby. The plush furniture had been removed. Papers were strewn across the floor. The entirety of its interior was rundown.

Alan pushed through the glass and entered. The momentary conflict between his body and the glass made him tense, but he didn't stop moving. On the other side, he saw a quarter inch of dust covering every surface. *It's been abandoned.* Tentatively, he walked across the lobby to the double doors. One of them had fallen off its hinges, and the other was hanging at a strange angle from only one hinge. Ducking under the loose door, he turned and made his way down the dark staircase. Though there was virtually no light at the bottom, Alan was able to see clearly. Many of the shelves that had lined the walls were disassembled and stacked in the corner opposite the stairs. The shelves still standing had been packed with boxes similar to the one in which his remains were placed so long ago. Alan walked through the cleared portion of the basement, around to the line of shelves, and along them, searching for his name again. The dates on the boxes ranged from the year 2156 to 2157. There was absolutely nothing to indicate the place his remains had been taken.

With no other leads to follow, Alan shrugged to himself and decided there was no need to stay on Earth any longer. He had witnessed countless souls leave this Earth and fly far into the reaches of outer space, and mapped out the movements of the constellation to which they had gone for at least a century and a half. Although it might have been longer, Alan was not bothered by how long it could have been. He was no longer interested in interacting with people, and flying around the Earth had become monotonous. *This must be why I have been left alive. Why else could I be virtually immortal than to be given the chance to do anything?*

Alan's curiosity for what space would be like had grown exponentially since his dream. He needed to go. That part of him which had pulled him back was still there in the back of his mind, but he ignored it. He didn't care if leaving Earth was a bad idea. He didn't care if there was even the slightest possibility of his body disintegrated into the vast vacuum of space. He had no ties to living. He had no ties to Earth. He had nothing but what lie ahead of him in his travels, and as far as he could tell, everything after his death had pointed him toward the stars. It was where he was meant to go. His mind had been cleared of the selfishness it once contained. He wasn't doing this purely because it would benefit him. This was the reason for his creation. This was the reason he couldn't die. If he had realized this sooner, he wouldn't have wasted time staying around Kaiya. He would not have aimlessly roamed the skies contemplating his own feeble emotions and their remedy.

Alan looked up at the blank concrete ceiling and imagined the night sky full of stars. In his mind, he could tell exactly where Pleiades would be from here. He reached toward the ceiling, longingly. *I know that's where I'm going. That's my final destination. But I'm going elsewhere first. The afterlife can wait.* Nothing was going to hold him back. He'd made up his mind. First stop: the moon. Next stop: infinity. The moon was at least an interesting change compared to everywhere he'd been on Earth. Even with his new found dedication, Alan sauntered toward the stairs. There was no hurry for him. Time didn't matter. He took the stairs slowly and found himself to be smiling. *This feels good.* He was actually excited about something for the first time in a very long time. Alan stepped carelessly over the fallen swinging door and crossed the lobby. A lump of anticipation formed in his throat and chest.

Outside the facility, Alan looked skyward and found the moon to be hidden behind a swelling storm front. The luminescence of the full moon was only barely visible through the deep, dark clouds. Nevertheless, his smile did not fade. Alan squinted, and his smile changed to a smirk of challenge. He rose through the air. Up until now, he had avoided large storm fronts. The electric field of energy surrounding the clouds had made him uncomfortable, but now, he was ready to face that fear. From now on, his life would be no holds barred. Arms outstretched, Alan punched his way through the clouds, leaving a plume of disturbance upon exiting. Higher and higher he rose until he could tell the air was thinning. His movements suddenly became easier. His flight was now faster and more effortless than before. He liked this feeling. It made him rich with newfound power. He'd been taking it slow, but he didn't feel the need anymore. He shot forward as fast as he could.

Before he had time to think, Alan was at the moon. Its dark splotched face approached him as he slowed. Alan landed on the moon's surface and dropped to his hands and knees. The ground was soft, like the desert sands from his dream. Around him, craters sizing from small to massive littered the surface and gave the moon a character unlike that of any place he'd ever seen on Earth. This new terrain was completely alien to him. Everything was new, from the color of the sandy ground below him to the way his body felt as though it were somehow freer. How hadn't he noticed that before? His movement was so unhindered by the lack of atmosphere that he was moving quicker and with hardly any effort. *This feels great!* He could get used to this. Even his body was urging him to go to the stars. He looked up at the Earth. From here, it appeared so tiny and frail. The sun was just beyond the Earth, and he noticed for the first time how brilliant it actually was. The white light pierced the boundless emptiness of space and brightened the opposite side of the Earth from him. As he watched, the Earth turned on its axis, creating a never ending sunrise. The effortlessness was calming. Peaceful. Alan flipped himself over to sit and stare upward. This was unlike anything he had ever seen before.

Clouds swirled in the air currents. Lights spread across the countries still in darkness. A film of atmosphere surrounded the outer rim of the earth and glowed from the penetrating white light of the sun. Alan could imagine all of the people on Earth just now getting up for breakfast or lying down to sleep after a long day. He wondered how many of them were going to die today. He wondered how many of them knew and how many would be caught unaware. He wondered how many would go through violent deaths, as he had. He wanted to know what their thoughts would be if someone told them it was their last breakfast or their last sleep. After having witnessed so many orbs fly into space, he supposed it would be a lot. For a moment, his thoughts went back to what that poor soul had asked him in his last dream. *Am I going to heaven?* At the time, Alan hadn't been able to answer. He hadn't the slightest clue. But now, he had a guess. Heaven did seem likely. Or some other form of afterlife. The souls had to go somewhere. What was heaven but a place beyond life? His mind went to Kaiya and Kayla for the first time in a very long time. He had had so much love for Kayla when he'd first seen her there in the desert. The thought of Kaiya and Kayla going somewhere after death was soothing. He'd always known they'd gone somewhere. But now he hoped that somewhere was heavenly. Alan's mind was so completely at ease that he closed his eyes and passed into a long and dreamless sleep.

Made in the USA
Columbia, SC
03 August 2022